Lavender Tide

Lavender Tide

Summer is Tomorrow Series

Book 2

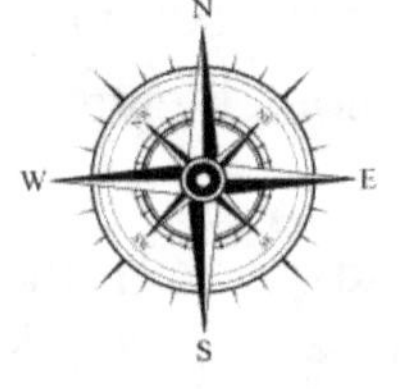

by

Starr Ayers

MBI

Lavender Tide
Published by Mountain Brook Ink
White Salmon, WA U.S.A.

The website addresses shown in this book are not intended in any way to be or imply an endorsement on the part of Mountain Brook Ink, nor do we vouch for their content.

This story is a work of fiction. All characters and events are the product of the author's imagination. Any resemblance to any person, living or dead, is coincidental.

Scripture quotations are taken from the King James Version of the Bible. Public domain.
ISBN 9781953957-65-8

The Team: Miralee Ferrell, Tim Pietz, Kristen Johnson, Alyssa Roat, Cindy Jackson
Cover Design: Indie Cover Design, Lynnette Bonner Designer

Mountain Brook Ink is an inspirational publisher offering fiction you can believe in.
Printed in the United States of America

*"Let us hold unswervingly to the hope we profess,
for He who promised is faithful."*

Hebrews 10:23 NIV

Dedication

To Jesus Christ, my Savior and Lord,
without whose inspiration I have no words.
I lift these pages to you and pray
you'll reveal your heart to all who read them.

To the brave men and women who served during the Vietnam War.
You wore the uniform with honor, gave your youth, and in many
cases, your lives. Your courage in the face of adversity, your
unseen sacrifices, and unwavering commitment must never
be forgotten. May your stories echo through time, reminding
us of the price of service and the power of remembrance.

Acknowledgments

*"Find a group of people who challenge and inspire you.
Spend a lot of time with them, and it will change your life."*
Amy Poehler

A huge thank you to my husband, **Michael**. Regardless of my artistic endeavors, you have always been my most ardent supporter. Whether critiquing a painting, assisting me with setup at craft shows, or helping me develop plotlines for my characters, you have been a valuable sounding board, have done the heavy lifting, and continue to be my most vocal admirer. Without your support, there would never have been one book, much less four. Yes…God knew what he was doing when he joined these two hearts. I love you!

To my publisher, **Miralee Ferrell,** thank you for opening the doors of **Mountain Brook Ink** to this fledgling author. I'm grateful for your editor's eyes, which make my stories shine. By pushing me out of my comfort zone while giving me the freedom to be myself, you have helped me refine my writing skills and believe in my abilities as an author.

To MBI's book cover designer, **Lynnette Bonner**, thank you for capturing my vision in all of your beautiful covers and for creating ones that draw the eyes and win the hearts of readers—and, yes—sell books.

To my critique partners in **Word Weavers, Page 3, and the four other Founding Erasers—Deborah Sprinkle, Sandra Hart,**

Linda Dindzans, and Denise Holmberg—thank you for your spot-on critiques and for the friendships that have grown throughout the years. I've found my tribe and wouldn't want to blaze this path without you.

Lori Marett, thank you for sharing your writing expertise and for your honest evaluations of my work. I value your input and am blessed to have you as a friend.

Jettie House, my precious Monday morning friend, thank you for all you do for me. Your listening ear, input, and words of encouragement mean more to me than you know.

Ashley Morris, who would have guessed that my visits to my nail tech would evolve into valuable brainstorming sessions, and one of them would produce the title for this book—*Lavender Tide*. What a blessing you are.

Thank you to my **endorsers** and **readers** who have purchased and reviewed my books. Your encouragement has launched me forward and inspired me to keep writing. Never underestimate the importance and power of your words to a writer.

Ultimately, I'm grateful to my **Heavenly Father** for the gift of story and the privilege of writing for You. The more I write, the more I'm aware of my dependence on You for Every. Single. Word. Like my chosen theme verse states, *"He who promised is faithful,"* and YOU have never failed me. Not. One. Time.

Chapter One

Sunday, March 19, 2023
Sunset Beach, North Carolina
Brooklyn Marshal

I handed my cousin, Olivia, her Boho-style maxi dress with its cropped jean jacket and lifted her wedding gown from the bed. "You were stunning today." Turning, I placed the off-the-shoulder lace dress with flared sleeves in the garment bag and hung it on the back of my bedroom door. "I couldn't stop watching Chase's reaction as you walked toward him. He is smitten. I'm so happy for you both."

"Thank you. He's everything I'd hoped for and more." She slipped the dusty-blue floral dress over her head, letting its soft fabric envelop her shapely figure, then turned her back to me and lifted her long blond hair from her shoulders. "Will you zip this?"

"Of course."

"Brooklyn, I can't thank you enough for helping me with the wedding preparations and for standing with me today. Your presence always quiets my spirit."

"I wouldn't have wanted to be anywhere else." I patted the zipper at the square neckline and helped her slip on her denim jacket. "Everyone had a wonderful time. After all of our fears about the storm, we couldn't have had a more perfect day for a beach wedding."

"I agree. Our prayers were answered." Olivia smoothed the fullness of her skirt. "But I'm afraid it's the calm before the storm." Looking in the dresser mirror, she picked up her comb and slid it through her hair, being careful not to pull out the waves. "Now, if God will hold back the winds long enough for us to board the plane tomorrow and get out ahead of it, I will be doubly grateful."

"That's my prayer too."

Olivia whirled around and fluffed her hair. "Well, how do I look?"

"Perfect. Just perfect. Like the beautiful, starry-eyed newlywed you are." I cracked open the door and peeked into the living room. Chase stood at the window watching the surf, his hands behind his back. "Ah-hem. Are you ready to see your bride, Mr. Evans?"

He turned and flashed his trademark circuit-breaker smile. "Past ready."

Stepping aside, I extended my arm and swept it toward the door. "Tada." Olivia drifted through and spun around, her breezy dress billowing and settling around her ankles.

Wolf-whistling, Chase moved closer, clasped her hands in his, and kissed her lightly on the lips. "Mrs. Evans, you take my breath away every time you enter a room." He offered his arm. "Are you ready to travel with me and stay by my side for as long as we both shall live?"

"Past ready." She gazed into his eyes and stroked the well-groomed stubble, which enhanced his jawline.

"Then what are we waiting for?"

"Here, let me get the door." I rushed past them as he picked up her suitcase and escorted her onto the porch.

Olivia and I said our goodbyes as we followed Chase to their new home next door. "Looks like you're traveling in style this morning," I said as he placed her luggage into the bed of Big Red.

Olivia pulled her sunglasses from her purse and slipped them on. "We wouldn't think of leaving Big Red behind. He's been an important part of our story since day one."

Chase brushed his hand over the fresh, shiny wax job of his '87 red Chevy pickup. "Yep. Red is at the top of his game. The old boy has never looked better."

Laughing, I hugged him. "Funny. That's exactly what I said to Liv about you earlier today."

He dismissed my quip and grinned. "You did, huh? I suppose I can live with that."

Holding his gaze, I stepped back and reached for Olivia's hand. "You take care of this precious lady now, you hear? If you don't, you'll have me to answer to."

"Now, that's scary…but no worries. I wouldn't think of doing anything else."

Olivia squeezed me and kissed my cheek, then moved toward the passenger side of the pick-up.

"Whoa." Chase held up his hand. "Not so fast there, missus. I have one more surprise for you before we leave."

She raised her brows. "You do?"

"I do." He chuckled and curled his index finger over his lips. "Hmm. Where have I heard those words lately?"

"Yes, Mr. Evans. You're mine now—all mine. I expect 'I do' and 'Yes, Ma'am,' will become your kneejerk responses in no time."

"Ha." He shifted his eyes toward hers and grinned. "You think so, huh?" He led her by the hand onto the screened porch of their cottage. Propped against the wall sat the lavender bike she'd rented from Surf Daddy the previous summer. Daisies spilled from its basket, and white and yellow ribbon streamers flowed over the front fender.

Olivia gasped. "Oh, Chase. You're such a charmer. You

think of everything." She slid her sunglasses into her hair and met his gaze. "Is it mine to keep?"

"Only for as long as you keep me." He chuckled. "As soon as you said yes, I purchased it from Kainalu. I wasn't about to let anyone else rent it." He patted the vinyl seat. "If it hadn't been for sweet old Iris here, we might never have gotten together."

"True. So true." She walked over and fingered the fresh flowers, then whirled around. "They're beautiful. Thank you."

Chase clapped his hands. "Okay. Enough of this. I've got more important things on my mind." He winked. "You comin', gorgeous?"

Olivia strolled across the floor, hips swaying, and took his hand. "Just try'n stop me."

Monday, March 20, 2023

Brooklyn yawned, lifted her cell phone from the nightstand, and noted the caller ID. "Good morning, Mrs. Evans."

"Morning, cuz. I'm happy to know you survived the night."

"Me too. It was a long one. When I peeked out about two this morning, the tide had washed into the yard. I can't remember a storm this brutal."

Throwing back the covers, I scooted to the edge of the bed and noted the second hand on my alarm clock stood still. "Looks like the power's out here." I rose and pushed open the sliding door to the porch. "Good grief, the yard is a mess. Palm fronds and seaweed everywhere. It looks like my work is cut out for me this afternoon. How did y'all fare?"

"It was definitely rough. Our hotel isn't on the oceanfront, though, so I'm sure you're feeling more beat up this morning than we are. Is it still raining there?"

"Yes, but it's tapering off, and the sky is brightening some."

"Good. Same here. I'm calling to let you know that our flight to Turks and Caicos has been delayed. The airline isn't sure when our departure will be. They're waiting for the outer bands of the nor'easter to move farther south. I'll call you as soon as we know something."

"Thanks. I've been concerned about your early morning flight. It's good to know the powers that be are cautious. Hopefully, you'll get out soon." I combed my fingers through my bedhead and plopped onto the chaise. "I wonder how the Kindred Spirit fared. Whenever the rain stops, I think I'll make a trip to the mailbox."

"Oh, yes, please do. I trust it's still standing. That box is stout. Despite numerous storms, it's only had to be replaced a couple of times. Let me know what you find."

"I sure will."

After hanging up, I slipped into my workout clothes, pulled my yellow rain slicker from the closet, and dropped it on the couch on my way to the kitchen. *Sheesh, a morning without coffee.* I dug through the wedding leftovers in the fridge and slid out my only caffeine option, a pitcher of tea. After filling my cup, I stepped onto the porch and eased into a rocker. If I couldn't share my morning with a cuppa Joe, I would at least experience the familiar comfort of holding my earthen mug. Although the temps were unseasonably warm, and the clouds still threatened to dump water like a wet sponge, the salt air energized me. Inhaling, I laid my head against the chair, then exhaled slowly and thanked the good Lord for bringing my 1950s cottage and me through one more storm.

Later, while slipping on my slicker and walking shoes, I

remembered Olivia's bike and toyed with the idea of riding it to the Kindred Spirit. Anxious to know the condition of the box, I walked next door. *Olivia won't mind.* Being careful not to spoil the thoughtful daisy arrangement Chase left, I lifted it from the wicker basket, set it on the cafe table in the corner, and pushed Iris onto the beach.

Olivia Houston Evans

Olivia sat across the table from Chase in the Pavilion Bar and Grill of Terminal B with her phone pressed to her ear and bit her freshly manicured nails. "Brooklyn still doesn't answer."

Chewing a mouthful of the grill's signature American Wagyu Beef burger, Chase held up his index finger and swallowed. "She's probably outside cleaning up the yard and doesn't hear her phone." He straightened in his seat and wiped his mouth with his napkin.

"You're probably right." She tossed her phone in her purse. "I'll try again after dark when I know she'll be inside." After making a trip to the ladies' room, Olivia walked to the gate with Chase and took a seat facing the tarmac. While he napped, she observed planes, eavesdropped on the young family behind her, and thumbed through travel magazines. Still, nothing could tamp down the uneasiness in her spirit. Jerking her purse from the seat beside her, she rifled through for her phone and dialed.

"Hello, Coffee Chronicles. This is Courtney. May I help you?"

"Hey. It's Olivia. I sure hope you can."

"Of course, girlfriend. What do you need?"

"I talked with Brooklyn this morning but haven't been able

to reach her since. Have you heard from her? Was she supposed to work today?"

"Yes. She was scheduled to work the evening shift at three but didn't show. I've called her several times with no luck. I know the power is still out on that end of the beach, but Brooklyn usually finds a way to let me know when she can't make it to work."

Olivia fought back tears and grabbed Chase's arm.

"What? What?" he hollered, jumping from sleep and grabbing his carry-on bag. "Are we boarding?"

"Shh." She shook her head and yanked him back down.

"Wow, Courtney. Now I'm really worried." She looked at the clock above the check-in counter. "We're due to fly out of MYR at 8:13 tonight, but I can't leave here until I know Brooklyn's okay. Would you call the police and ask them to go to her house? She usually leaves the kitchen door unlocked, so they should be able to get in. If she's not there, see if they'll check the beach between her house and the Kindred Spirit. She told me this morning that she wanted to make a trip to the mailbox to see if it weathered the storm."

"I sure will. I don't mind at all. As a matter of fact, I'll drive to the station and follow the police to Brooklyn's house myself. I'll be too antsy to be of any use around here. You hang on and try not to worry. I'll get back to you with news as soon as I can."

Olivia sighed. "Thanks. Thanks so much. In the meantime, I'll pray and wait for your call." She swiveled in her seat and looked into Chase's troubled eyes. "Honey, Brooklyn didn't show up for work, and no one's been able to reach her."

Grimacing, he pulled her to his side and kissed her cheek. "I'm sorry, Liv, but let's not think the worst. There's probably a good reason for all of this."

She redialed Brooklyn's number, then slammed her phone

into her purse and shrugged. "Straight to voicemail."

Chase released a deep, gratifying sigh and lifted his index finger. "Well, now, there's your answer. With no power, her phone's dead."

"I don't know. I hope you're right." She wiggled from his embrace. "I can't just sit here. I've got to work off this nervous energy. I'm going to walk around for a while."

"Sure, Babe. Go ahead. I'll stay here and watch our things."

Olivia slipped her crossbody bag over her head and walked through the terminal. After browsing at a couple of kiosks and an apparel shop, she strolled through Hudson News, purchased a Sherpa blanket for the plane, and stopped at the magazine rack. As she reached for the March issue of *Coastal Living*, she jumped at her phone's sudden ring. Snatching it from her purse, she blurted. "Yes, Courtney. Any news?"

"Umm…"

"What's wrong?"

Courtney groaned. "I'm sorry, I just—"

"What is it? Have they found Brooklyn?" She clutched the blanket to her chest, heart pounding.

"Not exactly."

In dread of what she might hear, she walked back across the terminal toward Chase. "What on earth does *not exactly* mean?" Her voice faded. "Have they found Brooklyn or not?"

"Olivia, I'm sorry. She wasn't at the cottage, and the police didn't need to go as far as the Kindred Spirit."

As if crushed in a vise, her chest tightened, and her voice dwindled to a whisper. "What? What do you mean?" Staring without seeing, she eased into the seat beside Chase. "Please…you're scaring me."

"I'm sorry to say that your lavender bike was found lying in the surf about three-quarters of a mile from Brooklyn's house, but—" Her voice cracked as she spoke. "Olivia…there was no sign of Brooklyn."

"What?" She jerked her head toward Chase. "No sign of Brooklyn? They found my bike, but not Brooklyn?" A bitter taste rose from the pit of her stomach.

"Yes. According to the direction the bicycle was facing, it looked like she'd been to the box and was on her way home. By the time the police found the bike, the waves had washed away any tracks or footprints that would have been left. They have no leads but are calling the hospital to see if anyone matching her description has been brought in. I wanted to catch you before you boarded, so I haven't heard what they found out. As it stands now, Brooklyn is…Brooklyn is missing."

Chapter Two

Myrtle Beach, South Carolina
Logan Corbett

Logan Corbett raked his fingers through his tousled hair and struggled to remain calm as he sat in the lobby of Grand Strand Medical Center. *Whatever you do, Corbett, don't look guilty.* A tall order as he sat across from Sunset Beach's lead police detective, Wilson Branson. Regardless of what he'd said, Logan had watched enough true-crime episodes on TV to know he was a suspect—correction...*a person of interest.*

The short and stocky, fifty-something detective scribbled in his notepad, then looked up and peered over his brown tortoise-shell glasses. "How old are you, Mr. Corbett?"

"Thirty-six."

"And you say you've been a resident of Sunset Beach for fourteen years now. Is that correct?"

"Yessir. About that."

"Where'd you live before that?"

"Conway."

He stopped writing, gave his ballpoint pen two hard shakes, and then jotted it down. "What do you do for a living?"

Logan swiped at the dirt on his khaki pants. "I'm a real estate agent with Harbor Realty."

"Worked there long?"

"Twelve years, sir."

With an assenting nod, he raised his eyebrows. "That's a

long time. You must be good at what you do.”

“I like to think so. Evidently, my agency does. I’ve received the Top Salesman of the Year award for the past three years.”

“Ya don’t say. That’s impressive. Congratulations.” He rubbed his hand over his balding head. “How long have you known the victim?”

“I don’t know her, sir.”

He looked up from his notepad. “Whaddaya mean you don’t know her? Aren’t you the one who called 911 earlier this afternoon?”

“Yessir, but as far as I know, I’ve not seen her before…” He swallowed hard as he remembered the moment. “…before today, when I found her on the beach. Or, I should say, my dog did.”

“Dog? Where’s your dog now?”

“Outside in my car.”

Detective Branson leaned back in his chair and crossed his legs. “So, tell me then how y’all found her.”

Logan sipped his energy drink and set the bottle on the table beside him. “I was walking my dog, and like usual, Murphy, my golden retriever, ran ahead of me to chase gulls. After a bit, he barked like he wanted to play, so I ran after him. I figured it was all a game until I saw something lying in the surf up ahead. When I stopped to shield the sun from my eyes and focus, I thought the object was a sea turtle or a small shark or something, but then I spotted something yellow.”

Detective Branson lifted his hand for Logan to stop while he wrote, then gazed over his glasses. “Go on.”

“Murphy must have heard or sensed I wasn’t coming, so he stopped and looked back, then kicked up sand and bolted. I took off after him. The closer I got, the more I realized what I saw wasn’t a sea creature.”

Logan rested his elbows on his knees, lowered his head, and choked out his words. "It was a body—a person. A young woman wearing a yellow rain slicker lying face down in the sand."

"What did you do then?"

He looked up and dropped back in his seat. "I froze and tried to process what I saw. I didn't know what to do. Should I touch her? Not touch her? But, there was no way I could stand there and do nothing." He cringed as the scene replayed in his head. "I knelt, turned over her body, and felt for a pulse." He straightened and looked into the detective's eyes. "Thank God. One was there. Faint—but there."

"…and then?"

"I called 911." Logan waited while the detective finished writing in his book. "Sir, do you think she's going to be all right?"

He shrugged. "Not my department, but I hope so."

Logan lowered his head again, stared at the floor, and nodded. "Me too, sir. Me too."

"Just a few more questions. You told me earlier that you have a house on the beachfront. How far was this from your house?"

He twisted his mouth and looked up at the ceiling. "Hmm…maybe a little over a quarter of a mile."

"Was there anyone else on the beach at the time?"

"The only people I saw were a long way down the beach, walking in the opposite direction. I live on the West end, close to Bird Island. It's pretty quiet down there. For the most part…" *Corbett, you're rattling. Cool your heels.* "Most are permanent residents, sir."

After jotting a few notes, Detective Branson slapped his book shut and locked eyes with Logan. "I think I've got all I need." He rose and shook Logan's hand. "Thanks for your cooperation, Mr. Corbett. Don't leave town until we find out more about the young lady."

His stomach clenched. "No. Of course not." Heat rose from his collar, and he swallowed hard. *Am I more than a person of interest?* "Could you keep me informed, sir?"

Sliding his glasses on top of his slick head, the detective tucked his small notebook and pen in the top pocket of his navy blazer. "I'll do what I can. I've got your number."

He smiled. "Thanks."

Detective Branson stepped to walk away, then stopped and turned back. "Oh, there is one more thing."

He moistened his lips. "Yessir?"

"Did you see anything else you think might help us with our investigation?"

He tipped his head. "Um…yes. Yes, I did. While I waited for the dispatcher to pick up, I noticed something in the waves."

Branson slid his glasses back onto his nose and pulled the notebook and pen from his pocket.

"It was a bicycle. A lavender one."

Logan slipped his bare feet into his well-worn top-siders, pointed the remote at the 55" flat-screen above the mantel, and clicked it off. Even though he was still unsettled by the day's events, it felt good to be home, back on Sunset Beach. Murphy's ears perked up. Lying on the opposite end of the sofa, Logan's five-year-old golden retriever shifted his dark eyes toward him and issued a muffled growl.

"What's it to you, fella? You weren't even watching it." He tossed his napkin onto his plate and carried his TV tray into the kitchen while Murphy raced past him and skidded to a stop at the door.

"Whoa, Murph. Not so fast. You know the drill." He put his plate in the dishwasher, pulled the carafe from the coffeemaker, and held it up. "After a day like today, I'm not going anywhere without this." He poured dark-roast coffee into his thermal cup, drizzled in a bit of honey and liquid creamer, then stirred till it was a rich caramel color. "Perfect." He snapped on the lid and slurped the hot brew. "Ah, yes. Now, we're good to go, big boy."

Murphy whimpered and crammed his nose into the doorjamb, wriggling his backside until his master flung open the storm door. Like a bull exploding from the chute, he bounded onto the deck.

Logan hollered, snatched his jacket from a hook beside the door, and followed him down the walkway toward the ocean. "You hang close, fella. I don't want to have to chase you down tonight." He slipped his phone into his jeans pocket and eased into one of the Adirondack chairs on the deck at the end of the walkway. Murphy had spooked a flock of gulls with his boisterous invitation to play in the surf. *That dog will never give up trying to bring home the prize.* He sipped his coffee and groaned. *Maybe I should take my cues from Murph and not give up.*

Logan breathed in the cool, salty air and listened to the waves breaking on the shore. He needed this. He looked back at the quaint two-bedroom cottage he'd dubbed The Shingle Life and had lived in for the last seven years. The possibility of having to let it go crushed him. *How can things look incredibly promising one minute and in the next—Snap! Gone.*

He shifted his eyes to the gray cedar-shake cottage next door and shook his head. What a day. Before his exploit on the beach, he'd spent the morning surveying storm damage, and it didn't look good. Although the other homes around his held firm, the storm surge had taken its toll on its older structure. He should have listened at the get-go to those who'd advised him to bulldoze the property and start over. Instead, he'd purchased it, invested his savings, and taken out a small loan on this fixer-upper. Now, after six months of hard work, the previous night's nor'easter had dropped the verdict. According to his inspector friend, it was too weak to salvage. His advice—raze it.

Only a few weeks away from a profitable closing with an out-of-state buyer, those were not the words Logan wanted to hear. He pulled his phone from his pocket and stared at it. How would he tell his client that the house he'd waited on for months and was about to sign on was now uninhabitable? He sighed. On the bright side for his client, the storm had come in days before the closing, not days after. But for himself, there was no silver lining. With no emergency fund to fall back on, he'd probably have to sell his home to pay for the razing and settle with the bank. *How could I have been so stupid? As a long-time, award-winning agent, I know better.*

Murphy bounded up the steps and barked, then paced back and forth in front of him.

Logan set his mug on the arm of his chair, rubbed the retriever's large, wet head, and combed tangles from his coat with his fingers. "So, have you decided to give the gulls a rest and come and pester me now?"

Murph shuffled backward, then ran to the top of the stairs and barked. "I can't help you with those gulls, fella. They're faster than both of us."

Whining, he looked back at the beach.

"Nope. I'm not taking you for a walk either. You've gotten me into enough trouble for one day. We'll sit here together and wait for sunset. At least maybe our day will have a beautiful ending."

Murphy lumbered back and plopped at Logan's feet with a

grunt.

"You've got that right, fella. That's the way I feel."

Chapter Three

Dancing with a leg brace isn't easy, but according to Patricia Malone's Granny Rogers, not much worthwhile in life is.

Careful not to scratch the record's shiny surface, she slipped it from the dust cover and placed it onto the center peg of her birthday present—a portable Motorola record player. Her first ever. After swiveling the tonearm over the turntable, she eased the needle onto the outer edge of the whirling vinyl surface and waited while it crackled. Once Chubby Checker's "Let's Twist Again" pulsed from the speakers, she snapped her fingers, grabbed the cannonball bedpost of her four-poster bed, and giggled. She liked to think that while dancing her version of the Twist, the rhythmic clicks of her leg brace provided additional percussion for the band.

Patricia, or Trish to those who knew her best, didn't allow polio to stop her from doing what most fourteen—now fifteen-year-old girls do. Although some activities presented more challenges than others, her parents had always told her she could do whatever she set her mind to.

Twirling and almost losing her balance, she steadied herself with the bedpost and noted the framed quote by Henry Ford on the wall. A gift from her Granny Rogers, it had hung beside her dresser since before she was old enough to read. But that hadn't kept her from knowing what it said—Granny made sure of that. *Obstacles are those frightful things you see when you take your eyes off your goal.* Then, her granny was always sure to add...*and your God.* Trish missed her. Up until last year, her grandmother had always been in the mix, cheering her on. She preferred to believe she still was. At times, she'd picture her granny standing several feet in front of her, arms outstretched, saying, "You can do it, babydoll, only a few more steps," ...all the while inching backward.

Trish's mother, Jane Malone, swung open the door and burst into her room. "Honey, turn that music down. I can hardly hear myself think." Dropping onto the bed, she pulled her gingham apron over her head, crumpled it in her lap, and patted the place beside her. "Come here, birthday girl."

She turned off the player, grabbed her mother's hand, and hoisted herself onto the mattress.

"Your daddy and I have a surprise for you," she said, patting Trish's frail leg. "Hurry up. Change from your nightgown and slip on some capris. You'll need comfortable shoes, too."

"But you've already given me a—" Her heart revved. "You mean there's more? What is it? Can you give me a hint?" Her mother's clear blue eyes crinkled at the corners as she laughed and walked toward the door. "Not on your life, sweet girl, but the sooner you get dressed, the quicker you'll find out."

Trish slid from the bed and opened her closet. *Did she dare hope it would be what she'd dreamed of for more than a year?*

When Trish reached the front door, her mother helped her down the steps and smoothed her daughter's auburn hair. "Now, wait right here, and let me see if your father's ready."

Trish's insides fluttered as she watched her mother's tall, slender figure walk down the stone path bordered with pink, white, and purple thrift.

Shielding her eyes from the sun, her mother looked up the drive. "Robert! Trish is ready. Are you?"

He hollered from inside the detached garage. "Hold on. Not quite."

She glanced back at her and giggled. "Are you excited?"

Trish rolled her eyes and placed her hands over her heart. "I can hardly stand it. Tell Daddy to hurry." She jolted as his booming voice pierced the still, muggy morning air.

"Okay. Bring the birthday girl around."

Her mother motioned and took her by the arm. "You're gonna love it."

Stepping into the driveway, Trish squealed and, despite her restrictive limp, ran toward her father. "Daddy, I can't believe this. I'm just not believing it. A bicycle—a lavender bicycle." She threw her arms around her tall, burly father's waist and squeezed him. Then, turning, she blew kisses at her mother before rushing to see the twenty-four-inch ladies' bicycle that stood in the drive.

Robert Malone chuckled as Trish walked around the bike and ran her hand over its polished fenders. "I think you're a wee bit excited, aren't you, Princess?"

She nodded, her smile spreading from ear to ear. "And it has a wicker basket. Just what I've wanted. Thank you both so much."

Her father and mother walked toward her, hand in hand. "Now, before you go giving us all the credit, you need to look in the basket."

Pressing her lips together, Trish laid her hands on her chest and peeked in at a lavender-colored envelope. "What's this?"

They both grinned and shrugged. Leaning over, her mother whispered. "Maybe you should open it."

She smiled and lifted the envelope to her nose.

"Mmm…lavender. Smells like Granny. Granny?" Her eyes widened as she choked out her words. "Is this from Granny?" She looked at her parents, who shrugged again in unison.

Trish's hands shook as she slipped the cream sheet of paper from the envelope and unfolded it. Once her eyes fell on the border of violets, there was no mistaking who the note was from. She stood silent, staring at the familiar scrawl, tears clouding her vision. She swallowed hard, wiped her eyes with the back of her hand, and read.

My darling Trish,

Happy 15th Birthday! I'm sure, by now, you've seen your gift. I'm tempted to ask you if you like it, but then that would be ridiculous. Of course you do. It's what you've chattered about for months. I only wish I were there to see your surprise. Who knows, maybe even as you read this, God will give me a glimpse of the joy on your face. All things are possible with Him, you know.

I hoped I'd make it to this day, but cancer had its way of letting me know I needed to plan ahead. Your momma and daddy offered to help with the cost of the bicycle, but I wouldn't let them. I wanted it to be from me. I told them no amount of money would keep me from giving you the bike you deserve. You've worked hard to get to this point, and I'm very, very proud of you. I hold your days of skinned knees and training wheels close to my heart. Seeing your drive and determination to accomplish each milestone was the joy of my life. Always remember your Granny believes in you and knows that you are capable of doing whatever your heart desires.

Now, a word of caution. Please be careful and don't do anything reckless. That is to say, at least don't do anything your Granny Rogers wouldn't do. (I'm laughing here.) Take care, my beautiful girl. Enjoy your special day and all the years that lie ahead of you.

I love you now and forever,

Granny

As the recollection of her grandmother's sweet voice faded in her ears, Trish slid the note back into the envelope. "I miss her so much," she said, looking up at her parents.

Her mother smiled, then sniffed and swiped a tear. "Now look behind the basket."

Mystified, Trish lifted the basket and read the engraved stainless plaque on the frame. *"Happy 15th Birthday, Trish. I love you! Granny Rogers."* Tears slid down her cheeks as she whispered. "I can't believe this."

Trish's mother pulled her close and blotted her cheeks with her handkerchief. "I pray God will give Mother a peek at your joy this morning. She would be thrilled."

Her father tilted the bicycle and raised the kickstand with his foot. "Okay, folks. Granny wouldn't stand for any of this blubbering. Let's turn that frown upside down and see how this beauty rolls."

Trish's mother unbuckled her daughter's brace and slipped it off. "There you go, honey. You're free to be. Climb up on your lavender chariot and spread your wings."

While her father steadied the bike, Trish straddled it and kept her right foot securely on the ground. Then, resting on the seat, she pressed down on the right pedal with her strong leg and pushed off. After coasting down the gravel drive, she turned at the end and powered back toward her parents, her good leg doing the work while her left leg tagged along. She brought the bike to a stop beside her father. "What do you think?"

"That looked good. How does it feel? Steady?"

"Yes. I'm surprised. It's much easier to ride than my twenty-inch bike. I can straighten my legs with this one. I love it." She climbed back on and rode several more laps around the drive. "Don't look so anxious, Momma. I'm good. Really, I am."

"I know you are, dear." She released a nervous laugh. "I think it's harder for me to watch you try new things than it is for you to do them. I suppose it comes with the territory of being a mom."

Trish stopped the bike again. "Can I go and thank Granny?"

Her momma looked at her daddy with worried eyes.

After cupping his hand around a match to light his cigarette, he nodded and blew a ring of smoke in the air.

"Okay," she said, rubbing Trish's back and issuing a reluctant assent. "Ride on, but don't stay long, you hear?"

Grinning, she hopped onto her bike and circled her parents. "I won't. I'll ride over and back in no time." As she pedaled onto the sidewalk, she waved at her neighbor. "Good morning, Mr. Satterfield."

"Hi, Trish." He leaned on his rake and wiped the sweat from his brow. "Looks like you've gotta cool new ride there."

"I do. It's a birthday present from my granny. I'm off to thank her."

"Ah, that's wonderful. Happy birthday, young lady. You be careful and be sure to look both ways at the corner."

Already halfway down the block, she hollered back. "I will."

She hurried to get to her grandmother's plot at The Old Smithville Burying Ground, two blocks away from her modest home on N. Atlantic Street. Maybe, just maybe, her granny would know she was there and sense her joy.

Within five minutes, Trish passed the small, dilapidated

wooden fence surrounding the historic cemetery and wound her way through its peaceful, shady grounds on the corner of Nash and Rhett Streets. She wiped her brow and peered up at the sprawling branches of giant live oaks draped with Spanish moss. Their sheltering canopy offered a welcome reprieve from this Carolina coastal town's sweltering summer heat. Her mother's ancestors, the Pearsons, had owned plots in this historic cemetery since the mid-1800s. As a cool breeze blew in from the mouth of the Cape Fear River, she was thankful her Granny had such a beautiful place to rest.

She stopped at the large plot where her great-grandparents and three of Granny's four siblings were buried, and propped her bike against a tall, long-leaf pine. Holding onto the back of a rusting wrought-iron bench, she limped around and eased onto the seat in front of her sweet granny's grave. Still unable to believe her granny was gone, reading her name etched in the granite headstone smacked of cruel reality.

Millicent Agnes Pearson Rogers
Born: April 21, 1901 – Died: May 3, 1962

"Well, Granny, have you been waiting for me? I'm sure you knew I'd be here to thank you for your amazing gift. I was so surprised when Daddy rolled the lavender bike out of the garage and even more surprised to find out it was from you." She plucked a couple of pine needles from her hair and chuckled. "I should have known it was from you, as many times as I chewed your ear off about it. "It rides great, by the way. I had no trouble pedaling here, but I am worn out now and very happy you thought to put this bench here.

"It's been a really swell birthday so far. Guess what Momma and Daddy gave me? A Motorola record player, and on top of that, they're taking me to your favorite restaurant for my dinner tonight. I wish you were here to go with us. I know how you always loved to sit on the wrap-around porch and look out over the Cape Fear, not to mention the chef's hot apple pie and ice cream you loved to devour." She lowered her chin and wiped a tear from her cheek with the back of her hand.

"Well, speaking of Momma, I promised her I wouldn't be gone long, so I'd better get back. You know how she is. She tries hard not to show it, but she's still not comfortable with me riding a bike. She doesn't have the confidence in me that you did. But that's okay. Before long, I'll make a believer out of her." Trish rose from the bench and maneuvered her way back to her bike. Straddling it, she glanced at her granny's grave. "Pretty cool, huh? Watch me as I leave." She pressed her hand to her lips, gave her fingers a loud smack, and flicked the make-believe kiss into the air. "You know I love you, Granny. I'll be back again soon. Promise."

She pedaled her bike onto the sidewalk lined with towering live oaks and rode through the close-knit neighborhood made up of modest clapboard houses. Noting a black plume of smoke rising above the trees, she sniffed the air and huffed. *Poor Momma. She's gonna be madder than a wet hen. Mr. Satterfield's leaf burning always messes with her sinuses.*

She pumped her bicycle harder, then slammed on the brakes at the driveway and almost lost her balance. As intense heat radiated from a blazing inferno at the end of the drive, she dropped her bike to the ground and stumbled her way to the porch. "Momma! Momma! Daddy!"

Holding onto the handrail, with eyes and throat burning, she dragged her weak leg up the steps and swung open the storm door. "Momma, Daddy, the garage is on fire. Where are you?" Panicking, tears streamed from her cheeks as she held onto the furniture and limped from room to room. Except for the soft strains of "Sweet Hour of Prayer" filtering from the Philco radio in the kitchen, the house was still.

Chapter Four

Wednesday, July 17, 1963

Trish sat drawing at the dining room table while her great-aunt, Mabel, cleaned up the kitchen. The events of the past month had been overwhelming for everyone. How would she have ever made it without Granny Rogers' only living sibling and the Martins next door? George Martin had taken over the lawn mowing, and his wife had helped with anything and everything—especially the grocery shopping.

Aunt Mabel entered the room while rubbing lotion on her hands and slathering it on her face. "Whew. The kitchen is closed." She peered over Trish's shoulder. "That's a swell picture you've got going there, darling. Didn't know you liked fishing."

"I don't, but Daddy did. This is for him. I'm gonna take it to his grave tomorrow and put it in the vase. It won't die like flowers." *Or people.*

"Whenever you finish up, why don't you get ready for bed and come watch the Lawrence Welk show with me?" She kissed Trish's hair, then walked into the living room and turned on the 19" black and white console TV. Heaving a big sigh, she plopped her rotund figure onto the couch.

"Okay. I'm almost done."

After scribbling, *I miss you, Daddy,* at the top of her drawing, she meticulously lined up the corners of the paper and folded it twice. Proud of her creation, she slipped it into an envelope, and dropped it into a dough bowl hewn by her daddy that sat in the center of the table. "Can I peek in on Momma before I get ready for bed?" She pulled open the bottom drawer of the sideboard and tucked her drawing tablet and colored pencils inside.

"If you promise to open the door quietly. I don't want you bothering her if she's asleep, you hear?"

"Yes, ma'am, I hear." Trish walked into the hall and eased open the door to her parents' bedroom.

Her momma looked up from her book, laid it in her lap, and reached out her hand. "Hi, pretty girl." She wiggled her fingers for Trish to come closer. "You all through with dinner?"

Nodding, she clasped her momma's hand, sat on the edge of the bed, and noted her plate on the TV tray. "Looks like you ate good tonight. You must feel better. Want some dessert? Aunt Mabel made a super duper custard pie for your homecoming. Your favorite."

"I know. She told me, and it sounds wonderful, but I think I'll save it for tomorrow and have a large slice—for breakfast, maybe." She giggled. "Does that sound good?" She smoothed Trish's hair. "Want to join me?"

"You bet."

She patted her daughter's hand. "Excellent. I'd love the company."

Trish peered into her momma's eyes. The second and third-degree burns over ten percent of her body were sure to leave permanent scars. But, despite her red and swollen skin, her crystal blue eyes sparkled. She was still beautiful.

Trish kissed the tip of her momma's slender nose. "I know you're tired. Aunt Mabel was afraid you'd be asleep, and I'd disturb you. I'm glad you weren't, so I could tell you goodnight. I love you, Momma, and I'm happy you're home. It's been hard here without you—and Daddy."

"I love you, too. It's good to be back where I belong. With you." She kissed Trish's cheek and squeezed her hand. "I know it's been difficult, but I'm proud of how you've pitched in and helped Aunt Mabel. I can tell you're going to make one fine nurse." She flashed a crooked smile. "Run along now and enjoy the rest of your evening. I'll see you tomorrow." She picked up her book and yawned. "After I finish this chapter, I'm calling it a night."

Trish laid her mother's empty glass on its side so it wouldn't topple, picked up her tray, and walked to the door. "You gonna be all right tonight without Daddy? I can sleep in here if you want me to."

"That's sweet, but I'll be okay. I need to adjust to him being gone. I might as well start now."

Trish nodded. "All right. Sleep tight."

"And don't let the bed bugs bite." Her mother giggled and waved. "Oh, and tell Aunt Mabel she can sleep in late tomorrow. Custard pie for two, it will be."

"Gotcha." She closed the door and thanked God for the flicker of light in her mother's eyes and for the soft sounds of laughter.

Trish placed her drawing in the vase in front of the granite headstone and sat on the bench across from it. "I sure hope you like it, Daddy. I did the best I could since I didn't exactly know what things looked like up there. I feel sure Heaven's got some huge fish, though. Have you caught the big one yet? I bet the big ones up there don't get away." Her smile faded, and tears bit at the rims of her eyes as she lowered her head and murmured. "I sure do miss having you down here." She swiped her wet cheeks, then lifted her chin and threw back her shoulders. "You'll be happy to know Momma came home yesterday." She paused. "Or maybe you already know. Anyway, she's got some healing to do, but she's gonna be fine." She nodded. "Yeah…just—"

"Is that you, Patricia Malone?"

Trish craned her neck and smiled at Billy Ray Jessup. "Sure is. What are you doing here?"

"Just cuttin' through from a friend's house. Headed over to the pier to see if they're catchin' any big ones today." He walked around the bench and smiled.

"Oh." Trish searched for words. Billy Ray would be a tenth grader, a year ahead of her in school. She'd noticed him several times in passing, but he never seemed to pay her any mind. The cute boys seldom did.

He smacked his bubble gum. "You havin' a good summer?"

She shook her head. "You haven't heard?"

"Heard? No, I guess not." He motioned toward the bench. "Care if I sit down?"

"Of course not." She slid over, heat rising in her cheeks.

Billy Ray took off his Southport ball cap, wiped the sweat from his close-shaven head, and plopped it back on. "What's going on with you?"

She motioned toward her daddy's gravestone. "We buried my daddy last month."

"Oh, no," he said, laying his hand on her shoulder. "I'm sorry, Trish. That's a bummer. What happened?"

She lowered her head and stared at the ground. "Our garage caught on fire, and he was inside. Momma, too."

His mouth gaped open, and his large brown eyes bulged. "What? You mean your momma's dead also?"

She shook her head. "No, but she was burned real bad. She just got home from the hospital yesterday."

"Wow. I'm glad she's home. That's some tough goin'." He kicked at a rock embedded in the ground with his soiled canvas sneaker. "How'd the fire start?"

Trish heaved a sigh. "Momma said Daddy was trying to start the lawnmower. She guessed ashes from his cigarette sparked the gas, and the mower blew up."

"Oh, no, that's horrible." He shook his head. "I really hate that for ya, girl."

"Yeah. Momma feels real bad because they were talking. She figures because she distracted Daddy, he forgot to stamp out his cigarette."

"What happened after the mower blew up?"

"Our neighbor tried to help, but the flames were too hot. The firemen pulled both of them out, but it wasn't soon enough for Daddy. Momma was standing farther away from the mower. She was unconscious when they rescued her, but alive."

"Gee. That's horrible. I don't know what to say."

"That's okay. There's not much to be said. It is what it is. With God's help, we're all just trying to make it through."

"God?" He snickered. "You believe in God?"

"Sure do. Don't you? I thought everybody did."

"Nah. Why would I? If there was a God up there who cares about us, he sure wouldn't have let something that terrible happen to your dad."

"Stop it, Billy Ray." She slapped her knee. "Don't say that. God's the only reason I'm sitting here today."

"Humph. So you say."

She shifted on the bench and glared at him. "He's also the reason you're here. God made us, ya know?"

He rolled his eyes. "Oh, boy. I suppose you think He made you have that crippled leg, too."

She dropped her chin and stuffed down words she'd never

thought of saying before.

Billy Ray scooted closer and put his arm around her. "I'm sorry, Trish. I didn't mean to hurt your feelins'."

She shrugged his hand from her shoulder and looked the other way. "Don't worry about it, okay?"

"It's all right, Trish. You can believe in your God if you want. You could be right, ya know. I just don't have time to stop and figure it all out. I'm doin' just fine like I am."

Trish sat silent.

He stood and wiped the sweat from his face with the back of his hand. "I guess I should be movin' along. See what's going on down at the pier and all."

She glanced up. "Okay. Nice of you to stop."

He nodded and threw up his hand as he shuffled off. "Maybe I'll see you at school this fall."

"Yeah. Maybe." Trish stared for a long time at her daddy's grave and listened to the warm breeze rustling the leaves overhead.

"Billy Ray *is* wrong, isn't he, Daddy? God *is* up there. Right?"

Chapter Five

Wednesday, March 22, 2023
Myrtle Beach, South Carolina

Olivia and Chase sat alone in an alcove a few doors down from Brooklyn's room at Grand Strand Medical Center. As they waited for Brooklyn's doctor to examine her, a nice-looking young man seated himself in a chair across from them. Within moments, Olivia struck up a conversation and asked if he had a relative in the hospital.

"No. A friend. Well, I can't say she's a friend, but I'm checking in on a young lady I found unconscious on the beach Monday. I want to make sure she's okay."

"Are you talking about Brooklyn Marshal?"

"I am."

"Oh, my goodness." Her eyes shot to Chase and then back to the man. "Are you Logan Corbett?"

He nodded. "I am."

Olivia jumped from her chair and extended her hand. "It's so good to meet you." She clasped his hand in both of hers and pumped it hard. "I'm Brooklyn's first cousin, Olivia Evans." She turned and graspedChase's arm. "And this is my husband, Chase."

"It's nice to meet you both."

Olivia moved to the chair beside him. "We can't thank you enough for finding Brooklyn. The doctors said if she'd lain on the beach much longer, she would have died."

"Wow. I'm glad I could be there for her." He lowered his eyes and continued with a quiet chuckle. "But if the truth is told, all credit must go to my golden retriever, Murphy. He led me to her." He peered into Olivia's eyes. "Is she going to be all right?"

She nodded. "Yes. Thanks to God and you…and, of course, Murphy."

He rubbed his forehead and sighed. "I'm so relieved to hear this. The detective called the day after he questioned me and said Ms. Marshal was going to live, but since I wasn't listed on her disclosure form, he couldn't give me any details. Do you mind if I ask what happened?"

"Not at all. After the nor'easter blew through the other night, Brooklyn wanted to check out the Kindred Spirit mailbox to see how it fared. Are you familiar with the mailbox?"

"I am. It's not far from my house."

"She'd ridden my bike, but—"

"A lavender one?"

"Yes."

"I saw it in the surf that afternoon."

"That morning, before Brooklyn left to go to the mailbox, she'd spent several hours cleaning the yard. About halfway to the box, she felt weak and remembered she hadn't eaten lunch or checked her blood sugar since breakfast. As a Type-1 Diabetic, she knew she needed to turn around and head home. She said she doesn't remember anything about passing out. Only remembers waking up in the hospital yesterday."

He shook his head. "Whew. I can't believe how close she was to death."

"I know. We're all so blessed." Olivia leaned back in her chair and crossed her legs. "So, Logan, you've not met Brooklyn, have you?"

"Other than seeing her that afternoon in the water, no. I'm sure I wouldn't recognize her now if I saw her." His dark eyes grew pensive as he blew out his cheeks. "She was a mess—soaked from head to toe, white as a sheet, and her hair was matted with sand. The whole experience was a nightmare." Shifting in his chair, he shook his head. "When I first saw her, I thought she was dead. I was relieved when I found a faint pulse and immediately called 911. This is the first I've heard that Brooklyn's a diabetic. Now, everything makes perfect sense."

Olivia laid her hand on his arm. "Well, Mr. Corbett, it sounds as if you deserve to meet my lovely first cousin."

His eyes widened. "Could I? I'd love to."

Brooklyn's doctor stepped into the waiting area. "You're free to go back in now. I'll let Ms. Marshal tell you what we discussed."

"Thank you, Dr. Reinhart," Chase said as the doctor hurried down the hall.

Olivia looked at Logan and motioned. "Come on. Let's surprise her. She'll be thrilled. She said she hoped she got to meet the man who found her." She tapped on Brooklyn's door. "Honey, it's me. Can we come in?"

Brooklyn

I scooted up in the bed and laid my book on the nightstand. "Of course."

Olivia pushed open the door of my room and entered with Chase and another man in tow. She tossed her purse on the chair beside my bed and gave me a warm hug. "You'll never guess who Chase and I found in the waiting room."

I studied the handsome stranger and smiled. "Hmm…I don't believe we've met."

Olivia grinned. "Sure you have."

It troubled me that I didn't recognize him. I rubbed my temples and wondered if the fog would ever lift. "I'm sorry, I don't recall. The best I can do is blame it on the bump to my head when I hit the ground." Embarrassed, I extended my hand. "Please, forgive me. My memory is still fuzzy."

The man clasped my hand with a firm grip and grinned. "Hi, Brooklyn. I think your cousin's playing a trick on you. You've never laid eyes on me—but I have you."

I peered into his dark brown eyes and dug deep into my thoughts. "Oh, are you…are you the man who found me? Are you Logan Corbett?"

He nodded and laughed. "Yep. All my life."

I chuckled and dropped my head back on the pillow. "Oh, goodness, I owe my life to you. I'm so grateful. If not for you, I'd be lying in a casket right now instead of this bed."

I was not only taken by this stranger's good looks but also by his quick sense of humor. "Why don't all of you have a seat? I'd love to hear Monday's events from Logan's perspective."

Logan and Chase sat on chairs at the foot of my bed while Olivia took the one beside me and laid her hand on my arm. "Before you hear his story, we want to hear what the doctor had to say."

I fluffed the pillow at my back and lifted my cup of water from the bedside table. "It's all good news. My numbers are stabilizing, and if I keep doing as well as I am now, I can go home tomorrow." Eyeing Olivia and Chase, I sipped my water. "And you two can leave for your honeymoon. Again."

Logan's eyes bulged. "Honeymoon? Again?"

I giggled. "Yes, poor things. The nor'easter and I made doubly sure they didn't go anywhere."

Olivia rolled her eyes. "Yes, there's nothing quite like

spending your honeymoon at Grand Strand Medical Center." While she explained the whole outlandish scenario to Logan, I observed my fine-looking visitor and noted he wasn't wearing a wedding band.

"Brooklyn? Are you still with us?"

I jolted and turned toward my cousin. "I'm sorry. My mind drifted. As I said, I'm still muddled. What were you saying?"

"I told Logan that I'm apprehensive about leaving the country after your episode."

I dismissed her comment. "Nonsense. My episode was totally my fault and could have been prevented had I eaten more that morning. I won't make that mistake again anytime soon, and I hope never. The last two days have opened my eyes to the seriousness of this disease."

"Good. We're glad to hear that. Chase and I have been worried sick about you."

"I'm sorry. I promise I'll be good from here on out."

Logan addressed Chase and Olivia. "What if I checked in on Brooklyn while you're away? Would that make you feel better?"

I blushed as Olivia was swift to approve. "Would you, really? That's an excellent idea." She cut her eyes to me. "Don't you think so, Brooklyn?"

I glanced at Logan and lowered my eyes. "I…I don't know what to say. Mr. Corbett is a very busy person, I'm sure."

He leaned forward. "You forget…it was my suggestion. Besides, I have a friend I'd like for you to meet."

Oh, perfect. My heart sank. *This guy's going to pawn me off to some lovelorn fellow who doesn't have enough nerve to ask for his own dates.*

"We met about five years ago and have been buddies ever since. I'm sure he'll love you."

But…will I love him? That's the better question. I squirmed.

"I don't know. I'm still not at my best. Maybe I could meet your friend another time."

The room erupted with laughter.

Feeling my face turn crimson, I took a long sip of my water and scooted down in my bed. "What?"

Olivia held her stomach and spewed her words. "Brooklyn, I'm sorry. We're being mean." She looked at Logan and smothered her laughter with her hand. "Go ahead. You tell her."

He shook his head and chuckled. "I'm sorry, too, Brooklyn. My friend's name is Murphy, and he's my golden retriever."

"Retriever? You mean a dog?" I slapped the bed covers. "You guys." I glared at Olivia. "Mean is not the word for it, cuz. Cruel would be more like it." I turned my attention back to Logan. "Seriously? Your dog?"

He nodded. "Oh, but Murphy is not just any dog. He's the hero of your story—the one responsible for saving your life."

Stunned, my mouth fell open. "What? You mean Murphy found me?"

Logan straightened in his seat and threw out his chest like a proud papa. "He did."

I sat mesmerized as he told me the story of that frightful afternoon and all of the events that followed. "Okay. You've convinced me. I must meet this amazing creature."

Logan nodded at Olivia. "There, that settles it. Murphy and I will pick up where we left off. We'll take care of Brooklyn while you're away. You two deserve a stress-free honeymoon." He shifted his eyes to me. "Deal?"

I grinned. "Deal. Please tell Murphy he's got a new forever friend, and I can't wait to meet him."

Chapter Six

Friday, March 24, 2023
Sunset Beach, North Carolina

"Good morning. Look at that baby." I walked across the porch, unhooked the screen, and swung open the door. "Come in. Come right on in here." Leaning over, I wrapped my arms around the big Golden retriever's neck and buried my face in his coat. "Murphy. You're beautiful." Taking his large face in my hands, I peered into his soft brown eyes and kissed his broad snout. "Muah. Muah. Thank you so much for finding me, sweet boy. Now, your wish is my command. Whatever you want, I'll get for you."

Logan laughed. "Wow, Murph. Aren't you the lucky one? I should have such an enthusiastic greeting."

Smiling, I straightened and offered my hand. "Let's see, sir, what was your name again?"

He gave me a limp handshake. "Corbett. Logan Corbett, ma'am. I belong to Murphy."

"Oh, yes. Forgive me. Any friend of Murphy's is a friend of mine." I tapped my finger on my lips. "Your name was right on the tip of my tongue, but…" I shrugged and pointed to my head. "Still fuzzy."

"Okay. We'll blame this one on brain fog, but next time, if you remember Murphy's name and not mine, I'm gonna be worried."

I looped my arm through his and led him into the kitchen.

"How about I make it up to you with a late-morning cup of coffee? I made a fresh pot."

"Would you happen to have cream and honey to go with it?"

"Yes. Wildflower honey in a squeezable bear bottle."

His eyes widened as he dropped onto the barstool. "Now that's class. How can I resist?"

I pulled the items from the cabinet, along with a large chew bone for Murphy, and passed it to Logan.

He held it up and laughed, "Whoa, boy. Look at this." As he stripped the cellophane from the bone, Murphy paced back and forth, his nails clicking on the hardwood floor. Logan handed it to him and rubbed the excited dog's head. "This should keep you busy for a while."

Murphy snatched the bone and trotted onto the porch. After dropping it at his feet, he lay in the sun and gnawed his reward while we fixed our coffee.

"Have you heard from Chase and Olivia?" Logan said as we seated ourselves in the porch rockers.

"Yes." I circled the rim of my mug with my finger. "We talked late last night. They had just checked into their hotel after a good flight. She said the weather should be sunny and warm there all week, so they're excited. Today, they go scuba diving. I'm jealous but really happy for them. They deserve it."

"They do." Logan sipped his coffee and gazed at the water. "This is a front-row seat to the greatest show on earth, don't you think?"

"I don't think…I know. Didn't you tell me you have an oceanfront house?"

"Yes. It's toward the end of West Main. Not far from Bird Island. I've owned it for seven years now."

"Where did you live before that?"

"In a small rental over on the mainland. I lived there for

five years after coming here from Conway. My cottage needed quite a bit of work before I could move in, but owning a place by the water was worth the wait."

"I know what you mean. Water is calming." She set her cup on the table between them and pointed to Murphy. "I believe he likes his bone, don't you?"

Logan laughed. "Yeah. He doesn't even know we're in the world right now."

"You mentioned Bird Island. I hate that I didn't make it to the Kindred Spirit the other day. I'm anxious to know if it weathered the storm."

"Well, that's an easy fix. We should go."

She shook her head. "Can't. Olivia put her foot down before she left. She said I was not to go to the box until she got back. When I told her that Dr. Reinhart ordered me to stay off a bike until after my two-week check-up, she was relieved."

Logan laid his head back on the chair. "We could walk. Murphy and I could go with you."

I scrunched my face. "I wouldn't have the strength. From here, it's close to three miles one way."

He drew a deep breath through clenched teeth. "Yeah, I'm afraid that would be too much of a hike for you right now. I wasn't thinking. I'm used to making the trek from my house." He hesitated, eyes widening. "That's it. My house. The Kindred Spirit is less than two miles from my place. Think you could handle that?"

I smiled. "I'm sure of it. Dr. Reinhart wants me to walk every day. Besides the distance, Olivia's main concern was me walking to the mailbox alone."

"I don't blame her, but it sounds like we just solved that problem. How about it? We could go today."

"I like the way you think, and the weather couldn't be more

perfect.”

He slapped his legs and stood. “What are we waiting for then? Let’s do it.”

Murphy jolted to his feet, grabbed his bone, and glared at us.

I laughed. “I don’t think we’ll have to twist his leg.”

“Nope. Big guy here is always ready for a road trip. Aren’t ya, Murph?”

The retriever shot to the door and shifted his eyes to Logan.

“You two go to the car. I’ll be right out.” In the bedroom, I dropped my phone in my fanny pack, slapped on my *Beach Hair, Don’t Care* ball cap, and grabbed my sunglasses. Catching my reflection in the dresser mirror, I winced and twisted my mouth. *Gloss.* After glazing my lips, I pursed them and slipped on my shades. “Okay…so I care.”

As Logan pulled his navy Jeep Grand Cherokee into the driveway, Murphy whined and paced from window to window. He barked, snapped up his bone, and wagged his tail. After Logan let him out, he opened my door. “Follow Murphy around to the back deck, and I’ll meet you there in a minute.” He ran up the front steps.

Before Murphy and I reached the top step, the back storm door slammed.

“That was quick.”

Logan lifted a metal detector and laughed. “I keep this baby locked and loaded by the door. I never pass up an opportunity to find hidden treasure after a storm.”

He handed me a mesh bag containing a stainless steel sand scoop and a small shovel. “Do you mind carrying this?”

"Not at all. I'll look like I know what I'm doing." I looped the bag over my shoulder and followed Murphy down the long boardwalk to the beach. As soon as Logan stepped onto the sand, he turned on the control box and slipped his arm through the cuff of the detector.

"I've never known a detectorist. Have you done this long?"

"Several years." He methodically moved the search coil back and forth over the sand as we walked. "When I was a kid, our family would come to Sunset Beach on vacation, and I'd treasure hunt with my uncle. After he died in 2019, my aunt gave me his detector. She said he wanted me to have it. I find looking for relics relaxing and entertaining, especially after a storm. You never know what the Old Man in the Sea will cough up."

As a gust of wind greeted us, I tugged on the brim of my ball cap and pulled it down tighter. "What kind of things have you found? Anything valuable?"

He chuckled. "Plenty of small change and a few rare coins, but most of the time, junk. Ring tabs from aluminum cans and stuff. I did help a friend find her silver anklet once. That was rewarding. It's a fun hobby, and it keeps me out of trouble."

Intrigued by my handsome new friend, I wanted to know everything about him. I was thankful for the distraction of our treasure hunt. It countered what could have been awkward pauses as we spent this time alone.

Logan stopped and looked up the beach. "We're not far now. You doing okay?"

"Yes. I'm fine. I love this."

He shielded his eyes from the sun and groaned. "I don't see the flag flying. I wonder if the wind took it out."

"Oh, no, don't say that. If that's true, I'm afraid the box will be down, too." I slipped off my sunglasses and squinted. "Maybe someone lowered it before the storm came through."

"Possibly."

I held my breath as we walked over the dune, then let out a sigh. "Look, Logan. It's standing. Thank goodness it made it through." I opened the mailbox, took out several journals, and plopped onto one of the benches. Logan sat beside me while Murphy sheltered underneath.

"Well, now ya know," he said, raking the sand with his shoe.

"Yep. Now I know, and it feels good." I laid my hand on his arm. "Thanks for coming with me. I can't wait to tell Olivia the Kindred Spirit is okay."

"I'm surprised, but I guess I shouldn't be. It's weathered a lot through the years." He pointed to the journal in my hands. "Interesting reading, huh?"

"Always."

"If you'd like to rest, you can sit here while I continue my search for pirates' treasure." He laughed, leaned over, and looked under the bench. "You going with me, big boy, or staying with Brooklyn?"

Murphy peered out with his dark, expressive eyes and whined.

"Yeah. Yeah. I know. The lady gives you one bone, and I now play second fiddle to her." He smiled. "Can't say that I blame him, though." He turned and walked toward the water. "I won't go far. Call my cell if you need me."

"I will. Good luck, Matey. I pray ye find yer fortune." My eyes followed Logan until he disappeared beyond the dune. Then, opening a notebook, I paged through and read. One entry in particular caught my eye and piqued my interest. I snapped a picture of it and lifted my eyes to the place where the sky touches the sea.

The last few years had been difficult. No…wrong. I'll be

honest. They'd been horrific. Never in a trillion years would I have dreamed my marriage would end in shambles—but then, I could never have imagined I'd find peace again, either. Coming back to my roots was the best decision I could have made. Sunset Beach will always be home, and my heart is truly at rest here. It's as if heaven came down and soothed my troubled soul. I wished the same for the person who'd jotted the entry.

After placing the journals back in the mailbox, I returned to the bench. Murphy poked his nose from underneath and snorted warm sand against my heel. "It's okay, fella. I'm not going anywhere. Your daddy will be back soon."

As the cool breeze brushed my skin, I yawned and stretched out on the bench. With my face to the sun, I welcomed its rays and allowed them to wrap me in their warm embrace. The tranquil lull of the waves cradled my worries, washed away my doubts, and reassured me that no matter how far my soul wandered, the sea would always be here to welcome me home.

Chapter Seven

When we returned to Logan's cottage, he propped his metal detector beside the door, hung his bag on a hook, and motioned toward the kitchen counter. "Have a seat at the bar while I feed Murphy, then I'll fix a couple of sandwiches. Does ham 'n Swiss sound good?"

"Sounds wonderful. Especially if you're making it."

"Yeah. Funny how even a sandwich tastes better when someone else makes it."

"That's so true." I nodded and looked around the open living space. "I love your house. It's beachy. Very comfortable. Did you decorate it?"

He chuckled. "Hardly. My sister did. She has a knack for it."

"I see that." I returned to the barstool. "Does she live at Sunset too?"

"No. Over on Bald Head. Her husband's a retired pilot."

"Awesome. I've always thought the island would be a wonderful place to retire."

"They love it, and I'm thrilled to have an excuse to visit." Logan placed Murphy's bowl on the floor, washed his hands, and made our sandwiches. "Wanna eat out on the deck?"

"Absolutely." I slid my stool under the bar and followed him to a wooden picnic table outside. "It's perfect out here."

He popped a potato chip into his mouth and sat across from me.

"Do you ever tire of living on the oceanfront?"

"Nope. The upkeep is tough, but this is where I want to be. To me, it's worth it." He sipped his soda. "Not sure how much longer I'll be able to stay here, though."

My spirit sank. "What? Are you moving?"

He wiped his mouth with his napkin and shrugged. "After Sunday night's storm, moving might be my only option." He pointed to the 50s cottage next door. "I also own that place The storm weakened its structure, and the inspector says that it would cost more to bring it up to code than to raze it and start over." He bit into his sandwich and talked around his chews. Murphy sat by his side and followed every hand-to-mouth movement, no doubt hoping a morsel would drop at his feet.

"I was set to close on it in a few weeks, but that's off now." He shook his head. "Just my luck. I bought it with the intention of selling it as soon as I renovated it. Had a buyer waiting in the wings, so I didn't take out insurance on the place. Dumb move. Now, I have an unlivable house, nothing left to invest, and a small loan to pay off. Unless I sell the house I live in, I can't even afford to level it without borrowing more money, and that's out of the question. At this point, I'm not sure what my next step is."

"Wow. I'm sorry. There appears to be more damage on this end of the beach. On our trek to the box today, I noticed quite a few houses lost their walkways. I'll pray you find a solution that doesn't involve selling your home."

He shook his head. "Thanks, but I don't know what that would be. I'll talk to my boss about it tomorrow. Maybe he'll have an idea." He stuffed the last of his sandwich into his mouth and chased it with soda. "Tell me about you. What made you decide to move to Sunset?"

I hesitated, then told him about my husband's affair. "The beach cottage has been a family vacation home since my childhood, and I'd intended to keep it that way until my marriage went south." Remembering better days, I chuckled. "My father used to say before we'd cross the bridge to the island, 'Drop your baggage here.' He wanted to keep our stays at Sunset as carefree as possible, so all of our troubles and worries were to be left on the mainland side of the bridge. "

"Smart man."

"I agree. Of course, we couldn't always honor his wishes, but for the most part, Sunset has been a place of respite and healing. It still is, but now, since it's my only home and all of my stuff comes with me, life isn't as simple as it used to be."

"I know what you mean, but an ocean breeze puts the mind at ease, right?"

I laughed. "Absolutely. Olivia did such a remarkable job remodeling the cottage that once I saw it, it was a no-brainer. I didn't want to leave. So…here I am."

His dark eyes pierced mine. "And I'm glad you are."

I smiled. "Thank you. Me too."

Our eyes remained locked until Logan stacked my plate on top of his and rose. "So…what now?"

"Wait," I said, reaching out. "Please sit back down. I have something I'd like to show you before we go in."

"Okay." He set our dishes back on the table and straddled the bench across from me.

I opened my phone, pulled up my last photo, and passed it to Logan. "I found this in one of the journals today."

Logan's eyes bulged, and his mouth fell open. "What is this?"

"A letter from a Ukrainian refugee."

He passed me my phone. "How do you know? Can you read it?"

"I went online and had it digitally translated."

"Ah…so what does it say?" He threw out his palm and shook his head. "No, wait. Let's sit where it's more comfortable, and you can read it to me." He led me to the chairs at the end of the walkway. Murphy followed.

I searched for the translation in my photos and read.

Thursday, March 16, 2023
Dear Kindred Spirit

I am a 29-year-old Ukrainian refugee who arrived in the United States in March of last year. After Putin invaded Ukraine in February, my husband Aleksander went to fight for our freedom alongside the Ukrainian military. He insisted that I use my active tourist visa to come to America and stay with his elderly cousin, Olena, who lives in the area. We believed that the war would be short and that I would soon return to Mariupol to meet him. This did not happen. The war in my homeland is still ongoing, and Russian troops took control of our beautiful city of Mariupol in May of last year. It is just a shell of its former self, and hundreds of thousands have either died or left the city.

Last month, I learned that my precious Aleksander was killed. I am so far removed from the reality of this war that it's hard for me to believe it's true. I am heartbroken and feel that nothing worse can happen, but it has. This week, Alexander's dear eighty-seven-year-old cousin passed away. I speak English poorly. She was my voice. My life. With a tourist visa, I am not allowed to work here. I don't have a social security number, a permit, or a driver's license, and I was evicted from the apartment where Olena

lived for several years. I have thirty days to find a place to live. I need a roof over my head and someone to help me learn to survive without my Aleksander, my Olena, and my homeland. Can you help me, indred spirit?
    Natalya

Logan lifted his eyes to mine. "Wow, that's heartbreaking."

"I know. I haven't been able to get her out of my mind since I read it. I wonder where she is and if she's found a home yet. I wish I could help her."

"Good luck. Her note gives you zero to go on."

"I know." I picked up my iced tea and followed Logan and Murphy into the house. Once again, the Kindred Spirit had played a role in connecting hearts.

Chapter Eight

Labor Day
Monday, September 9, 1963

Trish rose from her lawn chair, stepped to the edge of the Howe Street curb, and waved a small American flag over her head. "Look, Margo. Here come the majorettes. Isn't that your brother's girlfriend holding one side of the Dolphin banner?"

Her best friend, Margo Holmes, squeezed in next to her and staggered on her tiptoes. "Yeah, that's Cindy Chambers. Isn't she pretty?" Margo cheered and called out to her as Southport's band marched in formation to "When Johnny Comes Marching Home."

"Wow! Listen to those cool snares." Trish held her stomach. "I can feel the vibration in my gut."

Margo laughed. "I know. They're so good." She batted the air with her flag and sang at the top of her lungs. *"The girls will scream, the boys will shout, the ladies they will all turn out, and they'll all go mad when Johnny comes marching home."*

"That song always makes my soul sing." Trish loved all kinds of music, but patriotic songs were her favorite. She would give anything to play in the school's marching band but knew her limp would never allow it. She nudged Margo and pointed. "There. There he is. There's your brother."

"Yep. That's him." After spotting her older brother in the trombone section, she jumped up and down and hollered. "Way to go, Jamie." As the band passed, swinging their instruments from side to side, she whipped around toward Trish. "Doesn't he look handsome in his new uniform? And listen to them. They're the best, aren't they?"

"The best I've ever heard."

"Hey, Trish."

Feeling a tap on her shoulder, she turned, looked into Billy Ray's broad, toothy grin, and lowered her eyes. "Hey."

"You can do better than that, can't you?"

She shrugged and looked up. "What do you expect? You want me to jump up and down? The conversation we had a couple of months ago didn't go so well, remember?"

He nodded. "I do, and that's why I came over when I saw you here. After thinkin' about all that happened to you this summer, I felt like a heel for what I said. I'm sorry, Trish. I hope you'll forgive me."

She looked away. Then, knowing she needed to let go of her grudge, she blurted, "Yeah, I forgive you."

"Hmm. Doesn't sound convincing to me."

She lifted her gaze. "That might be because I've not convinced myself. Thanks for your apology, Billy Ray. It's hard for me to forget, but I promise I'll try."

"Would an ice cream cone help? They're selling them today over at Waterfront Park." His eyes pierced hers. "My treat."

She looked at her friend.

"Margo, you can come with us. I'll buy you both double scoop cones."

She smiled. "Thanks, Billy Ray, that's really nice of you, but I told Mom I'd come home right after the parade to help her get ready for the church picnic this afternoon." She smiled at Trish. "You go with Billy Ray. I'll carry your chair home."

"Are you sure?"

"Of course I am. Go on."

Trish hugged Margo. "Thanks. Tell Momma where I am, okay? And that I'll be home by three."

Billy Ray walked Trish to the corner of Howe and West Bay Streets and crossed over to the park at the mouth of the Cape Fear River—a saltwater estuary that emptied into the Atlantic Ocean. He pointed. "I see a swing by the waterfront. You grab it, and I'll get our cones. What flavor ya want?"

"Chocolate." She giggled. "Always chocolate."

"One scoop or two?"

"Well…I was going to say one, but since you're paying…" She tapped her index finger on her pursed lips. "Make that two," she said with a nervous laugh and limped toward the water.

Within minutes of her acquiring the swing, Billy Ray stood in front of her, holding a cone heaped with ice cream. "Peace?"

She grinned and nodded. "Peace."

He sat beside her and gave the swing a push. "It's pretty here, huh?"

"Yep. No matter what the weather, it always is. It's one of my favorite spots around here." She licked the melting cream from the sides of her cone and watched a colony of seagulls following a fishing trawler. The graceful scavengers took turns nosediving into the azure-blue waters for whatever morsel of dinner they could find. "What flavor of ice cream did you get?"

"Banana." Billy Ray gave the swing another push and let it go. "How was your first day of school on Friday?"

"Good."

"Whose homeroom are you in?"

"Mrs. Gray's."

He furrowed his brow. "Gray's? I had her in seventh. Didn't know she was teachin' high school classes now."

"Yeah, she switched. How about you? Who'd you get?"

He swallowed hard and wiped his mouth with his napkin.

"Mrs. Lockman."

"Oh." She shrugged. "Is she supposed to be good? I don't know any of the tenth-grade teachers."

"My brother had her. Said she was kinda strict, but he liked her okay. I guess I'll find out." He motioned toward her cone. "How's your ice cream?"

She widened her eyes and nodded. "Good. Really good. Thank you." She tilted her head, turned her cone, and licked it all the way around. "It melts fast out here in this heat, though, doesn't it?"

"You can say that again." He stuffed the last of his cone in his mouth and swiped at a drip on his shirt. After wiping his bulging cheeks and fingers, he wadded his napkin and tossed it into a nearby trash can.

She threw back her head and hollered, "Score. You're good. You gonna play basketball this year?"

"I'm gonna try out, but I don't think I'm good enough to make it."

"I bet you are." She finished her cone and handed him her napkin. "Here. Try this one."

He chuckled and wadded it into a tight ball. "Now you're making me nervous." He raised his arm and tossed it.

She clapped. "Slam dunk. See, I told ya. You're a shoo-in for the varsity team this year. Mark my words."

"Gee, I wish I believed in me as much as you do?"

"You practice. I'll pray."

He furrowed his brow. "You'll pray? About what?"

"That you make the team, silly?"

"Oh, yeah. Of course, you would."

She flashed a smile, then looked at her watch. "I suppose I should get back. Thanks for the ice cream. This has been fun."

"It has. You want me to walk you home?"

"Thanks, but I'm good. It's not that far, and besides, it's out of your way."

"Okay. If you're sure." He threw up his hand as he walked toward the street. "I'll probably see you at school. Hope you like your classes."

"Same for you." Trish watched until he turned the corner. *Billy Ray's not so bad after all. I'm glad we made up.*

Tuesday, September 10, 1963

Trish slid her tray from the lunch line and scanned the tables in the school cafeteria.

"Over here, Trish!"

She saw Margo waving her hands above her head and zigzagged her way past tables. Setting her tray on the table beside Margo's, she smiled at the girls across from her. "Hi, Elise. Rebecca."

"Hey," they said in unison.

Rebecca squirted ketchup onto her plate. "How do you like Mrs. Peace for English?"

"She seems nice. What do y'all think?"

Elise Phillips looked at her friend, Rebecca Cameron. "We like her. Rebecca's sister was in her class a few years ago and liked her a lot."

"That's good to hear." She turned to Margo. "How about you? Do you like her?"

She nodded. "I do."

Trish opened her carton of chocolate milk, dropped in the straw, and took a sip. "I'm starving." She looked at the fish sticks, mashed potatoes, and peas on her plate. "Not my favorite, but I'm so hungry I'll eat anything."

Rebecca swirled a fish stick in ketchup and bit into it. "I saw both of you at the parade yesterday. I was across the street in front of the barbershop. It was a great day, wasn't it?"

"Yes, and fun seeing Margo's brother in the band."

Elise elbowed Rebecca.

"Looked like you also had fun talking to someone else after the parade."

Trish felt a flush creep across her cheeks. "What do you mean?"

The girls giggled. "You know who we're talking about." Rebecca jerked her head a couple of times to the right and grinned.

Trish looked and saw Billy Ray sitting two tables over with a bunch of boys. "Oh, you mean Billy Ray?"

"Yes…Billy Ra-a-y," mimicked Elise.

"Oh, yeah. He came over to tell me he was sorry."

"Sorry?" they said, echoing one another.

"You know. About my Daddy and all." She looked at Margo, who kept her eyes glued to her plate.

Rebecca tapped her fork on her tray. "Well, he must have been really sorry to walk you to the park for an ice cream cone. You two got a thing for each other?"

"No." Grimacing, Trish blurted. "Good grief, he was just being nice. What are y'all doing spying on me, anyway?"

Elise looked surprised and shook her head. "We weren't spying on you. Just observing, that's all. Right, Rebecca?"

"Yep, that's right. Only observing."

Trish huffed and shoveled mashed potatoes into her mouth. "Well, quit making more of it than it was."

The girls glanced at one another, and Rebecca gave a quick, subtle nod.

Elise pushed her chair away from the table and tossed her napkin on her plate. "That's what you say. Maybe I should see what Billy Ray thinks."

"No, Elise, please." Trish moaned as she walked away. Turning to Margo, she pleaded. "Tell them."

Margo winced as she looked past her to the table full of boys. "I think it's too late."

Trish kept her head turned in the opposite direction and spoke through clenched teeth. "Why? What's she doing?"

Rebecca giggled. "She's whispering something to Billy Ray."

"Oh, no." Trish grabbed her water and gulped it, hoping to keep what threatened to come up—down. "What's he doing?"

Margo rested her elbow on the table, covered her mouth with her hand, and sighed. "They're all looking this way."

Tears flooded Trish's eyes as she grabbed her tray, and hurried toward the exit. Limping away with clouded vision, she failed to see a pile of books on the floor and careened face-first, hitting the ground with a crash. Her tray clattered to the linoleum floor, sending dishes skidding down the aisle.

An awkward silence crested like a wave across the cafeteria.

As if hollering from the bottom of a canyon, Trish heard Margo's frantic cry.

"Trish. Trish. Are you okay?" She collapsed beside her and pressed her cheek to the floor only inches from Trish's face.

Trish stared into her friend's frightened eyes and tried to focus. She winced as the skin on her forearms stung, and her good knee throbbed. She grasped Margo's hand, wishing she could melt into the floor. "I'm not sure, but I'm so embarrassed." She sobbed and felt a pat on her back.

"Trish, are you okay?"

At first, she didn't recognize the panicked voice, but when

asked a second time, she knew—*Billy Ray*. As he sat on the floor beside Margo, she could see the concern on his face.

"Do you think you can stand? Margo and I will help you up."

Inhaling, she winced. "I don't know. Maybe. Let me lie here a few more seconds." The soft rumble of voices around her increased.

Billy Ray stood. "Back up, y'all. Give her some air. We're gonna see if she can stand. You ready, Trish?"

"Yeah." She flinched as Margo and Billy Ray lifted her from the floor and brought her to a standing position. When he put his arm around her, she couldn't help but notice how good he smelled.

"Can you put weight on your feet?"

Trying to stand, she grimaced. "No, I don't think so. My good knee is really sore."

He looked at Margo. "Think you can help lift her?"

Billy Ray's friend, Paul McFarland, grabbed Margo's arm and pulled her aside. "Here. Let me do that. Trish, drape your arms over our shoulders, and we're going to carry you to the bench in the hall. Mrs. Donaldson, the school nurse, is right here. She'll take a look at you. Ready?"

She nodded.

As the two boys lifted her and carried her to the cushioned bench, whistles and applause exploded throughout the cafeteria. After settling her on the bench, Billy Ray sat beside her. "You're going to be okay, Trish. Margo and I will make sure you are."

"I wish I believed that as much as you do."

He looked into her eyes and chuckled. "I'll believe. You pray."

Chapter Nine

Wednesday, September 11, 1963

"I'll get it, Momma." At the chime of the bell, Trish limped from her room and opened the front door. A flush of adrenaline tingled through her body. "Billy Ray. What are you doing here?"

He stuffed his hands in his pockets and shuffled his feet as she unlatched the storm door and pushed it open. "I noticed you weren't at lunch today, so I thought I'd come by to see how you're doin'."

"That's mighty nice of you. Come on in." As he entered the living room, Trish stepped back and motioned toward her mother, seated on the sofa. "Momma, this is Billy Ray Jessup. He helped Margo pick me up yesterday when I fell in the cafeteria."

Jane Malone clicked off the television and extended her hand. "Oh yes. Come in and have a seat, young man. Trish told me all about how kind you were to her. Thank you."

"I was happy I could help, ma'am." He removed his Dolphin ball cap and sat in a chair across from her while Trish joined her on the sofa. He shifted his eyes to Trish. "So...you feelin' better?"

"I am. My knee is still sore, but it's lots better. I plan to be at school tomorrow."

He shook his head. "That's good."

The room fell silent.

Billy Ray coughed and cleared his throat. "Mrs. Malone, I'm real sorry about all that's happened to you. I mean, with your husband dyin' and all."

"Thank you, son. We're getting through it one day at a time."

"That's good." He nodded and fidgeted with his cap, then reached into his pocket. "I brought you something, Trish."

"Me? You did?"

"Yeah." He walked over and handed her a candy bar. "I know you like chocolate, so I stopped at the store on the way over and picked up a Mr. Goodbar."

She took the candy from him and smiled. "Thank you. Chocolate and peanuts are a match made in heaven. That's super thoughtful of you."

He glanced at Trish's mother. "I'm sorry, I didn't think to bring you one, Mrs. Malone."

"Oh, no. Don't worry about me. It's more than enough that you brought Trish something. You are a very kind young man."

He lowered his gaze to the floor. "Thanks. I was happy to do it, ma'am." He looked and motioned toward the door. "I guess I'd better be gettin' on home. Mom will be wonderin' where I am."

Trish rose and walked him across the room. As he pushed open the storm door, she said, "Billy Ray?"

He stopped. "Yeah?"

"Thank you. Thanks for everything."

"Sure." He gave her a quick hug, slapped his ball cap on his head, and stepped onto the front stoop. "I'll look for you in the cafeteria tomorrow. Maybe we can sit together."

Trish's stomach fluttered. *Did I hear right? Did one of the best-looking boys in the tenth grade just invite me to sit with him at lunch?* She smiled and nodded. "Uh, yeah. Yeah, sure. Maybe we can."

Thursday, September 12, 1963

Trish and Margo entered the cafeteria amid the scraping of dishes, clattering of trays, and the clinking of glasses and utensils. The shrill voices and high-pitched laughter of the lower-grade students rose as kids slammed their lunch boxes shut, scraped their chairs across the freshly waxed floors, and ran for the lines at the door. While boys pushed and shoved one another, prim and proper little girls waited and played rock-paper-scissors. Occasionally, an exasperated teacher's elevated voice would cut through the commotion with threats of staying after school and extra homework.

The two girls looked at one another and sighed. They welcomed their newly acquired upper-grade status as ninth graders and the opportunity to eat lunch in a more subdued atmosphere.

Trish scanned the room. As she grabbed a tray and pushed it along the stainless steel slider, she whispered. "I don't see Billy Ray, do you?"

"No, not yet, but once these screamin' meemie kids clear out, we'll find him." She reached for a bowl of peaches and cottage cheese.

Trish turned up her nose. "How do you stand that stuff? I gag just looking at it."

"Hush. Mind your own tray, and you won't have a problem." Margo waited and looked around the room while Trish picked up her dessert, then stopped beside her. She motioned with two quick tilts of her head. "Over there. Billy Ray's at a table by the windows. There's an empty chair beside him. I bet he's saving it for you."

Trish's heart fluttered. "You think?"

"Well, there's only one way to find out. I'll lead you by there and then sit a couple of tables over with Carrie and Mary Beth. I want to get to know them better, anyway."

Trish took a deep breath. "Okay. Go. I'm right behind you." She muttered to herself as they crossed the room. "You can do this, girl. You can. You really can." After Margo stopped to sit with the other girls, Trish put one foot in front of the other and walked on. Odd, the recurring clicks of her brace seemed louder than usual today. She stopped at the table filled with boys, except for the one empty chair, and squeaked out a greeting. "Hi, Billy Ray."

He looked up, and all eyes turned her way with looks of surprise. The table went silent. "Hey." His eyes shot to his friends, then back at Trish. "How ya doin'?"

"A lot better."

"Good. Glad to hear it." Tilting his chair back, he rocked and continued his conversation with a boy sitting across from him.

Trish backed away, her thoughts racing as she tried to make sense of her situation. "Have a nice day."

He threw up his hand. "Yeah. You too. Glad you're feelin' better." He glanced around. "Where's Margo?"

She motioned. "Over there."

"You not eatin' with her today?"

"Uh, yeah. I'm on my way."

"Good. Tell her I said hey."

"I will." Taking deep, steady breaths and trying not to cry, she squared her shoulders and walked toward her friend. Then, sliding her tray onto the table, she collapsed into the chair beside her.

Margo's eyes bulged. "What—what's with you? Why

aren't you eating with Billy Ray?"

Carrie and Mary Beth concurred. "Yeah, what happened?"

She shrugged. "I guess you'll have to ask him." Her insides trembled as she turned her back to the table of boys.

Trying to keep the appearance of their conversation low-key, Margo patted Trish's knee. "We're so sorry, Trish. What a jerk." She cut her eyes toward Billy Ray. "He seems unfazed that he might have hurt you. We won't let on that you expected anything from him." She motioned. "Go ahead, eat your lunch. We'll wait for you."

She shook her head. "I can't. I wouldn't be able to keep it down." She picked up her napkin and swiped a tear from her cheek. "I don't know why he bothered to come by my house yesterday and bring me candy. When we're alone, he's nice, but I guess it's all show. Let's face it, Billy Ray Jessup doesn't want to be seen with a crippled girl. Why would he when he can have any girl he wants? Especially if he gets on the basketball team. He'll have a whole squad of cheerleaders to pick from. I won't fall for his charade again."

"Hi, Trish. You mind if I sit here?"

She wiped her nose with her napkin, sniffed, and looked up into the clear blue eyes of Paul McFarland. "Paul. Uh, yeah. No…I mean, no, I don't mind. You can sit there."

He put his tray on the table beside hers, swung his leg over the back of the chair, and dropped into the seat. "It's good to see you. You feelin' okay now?"

"I'm still a little sore but lots better. Thanks for helping me the other day."

"Happy to." He tore open his milk carton, took several swallows, and wiped his mouth with his sleeve. "I've been wonderin' about you."

"You have?"

"Yeah." He devoured half his hot dog with one bite and mumbled. "That was a pretty mean fall. Lots of kids were worried about you."

"They were?"

He nodded and gulped down more of his milk.

Trish looked at Margo. "You know my friends, don't you?"

"Sure. Hi, y'all." He threw up his hand and then turned his attention back to Trish. "You coming to the football game tonight?"

"No. I help Momma get groceries on Fridays. By the time we get home, it's late."

"Oh. This is my brother's first year on the varsity team. Thought maybe if you were comin', you could sit with me and my parents."

"Thank you. That's nice, but I can't. Momma and I always listen to it on the radio when we get home, though. Tell your brother good luck and that I'll be listening for his name. I hope they win."

"Yeah. Me too." He wiped his mouth with his napkin and tossed it onto his tray. "Looks like it's about time for class. I'd better hurry." He looked at the other girls. "Bye, y'all."

"Bye, Paul."

Trish looked at Margo and widened her eyes.

Margo laughed. "Well, look at you. First, Billy Ray. Now, Paul." She looked at Carrie and Mary Beth and giggled. "Maybe we should all take a tumble."

Trish swatted her arm. "Hush. Next week, he won't even know I'm alive...just like Billy Ray."

"Oh, don't bet on it. Billy Ray had his eye on you the whole time Paul sat here talking. He was not happy."

She straightened in her seat. "Too bad. Serves him right." She looked at the clock on the wall and slid back her chair.

"Come on. We'd better get to class. We're going to be late." Trish stood, picked up her tray, and cut her eyes toward Billy Ray.

He smiled and waved.

She didn't.

Chapter Ten

Monday, April 3, 2023
Brooklyn

"Hey, lovebirds, are you home?"

Olivia swung open the door and put her index finger to her pursed lips. "We are, but Prince Charming isn't up yet. This is his last morning to sleep in before returning to Surf Daddy tomorrow."

"I'm sorry." I handed her a plate of my homemade chocolate chip cookies. "I can come back later."

"No, no." She waved me in. "Now is fine. I'm happy you're here." Olivia hugged me and set the cookies on the counter. "These look amazing, and so do you, by the way. You must feel better."

"Yes, lots. Thank you."

She lifted the carafe from the coffee maker. "I was about to pour myself a second cup. Will you join me?"

"Thanks, but I've had more than my share this morning." I slid a chair from the counter.

Olivia shook her head. "No. Not there. Let's walk on the beach. After spending most of yesterday in the air and in airports, I need the exercise."

"Sounds good to me. I'm always up for a stroll."

She twisted the top onto her mug and swiped a cookie from the plate. "Want one?" She pushed the temptation my way.

I twisted my mouth. "All right. Maybe one … since you insist."

Olivia eased the screen door shut, and we slid off our shoes. "Chase and I had a fabulous time on our trip, but there's nothing like coming home again. Nothing beats this Carolina blue sky and air." She kicked at the water as we walked in the surf. "How is everyone? Anything exciting happen on the island while we were away?"

"As per the island, I don't know. I've been a little out of the loop. When I go back to work on Wednesday, I'll hear it all, I'm sure. Courtney's been great. She wanted me to rest and take my time coming back, so I made the most of her offer. I've sorted through the last of Mother's things, plus…" I tilted my head and grinned.

"Plus, what?"

I waved her question off. "No. This isn't about me. I want to hear about your trip. Turks and Caicos must be gorgeous."

"Beyond gorgeous, and the weather was perfect. Eighty-two degrees with balmy ocean breezes. Truly a paradise."

Walking beside Olivia and listening to her share her stories swept me back to our teenage years—days when we'd walk along the water's edge and talk about our dreams for the future. Now, we were living that future. Some of it had been good, some not, and some better than hoped for, but one thing was certain…the ties between Olivia and me had only grown stronger.

"There now, I've talked enough. It's your turn to tell me what your *plus* meant."

I waded through the cool water, searching for the right words. "Now, I don't want you to make a big deal out of this. Well…not yet, anyway."

"What? Don't keep me in suspense. Spill it, girl."

"Logan walked with me to the box on Friday. He's super nice. Even made me lunch at his place afterward."

She shrieked and grabbed my arm. "Brooklyn, I—"

Stopping, I turned to her. "There you go. Settle down. We—"

"So, did he kiss you?"

I rolled my eyes and resumed walking. "Stop it. No, he didn't kiss me."

"Did you want him to?"

I slapped my hand to my forehead. "Good grief. We're just getting to know one another." I shook my head. "I knew I shouldn't have told you this soon."

Olivia put her arm around me and pulled me to her side. "I'm sorry. I promise I'll chill. I'm excited for you and want you to be happy, that's all. You've been through a lot and deserve a good man. Logan seems like such a nice guy, and do I even need to mention his looks? Goodness, Brooklyn, don't you dare let this one get away."

I pushed her into the surf and kicked the water. "Why, Olivia, if I didn't know better, I'd think you approve of this relationship. Believe me, I hear you, but it takes two to make it work. There are no guarantees here."

"I know, but I'm happy about the prospect." Olivia slipped her scrunchie from her wrist and twisted her hair into a ponytail. "Are you ready to walk back? Chase should be up by now."

"Yeah, and he's probably devoured the whole plate of cookies."

She grinned. "You know him well, don't you?"

A couple of days later, I slipped the last of the new books on the shelves, tossed the box in the storage room, and walked to the counter. "What's next, boss lady?"

Courtney turned and handed me a cup of my favorite brew.

"Pull up a chair on the porch and take a break. I'm afraid you're pushing yourself too hard."

"I don't think so, but thank you." I inhaled the chocolaty aroma as I made my way to the rockers. "Can you join me?"

"If no one else comes in during the next few minutes, I'll do just that. It's gorgeous out there."

"Wonderful. We need to catch up." After taking a seat on one of the rockers, I propped my feet on the rail and sighed. *And they call this work? How blessed can one girl be?* I sipped my coffee, laid my head back, and struggled to stay awake.

"Ahem."

My eyes popped open as I jumped and dropped my feet to the floor.

Logan laughed. "Wow! Asleep at your post again? Do they have any job openings around here? This looks like my kind of work." He slid over a rocker, angled it toward me, and took a seat.

I looked at my watch. "Wow, I guess I was more tired than I thought. Courtney felt I was overdoing it and insisted I take a break. I suppose she was right." I set my empty cup on the rail. "What brings you here?"

He grinned. "My ferocious appetite for reading?"

I cut my eyes at him. "Um…how long has it been, Mr. Corbett, since you even cracked open a book?"

"Oh…" He twisted his mouth and tilted his head. "I don't think I can remember back that far."

I laughed. "Now that rings true."

"Wanna hear another truth?"

"Sure." I pushed my feet against the rail and rocked.

"I came to see you."

I peered at him. "Oh, you did? What can I attribute my good fortune to?"

"You just being you."

My insides tingled as I felt heat rise in my cheeks. "Thank you. You're kind."

He leaned forward in his chair, laid his hand on my arm, and peered into my eyes. "I couldn't wait to tell you the news."

I stopped rocking and turned my chair toward his. "And I can't wait to hear it. What is it?"

"I don't have to move."

I clapped my hands to my mouth. "Seriously?"

"Seriously."

My heart raced. "Hurry up. Tell me everything your boss said."

He leaned back in his chair and rocked. "It couldn't have gone better. Rick, who knows the value of the property my house sits on, said that because of my loyalty and record with the company for the past twelve years, three of which I've been top salesman, he would stand with me and provide whatever I needed. He's offered to either buy the property outright or loan me the money, interest-free, to raze the house. He said we could settle up whenever the property sold."

I sat on the edge of my chair, my mouth wide open. "Oh, Logan. What a saint Rick is." I jumped from my chair and hugged him. "I'm so happy for you. I know his offer has lifted a huge weight from your shoulders."

He pulled me into his lap and laughed. "Yep! The weight has shifted for sure."

Taken off guard, I sat stunned.

"Sorry, Brooklyn. I couldn't resist the setup." He kissed me on the cheek. "Forgive me? I was out of line."

"Hmm…doesn't the Bible say if someone kisses you on the right cheek, you are to offer the other cheek as well?"

His dark eyes grew large as he tried to suppress a grin. "That's not exactly what my Bible says, but I like your version better." He leaned in and kissed my other cheek. "Forgiven?"

I smiled. "Absolutely." I returned to my rocker. "So, have you decided on which of the offers you'll take?"

He shook his head. "Gonna pray about it. I can't lose with either one. I'm to let Rick know by Friday."

"I know you'll make the right decision."

"Thanks. Your confidence in me means a lot."

Chapter Eleven

Friday, December 20, 1963

Trish approached the white frame building on Howe Street, swung open the screen advertising Hershey's Chocolate Syrup, and pushed on the weathered door, its faded green paint cracked and peeling. A small bell above her head jingled, announcing her entrance into Willie McKenzie's Ice Cream Parlor.

"Welcome, Miz Trish. How ya doin' today?"

"I'm good, Mister Willie. Even better now that I'm out of the cold. It's nice 'n toasty in here." She headed straight for the radiator, past tables of lunch customers and shelves lined with Miss Anna's homemade relishes, jellies, and jams. After pulling off her gloves, she stuffed them into the pockets of her wool jacket and warmed her hands.

"What brings you in all by yourself?" The aging Black man swiped a green and white checkered towel across the massive granite and white marble soda fountain, then draped it on a hook behind him.

"I slipped away to Leggett's to pick up a Christmas present for Momma." She flashed a broad smile. "Now I'm here for one of your grape sherbets, Mister Willie."

His large brown eyes widened. "Oh, ya are? What if I was to tell ya I'm slap out of grape syrup?"

Trish boosted herself onto the wrought iron ice cream chair, then pressed her hand against the marble counter and whirled herself around. "Oh, no. You can't be." She shook her head.

"That's not fair. I've looked forward to this all day."

He held up his palm. "Whoa. Hold yer horses, young lady, and I'll fix ya one." He scooped ice into the electric shaver and pressed the button.

Trish shouted above the whir of the machine. "Wait, Mr. Willie. I'm confused. I thought you said you were out of grape syrup."

He released the button and turned around. "When did I say that?"

She scrunched her face and shrugged. "Uh. A minute ago."

"Did not," he said, scooping ice into a paper cone.

"But—"

He turned and pointed to the bottles of colorful syrups lined up in front of a large mirror spanning the width of the mahogany storage cabinets. "What I said was, 'What *if*... I was to tell ya, I'm slap out of grape syrup?' Never said I was out." He tilted back his head and let out a deep belly laugh. "Guess I gotcha on that one, Miz Trish. Yep. Sure did."

She squinted her eyes and frowned. "That's not nice, Mr. Willie."

He drizzled grape syrup over the shaved ice and handed her the paper cone. "Merry Christmas, Miz Trish. My treat. Does that bit of nice make up for it?"

She grinned and chomped into the ice. "Mmm…yeth it does." She shivered as the cold ice slid over her tongue and down her throat.

"Better watch it there, missy. You'll get a brain freeze."

"I know, but it's so good." She reached across the counter, pulled a napkin from the stainless holder, and wiped the purple liquid from her mouth. "Thank you very much. I don't care if it is thirty-five degrees outside. It tastes as delicious in the winter as it does in the summer."

He took a lunch receipt from a customer and walked to the register. "That'll be $3.25, sir."

Trish filled her mouth with the last of her cold treat, sipped the syrup through the bottom of the paper cone, and crushed it. Then, sliding off the swivel chair, she steadied herself and moved toward the shelves, her brace clanking. Thanks to Mister Willie's kindness, she now had enough change to buy her momma her favorite treat—Brown Dogs, a chocolate and peanut confection straight from Miss Anna's kitchen.

After picking up a small bag, she returned to the counter. "Thanks again, Mister Willie," she said, handing him the change to cover the bag of candy. "This will be an added surprise for Momma on Christmas morning."

He laughed. "You mean if you can stay out of it for ten more days."

She shook her head and brushed off his comment with a dismissive wave. "It'll be hard, but I can do it. I hope you and Miss Anna have a Merry Christmas."

"Same to you, Miz Trish. Give your momma best wishes from Anna and me for a wonderful Christmas and a blessed New Year."

"Sure will." She turned to leave, then jumped back as the bell jingled and Billy Ray Jessup burst through the door. Her heart leaped as her mind raced. She swallowed hard.

The boy who made her head swoon stopped in front of her and smiled. "Hi, Trish. You headed out?"

She nodded and rushed past him.

He grasped her arm. "Please don't go. I saw your bike outside and came in specially to see you."

She slowly turned. "Momma will wonder where I am."

"I won't keep you long. I promise." He motioned. "Come sit with me for a few minutes. I need to tell you something."

She hesitated, then walked a smidge ahead of him as he laid his hand on her back and ushered her to one of the small round tables. As he pulled out her chair, she eased herself into the seat and followed him with her eyes. Her throat tightened. *What on earth....*

He sat across from her and leaned back in the wrought iron chair that appeared much too small for his large frame. "How ya been doin'?"

"Okay," she said, laying the small bags containing her mother's gifts on the table.

"I know you don't know what to think of this, seeing as how I was rude to you a couple of months ago."

She glared at him.

He fiddled with the salt and pepper shakers, circling one around the other. "That's why when I saw your bike propped against the wall outside, I made a point to come in. No mistakin' that lavender bike." He released a nervous laugh.

She didn't move.

"Trish, you're not making this easy." He squirmed. "I want to apologize and explain."

She smirked. "You're getting rather good at this apologizing thing, aren't you? Have you ever thought that being nice might be a better idea? Then no apologies would be necessary?"

He lowered his eyes and brushed salt from the table.

"I know you're ashamed to be seen with me when you're with your friends. That's pretty apparent."

He shook his head. "No. No. That's not it. That's not it at all."

She rolled her eyes. "Seriously? I wasn't born yesterday, you know."

He slid the shakers back in their place, straightened the

napkin holder, and leaned in. "I'm sure it seems like that, but the real reason I brushed you off that day was because my mother told me not to get involved with you."

She pressed her lips together and nodded. "Oh. And that's supposed to make me feel better?"

"No. It's to say I'm sorry and that I need to do what my mother says. If the guys see me talking to you and think I like you, it could get back to her."

"So why doesn't she like—oh, that's a stupid question. She doesn't want her handsome, athletic son to be seen with a cripple."

He winced, then shrugged. "Her reasons aren't good, Trish, but I want you to know I like you. I like you a lot, but I have to obey my mother. After all, I live under my parents' roof."

Trish lowered her head.

He inched his hand across the table and touched her fingers. "I'm sorry. It stinks, but I didn't want you to think it was what I wanted. You're the kindest and sweetest girl I know. Pretty too. I want to get to know you better, but for now, I can't let on like I care about you."

She lifted her eyes to his and nodded. "I understand. Thanks for telling me. It does make me feel better about you. I like you, and I couldn't figure out what I'd done to upset you."

"Maybe someday Mother will change her mind."

"Yeah, but by the time she does, you'll probably have changed yours. Found some cute, perky cheerleader or something." She leaned back in her seat and folded her arms. "I saw you made the basketball team."

His eyes reflected his pride as a broad smile spread across his face. "Yeah, I did."

"See. I said you would."

"I know. I thought about that when the coach called my name."

"You did?"

He nodded, his dark eyes meeting hers. "I love how you believe in me, Trish. It means a lot. I believe in you also. Thanks for sitting with me and giving me a chance to explain."

"I'm glad I did." She squirmed and picked up her purchases from the table. "I really need to go. Momma will be worried."

Billy Ray walked her outside. "I hope you have a good Christmas."

She pulled her bike away from the wall and put her bags in the basket. "Thanks. The same to you."

He stepped away, then stopped and turned. "Hey, Trish?"

"Yes?"

"When school starts back, I'd love for you to come to a game and watch me play."

Her eyes widened. "You would?"

"I would."

She smiled. "Thanks. Maybe I can do that." She straddled her bike and pushed off. "Merry Christmas, Billy Ray."

"Merry Christmas."

Dazed by her unexpected conversation with Billy, she replayed his sweet words and remembered the warmth of his fingers on hers. Pedaling to the intersection, she glanced both ways and pushed through. Then, looking again to the left, she shrieked. Every muscle in her body tensed as tires squalled, metal crunched beneath her, and the car's impact sent her skidding across the pavement and crashing into the curb. Screams erupted, then melted into the distance.

All went black.

Billy Ray thrust his balled fist in the air and yelled as the car sped away, then gasping, pressed through the crowd surrounding Trish. People froze, mouths gaping, eyes bulging. "For goodness sake, somebody call for help." Horrified, he fell to his knees and hollered her name as blood spilled from her head to the pavement and color drained from her face. He grimaced, grabbed her hand, and dropped his chin to his chest. *Lord, if you're real. If you can hear me. If you care about us down here at all. Please...don't let Trish die. Help her to be okay. She doesn't deserve this. I should've— I'm the one who—"*

"Move. Get out of the way, son."

He jolted and looked up, tears streaming down his cheeks. Through clouded eyes, he peered at two rescue personnel. "Oh, sorry—" He backed away and dropped onto the curb. Swiping his cheeks with trembling hands, he closed his eyes and took long, deep breaths.

"You all right, boy?"

He jumped as a hand squeezed his shoulder. "Been better," he mumbled, looking up into Mister Willie's troubled and compassionate eyes.

The broad-chested man put his arm around Billy Ray and dropped to the curb beside him. "I saw you come into the shop and sit with Trish. So...she's a friend of yours? A relative?"

"A friend, sir—a very special one."

"I understand. Everyone who's had the pleasure of meeting Miz Trish knows how special she is." He rubbed Billy Ray's back. "Want you to know...Miz Anna and me...we'll be prayin' for her."

"Thanks. I'm not convinced the Lord hears mine." His words that followed were low and muffled. "Can't say that I blame Him, though."

They both sat stunned as the attendants placed Trish's motionless body onto the gurney and slid her into the ambulance to carry her to Dosher Memorial. One of the men stooped to get information from Billy Ray before climbing in behind her and closing the door. Afterward, the other attendant jumped into the driver's side of the vehicle and sped away.

Billy Ray followed the flashing red light with blurry eyes until the ambulance turned off of Howe Street. Sighing, he rose and picked up Trish's bags from the pavement.

Willie followed him. "Did you walk here, son?"

"Yes, sir."

"You gonna be okay? I'd be happy to close the shop for a bit and take you home."

"Thanks. That's mighty kind of you, but I'll be fine. You've got a business to run, and besides…I could use the time to sort through my thoughts." He stooped down and examined the bent wheel on Trish's bike, then walked over to one of the law officers. "Do you mind if I take my friend's bicycle home with me, sir?"

The broad-shouldered, middle-aged policeman smiled. "Can't yet. We're still examining the scene. Tell your friend we'll keep it safe for her at the police station. Whenever she's ready for it, it'll be there."

Billy Ray nodded. "Good enough, sir." He stepped away, then turned and held up the small bags. "Oh, is it okay if I take these with me? They were in her basket."

The police officer took them and looked inside before handing them back. "Sure. You're free to take her personal things." He locked eyes with Billy Ray. "I hope your friend gets along okay, son."

He nodded. "Thank you. I'm believin' she will—and prayin'."

Chapter Twelve

Wednesday, April 5, 2023
Brooklyn

Unwinding after my first day back at work, I laid my book on the towel, drew my knees to my chest, and inhaled the evening's fragile beauty. As the sun sank in the lavender sky, the sea mirrored its delicate hues while wispy white clouds tinged with pink danced above as if taunting the sea with their beauty. My eyes followed the graceful movement of a lone gull. Its wings caught the last rays of sunlight as it dipped near the water's edge, where a couple strolled hand in hand. Surrendering to the gentle lap of waves, I closed my eyes, dug my toes into the moist sand, and listened to the soft, melodious sounds of nature's lullaby.

As day slipped into twilight, a Psalm resonated in my spirit. It had kept me afloat and rocked me to sleep more nights than I could count. *Weeping may endure for a night, but joy comes in the morning.* My life had taken a dramatic turn, a course I welcomed. Yes, morning *had* come accompanied by joy. I loved this new season of my life, a sharp contrast to the turbulence of my past.

Thinking I heard my name filter through the breeze, I turned my ear to the houses behind me. Twisting my body, I saw a lone figure, silhouetted by my yard light, walking toward me. Still unable to make out the person's features, I recognized their stride, and the hair on my arms stood on end. Then came the voice. One I hadn't heard in a while. One I didn't want to hear now and one I hoped I would never hear again. I turned my head toward the water and tried to push back dark images that invaded my mind. *Jesus, why? Why now? What do I do? Where do I run? Olivia and Chase are in Wilmington.*

The repugnant stench of alcohol filtered through the balmy breeze and penetrated my space. My most dreaded nightmare had emerged from the mist. Wes dropped onto the sand beside me and leaned in. I jerked my head in the opposite direction. His hot breath, reeking of stale beer, brushed the nape of my neck and sent chills down my spine.

"Brookie"

I hated it when he called me that. There was something about the way he said it. I despised him.

"I hoped you'd be happy to see me."

My body trembled as he placed fingers like a talon around the top of my head and turned my face toward his. His eyes, now only inches from mine, were blacker than I remembered. Their only spark was the glint from the yard light. My insides roiled at the familiarity of the moment, and I bolted.

As I dashed toward the house, he blocked me. I spun on my heels and ran down the beach, my eyes searching the darkness for someone, anyone, who could rescue me from this beast. We were alone, and I could hear and feel his heavy footsteps pounding the wet sand behind me. When he grabbed my arm, my knees buckled, and I squealed. He pulled me into the dry sand and pushed me to the ground. Dropping beside me, he squeezed my arm tighter, making it impossible for me to pull away. From past experience, I knew it would be best if I froze. I tried to catch my breath and prayed my heart wouldn't rupture.

He ran his fingers through my hair, combing it away from my face. "There, now, isn't that better? We can have a nice little chat in the moonlight." He stroked my cheek.

My skin crawled at his touch, and I said nothing.

He turned my face toward his. "Brookie, has the cat got your tongue?"

I closed my eyes and swallowed hard.

"Really, I'm not here to hurt you. I just needed to see you. I miss you, Brooklyn."

I stared out at the water and prayed for a tsunami to carry me away.

He stroked the top of my hand and lifted my ring finger. "I guess it was silly to think it might still be there."

I glared at him and spoke through clenched teeth. "We're divorced. Remember?"

"I'm afraid I do." His voice broke, and he brushed his cheek with the back of his hand. "My biggest regret. I've never loved anyone like I love you, Brookie."

I grunted. "I would certainly hope not. No one deserves your kind of love." I blasted him. "And you certainly don't deserve mine."

As I tried to wriggle my hand from his grip, he squeezed it tighter and pleaded. "No, please, just give me a moment. I want to apologize."

"What? For the trillionth time? Your words mean nothing to me. Besides, you're drunk as a skunk. You won't remember anything you say tomorrow and will fall right back into the gutter where you've lived for years."

He let go of my hand and sat up, sullen. Then, pulling his legs to his chest, he wrapped his arms around them and dropped his forehead to his knees. "I know you're right. You always were. You said I'd regret losing you, and I do. You were the best thing that ever happened to me." He lifted his head and turned his body to face me. "Brooklyn, will you give me another chance?"

I sat stunned, then laughed in his face. "You've got to be

kidding me. Did you come all the way from Raleigh in your condition to ask me that?"

He nodded. "I did."

"You should have called first. I could have saved you the gas."

He reached for my hand, and I smacked it.

"Ouch!" He said, yanking it away. "That hurt, but not as much as your unkind words."

I rolled my eyes. "Do you think I care? Wes Marshal, pick your body up from this beach and don't ever come back. This is my home now. I came here to get away from you, and I don't want your stink anywhere near it."

He straightened his back and glared at me without saying a word for what seemed like forever. "Okay," he said, rising to his feet. "I'll leave."

I stood and walked toward the house, feeling his ominous presence as he followed. When I reached for the screen door, he grabbed my arm. "You are going to invite me in, aren't you?"

I sneered. "Are you serious? Why would I do that? Didn't you hear what I said? I told you to leave."

"I know. I will, but can I use your bathroom first?"

I twisted my arm from his grasp, yanked open the screen, and slammed it behind me. Latching it, I said, "The great outdoors is behind you. Figure it out."

I opened my eyes, stared up at the rotating ceiling fan, and questioned why I was not in my bed. Within moments, the horror of the previous night flooded in, and my heart pounded. I shot from the sofa and rushed to the window. After peeking through the blinds, I raced through every room in the house and did the same. Although the sun was shining, the storm in my spirit raged on. There was no external sign of Wes Marshal, but he remained alive and well in my head. *Where did he go? Did he go home? Would he come back?* I called Olivia and asked her to come over. Within minutes, she was by my side.

"Here, drink this." She walked from the kitchen and handed me a mug of hot Chamomile tea. After covering my legs with a throw, she sat beside me on the couch. "I'm so sorry we weren't here for you, honey. It was past midnight before we got home. I can't imagine how afraid you were."

I shook my head and stared out at the sea. "I have felt so safe here. Now…now, I don't know."

She stroked my hair. "It sounds like you handled things well and made yourself clear. I doubt Wes will return."

"I hope you're probably right." I sipped my tea and held the warm mug to my chest. "Mmm. This is so good. It's just what I needed. Thank you."

"What are your plans for today? Are you working?"

I looked at my watch. "Yes. I go in this afternoon at three, but Logan asked me to come by his house first. He's made a decision about his property next door and wants to tell me about it."

"Good. I'm glad you have something to occupy your mind today. It will be challenging at first, but I believe you'll feel better with each passing day. And you know, we're right next door. You can stay at our house anytime you want."

I smiled. "Yes, I know I can. Thank you."

Chapter Thirteen

"Brooklyn, I'm over here."

From Logan's front porch, I looked into the yard next door and waved. Murphy bounded toward me and met me at the foot of the steps. After he nuzzled my hand, I gave him a kiss on his noggin, and he accompanied me across the drive toward Logan. "What's up? I can't wait to hear?"

Logan hugged me and led me to a glider swing in the backyard, facing the ocean. "Have a seat, beautiful. I have something I want to show you. I need your opinion." He sat next to me and passed me his clipboard. "Take a look at these and tell me which one you like best?"

As I fingered through several one-story beach house plans, he reached over and yanked a sheet from the board.

"Oops," he said, wadding it up. "I didn't realize I'd left that one in the mix. It's no longer in the running."

After narrowing the stack down to three favorites, I struggled to make a decision. "Hmm…it's a hard choice, but I believe I'll go with this one." I passed Logan the sheet showing the 1500-square-foot Windjammer with three bedrooms and two bathrooms. "How'd I do?"

He grinned and patted my back. "Excellent. That's one of my favorites, too. A spacious open floor plan, yet modest and affordable." He gave the glider a push. "I like your style."

I passed him the clipboard. "Well, in light of what you showed me, I assume you took Rick up on his loan offer."

"I did. Starting from scratch on this place will be a huge task, but I've never shied away from hard work, and I'm ready to go. I'd rather rebuild than not get full value for my property."

"I understand that. Sounds like you've made a wise decision."

"Hope so." He lifted his ball cap, wiped the sweat from his forehead with the back of his arm, and plopped his cap back on his head. "It's steaming out here. Let's walk over to my place and get something cold to drink."

I checked my watch. "That sounds good, but I'm expected at Coffee Chronicles in about forty-five minutes."

He offered me his hand. "That's doable." As we walked toward the driveway, Logan raised his arm and pulled it back over his shoulder.

Murky images exploded in my mind. I screamed and ran— then stopped. Embarrassed, I dropped my head in my hands and breathed deeply. Murphy whimpered at my feet.

With a tender grip, Logan clasped my shoulders and turned me around. "Brooklyn, what's the matter? I was aiming for the trash can under the house. Just throwing away the sketch." He lifted my chin. "What did you think I was going to do? Hit you?"

I fell against his chest and cried. "Logan, I'm sorry. I don't know what to say. I didn't think. I just reacted."

He stroked my hair. "Sweetie, I'm so sorry. Come on. Let's go inside where it's cool, and I'll get us something to drink. Then, if you want, you can tell me about it." He led me across the drive and into the house.

I grappled with my emotions as I eased myself onto the sofa and watched Logan pour two tall glasses of tea. My physical attraction to him was understandable, but did my affection for him run deeper than his appearance? Was it greater than my intense gratitude for him saving my life?

My experience with Wes on the beach had caused me to second-guess my readiness to move into another relationship, and my reaction to Logan moments ago confirmed my suspicion. In my heart of hearts, I believed he was a safe place to fall, but my emotions had betrayed me before. It wasn't easy for me to trust again, but I chose to remember Olivia's advice and tried to cling to it. *You don't have to build a fortress, only a shelter—a place where love can take root and thrive.*

Logan sat beside me and handed me a glass of tea wrapped in a Pittsburgh Steelers napkin. "It's probably not as good as yours, but at least it's cold."

I sipped it and smiled. "It's perfect." I turned to face him, subtly widening the space between us.

"Do you want to talk about what happened outside?"

"Not really, but I know I should." As a painful lump rose in my throat, I took a deep breath and peered into his kind eyes. "I know my reaction startled you. I'm sorry. It stunned me. When it comes to healing from my disastrous marriage, it appears I have more work to do than I thought."

Logan listened as I shared about Wes's affair and his need to control every aspect of my life. Even as I spoke, my insides shuddered. "I'm not sure I— Oh, no." I scrambled to grab my glass of tea as it slipped from my hands and crashed to the tile floor. When I burst into tears, Murphy jumped from his position at Logan's feet and rushed to my side.

"I'm so sorry."

Logan reached for me and pulled me closer. "It's okay. It's okay, Brooklyn. Don't worry about it."

I moved to rise. "Here, let me…"

"No. I'll get it." He pulled me back, patted my hands, and rose. "Sit here. I don't want you to step on glass."

While Logan cleaned up the floor, I buried my face in

Murphy's coat, then held his face and looked into his brown eyes. "Murph, you're such a good boy. You make me wish I had a dog, but I suspect there's not another one out there like you."

As Logan finished with the floor, I glanced at my watch. "I'm sorry to wreck your house and run, but Courtney's expecting me at the shop."

He walked me to the door and kissed me on the forehead. "Are you going to be okay?"

I nodded. "I will. Thanks for your ear and for all you've done. By the time I get to work, I'll be fine."

"I'll call you later tonight to check on you, okay?"

"Sure. Thanks." I slid from his embrace. "It seems like all I do is keep you and your wonder dog busy taking care of me."

He looked at Murphy and laughed. "I think I can speak for us both when I say…it's our pleasure."

The aroma of freshly brewed coffee, mingling with the scent of new and old books, lifted my spirits and helped me to dismiss thoughts of my frightening encounter with Wes. Working the evening shift on the first Thursday of every month was one of the highlights of my job. The gathering of The Plot Twisters Book Club in the bookstore's meeting room was a delightful blend of literature, caffeine, and community. Usually, several members would arrive early to scope out titles for the club's future reads. The enthusiasm the group brought with them was palpable, and after serving them coffee and pastries, I had the pleasure of sitting in on their discussions.

After the meeting, I helped Ella, our young barista, check out those who stayed behind to browse the shop. When the club's president handed me a couple of books at the register, I greeted her. "Great discussion tonight. As usual, I enjoyed it."

"I'm glad you did. We're so appreciative of this cozy space. Thanks for all you do for our group."

"Our pleasure. You had a room full tonight." After taking her money, I handed her the purchase.

"We did. Most of our members were here, and we had a few guests, which is always exciting." She motioned for a striking, dark-haired young lady waiting on the couch to join us. "I'd like you to meet my new friend."

I smiled and extended my hand.

"This is Natalya Shevchenko. She's from Mariupol and is staying with me for a while."

Thoughts of the mailbox swirled through my head as I shook her hand. "It's nice to meet you."

With a sweet smile, she nodded and greeted me in broken English.

"I'm Natalya's sponsor while she's in the States. Last week, I connected her with Refugee Services so that she can receive assistance. Her case manager is searching for a suitable job for her."

"Hmm…I'll mention her to Courtney. She's in the process of reviewing applications for summer help. Maybe something will work out."

"That would be wonderful. Thank you. Courtney has my number on file. Tell her I'll bring Natalya in if there's the possibility of a position here for her."

"I certainly will." I looked at Natalya and waved goodbye. As the door closed behind them, I shook my head in disbelief. I couldn't wait to tell Logan.

Chapter Fourteen

Tuesday, February 18, 1964
Billy Ray

Amid the roar of passionate Southport basketball fans and squeaking sneakers on the freshly polished gymnasium floor, Billy Ray followed the opposing team to the opposite end of the court. The game hung in the balance, with Leland's Tigers in possession of the ball and Southport's Dolphins trailing by one.

Southport's cheerleaders waved their pompoms in the air and led the frenzied crowd in, *"Hey, hey, what do you say? Take that ball the other way. Hey, hey, what do you say? Give that ball to Billy Ray."*

As one of the home team guards intercepted the ball, the thunderous pounding of feet raced to the end of the court. As the ball streaked toward Billy Ray, he leaped and snatched it from the air. When he turned to hurl it farther, Leland's #44 slammed into him and sent him careening across the floor. A diverse roar spilled from the bleachers as a shrill whistle pierced the air, and a red-faced referee called, "Foul." Billy Ray lifted himself from the floor and limped toward the free-throw line while exuberant fans rose to their feet, shouting, "Billy, Billy, Billy." With less than a minute left in the game, the team's fate rested squarely upon his shoulders. His #23 jersey clung to his sweat-drenched skin as he tucked the ball in the crook of his arm and wiped his forehead with the back of his hand. Adrenaline pulsed through his veins as he locked his eyes on the hoop and mouthed words to encourage himself. His heartbeat synced to the bounce of the ball at his feet. Slowly raising it to eye level, he launched it into the air. He traced the orange orb's perfect arc with unwavering eyes as it soared toward the goal and kissed the rim. As the crowd held its collective breath, Billy Ray willed it to happen. Then— *swish*, came the welcome whisper of nylon threads. Dolphin fans erupted into a jubilant cheer as the scoreboard lit up 65-65.

"One more. Just one more," Billy Ray muttered as he caught the returning ball. After repeating his previous movements, he released the ball. The minute it left his fingers, he knew. *Wrong. It was wrong.* He stood frozen and unable to breathe as the ball circled the rim and rolled to the outer edge of the hoop. Then, like a shot out of nowhere, Dave Dawkins, last year's MVP, sprang from the side and tapped it into the basket. Billy Ray rushed his friend and grabbed his neck just as the board flashed a 65-67 score. With the clock counting down the final seconds of the game, Billy Ray's teammates mobbed him, celebrating the Dolphin's win split seconds before the official buzzer sealed the outcome. Fans poured from the bleachers to join the winners on the floor, but Billy Ray's eyes combed the crowd for one.

"Billy. Billy Ray, you did it. You did it." Susie Yearmont, the Dolphins' chief cheerleader, pressed her way through the crowd, threw her arms around him, and planted a kiss on his cheek. "I'm so proud of you."

Pride welled in his spirit as Susie, voted the best-looking girl in the senior class, showered him with accolades and clung to his arm with an unrelenting grip. He savored the moment and basked in the thrill of another Dolphin victory.

After the team shook hands with the Tigers, they walked toward the locker rooms. Billy Ray was about to leave the floor when someone called his name. He turned and saw Trish smiling and waving as Margo pushed her wheelchair closer.

She did come. He greeted Margo, then wrapped his arms around Trish and squatted beside her chair. "Have you been here the whole time?"

"Yes. It was a great game."

"I looked for you afterward, but when I didn't see you, I assumed it was wishful thinking on my part."

"Why do you say that? I told you I'd try to come to one of your games."

"I don't know." He shrugged. "I figured maybe you'd changed your mind by now. Where did y'all sit?"

Margo pointed across the gym. "We were with my parents in the corner at the end of the first row. I'm surprised you didn't hear us yelling. I kept having to push Trish down in her chair. I was afraid she was going to re-injure her good leg."

He chuckled and looked at her. "Well, I appreciate your enthusiasm, but I'm happy Margo saw that you stayed seated."

"We came over to congratulate you right after the game, but there were so many people around we decided to wait."

Remembering Susie's uninvited attention, he changed the subject. "How are you getting along?"

Her eyes grew large and round. "Good. The doctor said he hopes to remove my cast in a couple of weeks, and with a bit of therapy, I should be as good as new by spring."

Billy Ray clicked his tongue and patted her hand. "That's super. When I saw you lying in the middle of the intersection that day, I wasn't sure what to expect. I thought maybe I'd lost you. I'm happy you're better."

"Thanks. It's been a hard road."

He turned and looked at the large clock above the entrance. "Well, I'd better hurry. The team's going out to celebrate, and we're to be on the bus in thirty minutes." He gave them both a hug and then peered into Trish's eyes. "We'll catch up soon, okay?"

She nodded. "Yeah, I'd like that." She lifted her hand. "Oh, before I forget, thanks for taking my bicycle over to Cedric's repair shop last month. He called to tell me he'd have it done by Saturday. When I told him I still couldn't ride it, he said he'd hold it for me till I could."

"Great. Let me know whenever you're ready for it, and I'll pick it up and run it by your house."

Her face lit up. "You would? That would help Momma out a lot."

"I got ya covered," he said, hurrying toward the boy's locker room.

Susie, walking with several cheerleaders toward the exit, hollered across the floor. "You'd better hurry up, Billy Ray. You're going to miss the bus."

He shook his head. "Don't worry. I'll make it."

"Okay. I'll save you a seat, and if you're late, I'll tell the driver to hold up."

He dismissed her comment and looked around for Trish. The door closed behind Margo and Trish as Susie and her friends reached the exit. Billy Ray winced and descended the stairs. *Had she heard their conversation?*

Billy Ray climbed onto the Dolphin's activity bus, caught Dave's wave from the back, and strode down the aisle. Feeling a tug on his jacket, he glanced down.

Susie patted the seat beside her. "I saved you a seat like I said I would, Mr. Basketball."

He dispensed a polite smile. "Thanks, but it looks like Dave's got me covered in the back." He brushed past her, tossed his athletic bag on the overhead rack, and dropped into the seat beside his friend.

"You had me worried, big man. I thought you weren't gonna make it."

"You kiddin'? You've known me since the first grade. Have I ever let you down?"

Dave raised a finger. "Well, there was—"

He slapped his hand. "You jerk. Let's talk about the game. Thanks for saving my shot tonight. Everyone's giving me the credit, but tonight's win belongs to you."

He shrugged. "Thanks, but it's just one more for the team, right? Dolphins did it again. That's all I care about."

"I know. One more win, and we'll make it to the regional championship." He punched the air with his fist. "Go, Dolphins!"

Whenever the driver closed the door, flipped off the lights, and pulled away from the curb, a loud chant erupted from the seats. The team was pumped and ready to celebrate.

Dave slid down in the seat. "Hey, man, I gotta ask you somethin'."

"Sure. Fire away."

"I saw you talking with Trish Malone a while ago. What's going on there? Y'all looked mighty chummy. Anything I should know about?"

He shook his head and pulled the bill of his ball cap lower. "Nah. We were just chattin'."

I was there in December when she got hit by the car, remember? I wanted to know how she was doin'."

Dave shook his head. "Oh, yeah. She's had some tough breaks this year. Nice of you to be kind to her."

He huffed. "I'm not doling out charity. She doesn't need anyone's sympathy, just people who care about her as a person. You should take time to get to know her. She's a swell girl."

"I'll take your word for it. She may be nice, but she's not my type." He pointed to Susie, who'd moved to sit with a friend. "Now that girl right there, if she had offered me a seat tonight, I'd be sayin', adios amigo."

"Gee, thanks. So, you'd leave me sittin' here all by myself, huh?" He punched him on the arm. "Maybe I don't know you as well as I thought."

"Well, don't lose any sleep over it. You haven't seen her makin' tracks my way, have ya?"

"Can't say that I've noticed." As the bus rolled to a stop in front of the local hangout, Billy Ray straightened in his seat and slapped on his cap. "Right now…all I've got on my mind is a juicy cheeseburger, fries, and a chocolate shake. Let's move out. I might have been the last one on this party pony, but I'm not about to be the tail when it comes to biting into a big fat burger."

Dave hopped up. "Now you've got your priorities straight, sport. Head on out."

Chapter Fifteen

Thursday, May 21, 1964

"Hey, wait up." Billy Ray trotted down the sidewalk at Southport School and grabbed Trish's arm. "Hi. It's been a while."

She stared straight ahead. "It has."

"How've you been? You look like you're doing good."

"I am. It took a while, but I'm no worse for the wear since my accident."

He searched for words and rubbed the back of his neck. "I hate that our paths haven't crossed as much this year. Sports and homework take up most of my time."

She cut her eyes toward him. "I'm sure."

"I've thought about you a lot."

"Good things, I hope."

"Always." He shoved his hands in his pockets and kicked a small rock into the gravel parking lot. "Did you remember I turned seventeen this month?"

"I did. It was the seventh, right?"

He smiled. "Yeah."

"Well, happy belated. I hope it was a good one."

"Thanks. It was. My best so far."

"Great. Did you do anything special?"

"I guess you could say that." He stopped. "Are you walking home?"

She turned around and nodded.

"Well then, how about I give you a lift?"

"A lift?"

"Yeah. That's what we did for my birthday. My parents took me car shopping. I've got my own wheels now."

Her eyes grew large. "You do? That's awesome. What color did you get?"

"Color?" He chuckled. "Cherry red. Wanna know what make it is, as well?"

"Sure." She blushed. "I was just fixing to ask that."

"I got a red Empire."

"Oh, yeah? Those are real pretty."

"You think?"

"I do. Good choice."

Billy threw back his head and laughed.

"Why are you laughing?"

"There is no such car as an Empire."

Trish whipped around and walked toward the street.

"Wait. Wait, Trish. I'm sorry." He clasped her shoulder and turned her around. When she lowered her eyes, he lifted her chin. "I'm sorry. Really, I am. I just couldn't help myself. You were so innocent. It's such a girl thing. Please. Please, forgive me."

She narrowed her eyes and shook her head. "Some things never change. You're always having to ask for forgiveness."

He exhaled. "Bummer. You're right. I promise I'll try to straighten up. I just need a good girl to keep me in line."

"You shouldn't have any problem in that department. I imagine you have a long line. Most girls go for a star athlete."

"Most? Would that number include you?"

"Probably not. Status doesn't impress me. Nice does."

He winced. "I can be nice."

She pressed her lips together and tilted her head from side to side. "Hmm…I suppose."

"So, do you take me up on my *nice* offer for a ride or not? I'll even take you over to Willie's for a sherbet."

"Oh, now you're turning the screws."

"Is that a yes?"

She grinned. "It is."

"That's more like it. Here, give me your books." He stacked her books on top of his and motioned with his head toward the parking lot. "I'm over this way."

"You never said what kind of car you got?"

"A 1958 Bugeye Sprite."

She stopped, threw back her shoulders, and huffed. "I'm not falling for that. Bug-eye? Sprite? I don't think so."

He laughed. "No. No. I'm telling the truth. Honest. It's a British car made by Austin Healey." He pointed as they approached. "It's right here."

"Oh, wow. Cute. You're right. The headlights do look like bug eyes."

He put their books behind the front seats. "Do you like it?"

"What's not to like? It looks like a fun ride."

He opened the car door. "Hop in. I'll let you be the judge."

Trish lowered herself into the car and pulled in her braced leg. She ran her hand over the dashboard and looked around. "This is so cool."

He dropped behind the wheel.

"I'm surprised you fit," she said, giggling.

He looked at her and grinned. "Why do you think I have the top down?"

"Oh, no…that could get pretty icy in the winter."

He turned the key in the ignition. "Speaking of icy, let's go get your sherbet."

Billy Ray pulled into Trish's driveway, cut the engine, and smiled. "Thanks for taking me up on my offer. This has been nice."

"I agree. It has. Thanks for treating me."

He nodded. "Happy to."

When Trish moved to get out, Billy Ray clasped her arm. "Wait. Can we do this again soon?"

"I don't know. Can we? I thought your parents disapproved of me."

"They're lightening up a bit since I turned seventeen. More than the problem being you, they thought we were too young and didn't want me to be distracted from my homework and sports. But time hasn't changed my feelings for you."

Trish smiled. "Mine either. I've always hoped you'd like me, but I didn't really think it would happen."

He cupped her chin in his hand and peered into her eyes. "Trish, don't let your disability color your future. I see you. Not your disability. All I want is to know you better, and now that I can drive, I plan to. If it's okay with you, that is—and your mother, of course."

"It shouldn't be a problem. Momma's always thought a lot of you. She trusts you, Billy Ray, and so do I."

He put his hand on his chest. "You don't know how good those words make me feel. I'd be happy to bring you home after school on the days I don't have ball practice. How about it?"

"I don't know. That would be a lot."

"No, it wouldn't. What is it…a half a mile?"

She laughed. "You're right. I just don't want you to feel tied down. It has been a little harder since I lost my bike, but the school's close enough to walk, and the exercise is good for me."

"You can exercise another time. I'm saying I'd like to bring you home each day."

She nodded. "Okay. I'd love that. Thank you."

"I've meant to ask about your bike. Whatever happened to it?"

"We don't know." She laid her head back on the seat and watched the sun's rays filter through the canopy of leaves. "Cedric said it simply disappeared. As you know, he was holding it for me in his storage shed until I could ride it again. He's not sure when it disappeared. There have been no clues. It just vanished."

"Wow. I hate that for you. I know, since it was a gift from your granny, it was more than a way for you to get around. It was sentimental."

"Very much so. That's what hurts worse than anything, but I'm working through it."

He shook his head. "Life's not fair, is it?"

She scooted up in her seat. "Nope. It certainly isn't."

"I've got something else I want you to think about. You can ask your mother. After school's out for the summer, I want to celebrate by driving to Sunset Beach for the day." He tapped the woodgrain steering wheel with his palm. "Drive this baby somewhere besides around town. Wanna go with me?"

Her face lit up. "Yes. That sounds like fun. I've not been to Sunset. I'll ask Momma and let you know."

"Terrific." He hopped from the car, opened Trish's door, and helped her out. Then, gathering her books from behind the seat, he asked, "Want me to take these to the house for you?"

"Thank you, but I'm good." She reached for them and pulled them to her chest. "Thanks for the nice afternoon, Billy Ray."

"You're welcome. It has been nice." He hugged her and hopped in the car. "I'll see you tomorrow. Meet me on the sidewalk, okay?"

She smiled. "I'll be there."

After backing onto the street, Billy Ray shifted into first gear and glanced back at Trish.

She lifted her hand and waved.

He tapped the horn and stepped on the gas. *No, life's not fair. Today—it's more than fair.*

Chapter Sixteen

Monday, June 15, 1964

Trish laid her head back on the seat of Billy Ray's cherry red convertible and watched wispy clouds float across clear blue skies—the precursor of a perfect day. As the car sailed down Highway 211 toward 17 with songs like Del Shannon's "Runaway" blaring from the speakers, Trish danced from the waist up and later sang along with the more subdued lyrics of Patsy Cline's "I Fall to Pieces." She couldn't recall a happier moment since the garage fire or a time when she'd felt more free. "What a super way to kick off summer vacation."

Billy Ray looked over and flashed a toothy grin. "Pretty cool, huh?"

"The best." She scooted up in the seat and shifted to face him. "Thank you for inviting me to come with you."

He shouted above the wind. "I've thought about this day for a long time and wouldn't have it any other way. Your excitement is contagious."

She brushed her chin-length hair away from her face, knowing it was a losing battle, and smiled. "Next time, I'll remember to bring a scarf."

He removed his Dolphin cap and handed it to her. "Here, try this."

Her eyes questioned his. "You sure?"

He ran his fingers through his crewcut. "I know mine will be in tangles by the time we get there, but I'll make the sacrifice."

She punched him on the arm and giggled. "Well, what do you know, chivalry isn't dead, after all." She tucked her hair behind her ears and pulled his cap down as tight as she could. "Voilà," she said, framing her face with her hands and grinning.

"There you go. It suits you."

"Thanks. It does help." She leaned back in her seat. "So, what's the plan for today?"

He shrugged and turned down the radio. "Don't have one. Thought we'd play it by ear. I've always heard Sunset Beach was nice, so I figured it was time to see it for myself."

After exiting Highway 17, Billy Ray drove over winding roads through rich green swampland and eventually arrived at the single-lane Sunset Beach swing bridge. They took their place in a long line of cars while the tender swung open the bridge, allowing boats on the waterway to pass through. Trish's heart pulsed in her throat as she observed the unique operation. While they waited, Billy Ray tried to answer her questions and shared what little history he knew about the newly developed island.

"In 1955, local World War II veteran Mannon Gore bought the undeveloped island across the waterway, which was then called Bald Beach. Later, he sold his farm and opened a dredging business that helped him finance and build this bridge. They finished it in 1958. Can you believe he built this pontoon swing bridge from a World War II surplus barge?"

Mesmerized, Trish shook her head as she watched boats pass through the open channel. "That is the most amazing thing I've ever seen. This was worth the trip, and we've not even driven onto the island yet." She reached over and squeezed his arm. "Thanks again, Billy Ray, for bringing me. I can't wait to tell Momma."

He pointed to a small white tender house that sat on the right side of the bridge. "I hear Mr. Gore is the tender who opens and closes the bridge every hour on the hour so boats can pass through. They say he lives in a house close by." Straightening in his seat, he stretched his neck, looked up and down the waterway, and then motioned. "Probably that one over there on the waterfront. Wow, he has some view, doesn't he? Can you imagine the sunsets along this body of water? Mr. Gore was so impressed by them, he renamed the island Sunset Beach."

"No. I can't imagine any of this. I've lived in Southport all my life, but I've never seen a swing bridge or a place this peaceful and beautiful. It's more than I can take in."

At the chugging diesel sound of the bridge closing, Billy Ray started the car. "We'll be moving soon. You ready to cross?"

"I'm so excited I can't stand it."

After a long stream of traffic leaving the island crossed to the mainland, Billy followed the cars in front of him and drove onto the bridge. As their tires rolled over the wooden planks, there was a rhythmic clacking sound, similar to that of a train on its tracks.

When they drove past the tender house, Trish waved at Mr. Gore sitting at the open window, then looked down the waterway and squealed. "Gorgeous, simply gorgeous."

Billy Ray reached over and clasped her hand. "That's what I say—gorgeous. You make me so happy, Trish. I'm glad we're experiencing this first together."

Feeling heat rise in her cheeks, she lowered her eyes. "Me too."

As they drove onto the island, Billy Ray pointed out the new fishing pier, which opened the year before. "I hear they've got a snack bar inside the green building. Are you hungry?"

She nodded. "Yes. I was so excited I couldn't eat before we left this morning. How about you?"

He chuckled. "Are you kidding? I'm always hungry. A

burger or hot dog sounds good to me. We can eat inside, or if you'd like to eat on the beach, I brought a couple of chairs. What do you think?"

"Lunch by the water is a fantastic idea. Yes, let's do that."

Billy Ray grabbed the chairs from the trunk and followed Trish into the wooden building. After checking out the menu that hung above the lunch counter, they ordered two Barnacle Burger Baskets with curly fries and sodas. While they waited for their orders, Trish purchased a hat, and Billy Ray checked out some vacation pamphlets. Seeing one he wanted, he tucked it in his shirt pocket. "We can look at this later. It's the history of the pier."

Trish plopped Billy Ray's cap back on his head, then tied her wide-brimmed sunhat under her chin and twirled around. "So what do you think?"

"I like it. You'll pass for an islander, now."

Trish giggled and followed Billy Ray with their lunches as he carried the chairs to the water's edge. After putting the lunch bags on the ground, she placed her hands on her hips and scanned the horizon. "Ahh. This is heaven," she said, turning and lowering herself into one of the chairs.

Billy dropped into the other beside her. "You talkin' about the view or the smell of burgers?"

She cut her eyes at him and smirked. "The burgers, of course, silly." Laughing, she handed him his sack.

They inhaled their meals, then shared a few curly fries with the gulls. Trish shrieked with delight as the scavengers squawked and swooped in to fight for the tiny morsels of food. After tossing them the last of their fries, she splashed one foot in the surf, then leaned back in her chair and allowed the warmth of the sun's rays to caress her face. "This is so nice. I could get used to this." She sat up and looked at the row of houses behind them. "Wouldn't it be nice to live here one day?" She abruptly dismissed the far-fetched idea as quickly as it came. "Hmph. I can only dream."

"I don't know, Trish. It could happen. What was it your Granny used to say?"

She twisted her mouth and nodded. "You're right. She believed anything was possible if we'd keep our eyes on the goal…and our God."

"So, there you have it." He extended his arm and swept it toward the houses. "Which one of these beauties do you want?"

"Hmm….let me see." She held her finger to her lips as she surveyed the colorful row of homes. "Oh, gee, I don't know. I'm not picky. I'd count myself blessed to have any one of them."

"Okay. Only time will tell. I just hope I get an invitation to visit." Billy Ray laughed, leaned back in his chair, and closed his eyes.

Trish followed suit and allowed her thoughts to drift in the cool, crisp breeze that brushed her warm skin. *Oh, Granny. If you could see me now…and the handsome boy I'm with. I'm sure you'd like him lots. He's a real gentleman. Even opens the car door for me, like you said Gramps did for you. And the car— wow. You wouldn't believe it. Nothing like—* She jolted at a light tap on her arm.

Billy Ray choked back a laugh. "I'm sorry, Trish. I didn't mean to scare you, but the day's getting away from us."

She inhaled and let out a long breath. "You're right. It's just so peaceful here. I guess the waves lulled me to sleep." She straightened her chair and started to stand.

He swung out his arm. "Nope, wait. I've got something for you."

She scrunched her face. "Me?"

He reached into his pocket and held out a small box tied with a lavender ribbon. His dark eyes sparkled as he smiled.

"Happy 16th Birthday, Trish."

Her mouth fell open as her eyes widened. "What? How did you know it was my birthday?"

He chuckled. "I guess the same way you knew it was mine last month."

"Yeah, but I didn't get you anything."

"I didn't know giving was a prerequisite for getting." He waved the box. "Are you going to accept it or not?"

"Yes. Yes. I'm sorry." Taking it, she admired the paper covered with tiny purple flowers, untied the lavender ribbon, and tore off the wrapping. Her breath caught. "Southport Jewelers?"

He grinned and moved his chair closer to hers.

With trembling hands, she lifted the lid and took out a small velvet box. She hesitated and shifted her questioning eyes to Billy Ray's.

He motioned her on. "Go ahead."

She breathed deep, opened it, and gasped. "No way. This is my birthstone." Her eyes shot to Billy Ray's as she rubbed her fingertip over the pearl set in a thin gold band.

He grinned. "Do you like it?"

She nodded. "Oh, yes, but you shouldn't have done it."

"Says who?"

"Uh…

He held out his upturned palm and wiggled his fingers. "Here. Let me see it." He slid the ring from the box. "Now, give me your hand."

She offered her right hand, and Billy Ray slipped it on her trembling ring finger. "Looks like a good fit to me. What do you think?"

"I love it." She slid it back and forth, then held her hand out in front of her. "It's perfect and so beautiful." She turned to meet his eyes. "Thank you."

"You're welcome." He leaned closer.

Her heart raced as she leaned in to meet him and closed her eyes. Their lips brushed and then found each other again. Her insides tingled, and for a brief moment, time ceased. As the cry of gulls and the gentle lap of the waves faded into the distance, she knew that Billy Ray was all she'd ever wanted or needed. Someone who looked past her limitations and saw her for the girl she was within.

The ring was beautiful, but Billy Ray Jessup was the gift.

Chapter Seventeen

Monday, April 10, 2023
Brooklyn

I pulled into Logan's driveway and parked beside an Island Home Builders van. While Murphy bounded toward me, Logan waved and continued his conversation with a man in the backyard of his house next door. I decided to give them their space and sat on the steps of Logan's cottage. Murphy plopped at my feet, and it wasn't long before Logan joined us.

"Good morning, Sunshine. To what do I owe this early morning visit?"

"I work the day shift today, but wanted to stop by and fill you in on who I met Thursday night. Wanna guess?"

"Hmm… He looked upward. "Someone famous?"

I shook my head.

"I haven't a clue."

"Natalya."

"Who?"

"You know…the Ukrainian lady who left a note in the Kindred Spirit mailbox."

He tilted his head back. "Oh, yes. Where did you run into her?"

"At the Plot Twisters' meeting." I shared with him the events of the evening and my plans to tell Courtney today that Natalya was searching for a job.

"Does she speak English?"

"We only greeted one another after the meeting, but I spoke on the phone with her sponsor again yesterday. She said Natalya has taken English classes over in Supply for several months and has caught on quickly. She wants to remain in the States and has applied for a green card."

"Good. I know you've had her on your mind ever since you read her note at the mailbox. So, now you know."

I nodded. "I hope Courtney hires her. She seems to have a sweet disposition. I'd love to get to know her." I laid my hand on his arm. "So what's the story on your house?"

"We're about to get the ball rolling—or I suppose I should say the wrecking ball flying. A demolition crew will come next week."

"That's fantastic. Which house plan did you decide on?"

"The Windjammer. Figured the smaller size would be an easier sell. Newer small homes on the oceanfront are hard to come by. It will make an affordable single-family dwelling or rental property."

I straightened. "Well, congratulations! I'm glad it's worked out for you to keep the property. I see the gleam in your eyes."

"Really?" He wrapped his arm around me and pulled me closer. "Maybe the gleam is because of the lady sitting beside me."

I wasn't sure how to respond. I knew how I wanted to, but I was still conflicted. "You're kind." I giggled and gave him a quick hug. "I should be on my way. I open up today."

Logan cast me a questioning glance as we rose. "Sure. I hope you have a good one."

"You too. We'll catch up later."

"Sure thing."

I felt terrible as I backed out of the driveway. I knew I needed to be upfront with Logan, but I couldn't until I could be honest with myself.

Wednesday, April 12, 2023
Brooklyn

Courtney poked her head around the office door. "Brooklyn, the young lady you spoke to me about on Monday, is coming in for an interview after a while. Tap on my door when she gets here, okay?"

"I sure will. I think you'll like her."

A smile eased across my face as I returned to pulling books for the sale table. I couldn't imagine the pain Natalya had experienced since the Ukraine war had begun, and I hoped she'd found the States a welcoming, safe harbor. Maybe Sunset Beach and a position at Coffee Chronicles would be a good fit for her.

When the bell on the front door chimed, I walked from the storage room and was surprised to see Logan at the counter ordering a mocha latte from Ella. Sneaking up behind him, I placed my hands over his eyes. "Guess who?"

"Hmm…let me think." He whirled around. "I don't know. Who?"

I laughed. "Oh, I'm so sorry, sir. I mistook you for someone else."

His eyes twinkled. "Well, you look like someone I'd like to get to know."

"Oh, really now. Well, this may be your lucky day." I checked my watch. "It just happens to be my break time."

I looked at our barista, who was giggling at our silliness.

"I'll take my usual, Ella, and you can put the gentleman's latte on my tab."

"You've got it," she said, pulling a cup from the stack.

I looked at Logan. "It's a beautiful day. Let's sit on the porch. If you want to go out, I'll bring our coffees when they're ready."

He nodded. "I'm going to let you do that. I'm about to drop."

Minutes later, I handed Logan his latte and sat in the rocking chair beside him. "So, what brings you my way?"

"I needed an afternoon pick-me-up, and it looks like my plan worked—I got picked up." He lifted his cup in the air. "And got free coffee. Can't beat that."

I swatted my napkin at him. "Nope. I don't think you can." I sipped my caramel macchiato and rocked. "Seriously, was there a reason for your visit besides coffee?"

"None other than to hopefully get a glimpse of my favorite girl and see how she's doing."

I rocked harder. "I'm good."

His eyes questioned mine. "You sure?"

"Yeah. Why do you ask?"

"You seemed nervous when you dropped by Monday morning, and I wanted to make sure you're okay."

I sighed. "Thank you, that's sweet."

We sat silently.

"After my experience with Wes last week, I've had to assess where I am emotionally. I like you a lot, Logan, but I need to give myself more time to heal."

He nodded. "I understand, and I'm willing to wait, but I certainly don't want to give up on us."

I turned at the sound of a car pulling into the parking lot and rose. "I don't want to give up on us either."

"We'll move at whatever pace you want. Good?"

I leaned over and hugged him. "Thanks for understanding." I straightened and watched as two ladies stepped from the car. "Logan, that's Natalya. Let me run and tell Courtney she's here. I'll be right back."

I stepped into the house and knocked on the office door. "Natalya just pulled up."

"Sounds good. I'll be there in a minute."

When I turned, Natalya walked through the door accompanied by her sponsor. Natalya was a lovely young lady with blonde hair, translucent skin, and high cheekbones.

"Hi, ladies, it's good to see you again."

"Thank you. I'm here to speak with Miss Bowers," she said, her light blue-gray eyes sparkling.

I smiled. "Yes, she told me you were coming today. I just let her—"

"Hello," Courtney entered the room, greeted them both, and then motioned toward the coffee counter. "Would you like something to drink before we go back to my office?"

Natalya smiled as they politely declined and followed Courtney.

"That's her," I said, returning to my seat beside Logan on the porch. "She seems really nervous. It must be hard to be in a strange land with a different culture and have to start over alone. It was hard enough for me to give up my home in Raleigh."

"But you're glad you did, right?"

"Yes. I'm happy here."

"I don't think I have to tell you I'm pleased you're here, too." He stood. "I'd better get back home. Murphy will be worried about me." He chuckled. "Well, probably more worried about his dinner than me."

I walked him to the steps. "I'm glad you stopped by. Thanks

for being so understanding." I kissed him on the cheek.

He lifted his hand and walked toward his car. "I'll call you after my meeting at the agency tonight to find out what happened with Natalya."

"Okay." I leaned against the column, sipped my coffee, and watched until his car was out of sight.

I snatched my phone from the nightstand and noted the caller ID. "Hey. I was worried about you but didn't want to call in case you were still in your meeting."

"I'm sorry. I should have let you know earlier what was happening, but time got away from me. I didn't realize it was so late."

"So, where are you? Home?" I turned my book facedown beside me on the bed, pulled my knees to my chest, and leaned against the headboard.

"Yes, I've been here about fifteen minutes. Of course, I couldn't do a thing until I fed Murphy. He was frantic—more so about his meal than me, I'm sure. I hope I haven't kept you up."

"No, it's fine. I was reading. I'm happy to know you're okay. So, your meeting ran long, huh?"

"No. It didn't. We had a great meeting. One of the shortest in a long time. It was after we met that my night went south."

"Oh, no, what happened?"

"I'd parked my car on the curb in front of the agency, and when I unlocked it to come home, I noticed someone had hit it. My taillight and back quarter panel were smashed."

I sat straight up and clapped my hand to my mouth. "No way. Did the person leave a note?"

"Nope. Just a streak of white paint on my navy Cherokee."

"You mean it was a hit and run?"

"Yep! That's what I'm saying."

I could feel the depth of his angst through the phone. "Logan. I'm so sorry."

"Yeah. Definitely not the way I wanted to wind down my day." He sighed. "Because the panel was pushed into the tire, I couldn't even drive home. Had to have the car towed to the repair shop."

"Wow." I shook my head. "It's always something, isn't it?"

"Sure seems that way. At least Rick was there and brought me home. I'll have to call for a rental tomorrow."

"Okay. I work the afternoon shift at the bookstore. Let me drive you there in the morning."

"Deal. That would help a lot. I'll call you whenever I have a car lined up."

"Great."

"So now, before we go, what happened with Natalya?"

"Courtney hired her. She starts on Monday."

"Awesome."

"Yeah. She's going to shadow Ella in the coffee shop next week. She was really excited. Such a sweetheart. I think we'll enjoy having her there."

"Good. I'm glad things went well." He yawned. "I don't know about you, but I need to turn in. It's been a day and a half. I'll call you as soon as I know something tomorrow."

"Okay. I hope you rest well."

"You too, sweetheart."

I hung up and shook my head. *First, his house. Now, his car. Lord, bless him.*

Chapter Eighteen

Saturday, May 13, 2023
Brooklyn

Natalya has worked at Coffee Chronicles for about a month, and it didn't take me long to know I adored her. She was soft-spoken and possessed an innocence and charm that could melt the hardest of hearts. Her broken English made her even more endearing.

Although I was only a few years her senior, I wanted to take her under my wings and shelter her like a mother hen provides a safe haven for her chicks. The world had dealt Natalya devastating blows. She'd lost her homeland and her husband. She had no news of her family and friends. Sunset Beach was ground zero for her. I wanted her to find true love and happiness here, to experience peace—not only external calm, but also freedom from internal turmoil. I wanted that for everyone. We all had personal battles, but Natalya's appeared weightier than most.

Contrary to how one would perceive her due to her sweet nature, Natalya was a strong woman. The hardships she'd endured had tested her mettle. She'd exhibited profound courage and resilience beyond her years. She wanted to be independent, to make her own way. Although I admired that attribute, I saw her need for guidance just as I would need it if I were in a foreign land. So…I had an idea.

"Olivia." I peeked inside the open kitchen door from the porch. "It's me." I heard footsteps coming from the end of the hall.

Chase walked into the kitchen and greeted me with a warm hug. "Liv drove to the Home Goods store in Myrtle Beach to pick up several things for a client. Can I help?"

I weighed my answer and nodded. "Yes. I believe you can. I'd hoped to bounce my idea off of Olivia first, but since you'll have the final say anyway, I should speak to you. Have you got a moment?"

He laid his book on the counter and motioned toward the porch rockers. "I'm all ears. And for you, Brooklyn, I have more than a moment."

I smiled and chose my favorite rocker, the one I'd always sat in when chatting with Winnie. I shifted it to face him. "Thanks. You know me, Chase. Whenever I have an idea, I want to execute it right away."

"Do I ever. You're a carbon copy of your first cousin." He leaned back in his chair and crossed one leg over his knee. "Don't leave me in suspense, gal. What do you need?"

I inhaled and searched for the right words to present my case. "I know you haven't met my Ukrainian friend, Natalya, but I'm sure Olivia has told you about her."

He nodded. "She has."

"She's lived in the States for over a year now and has a wonderful sponsor who does all she can to help her adapt to life here. She's more than willing for Natalya to continue to live under her roof, but Natalya wants a place of her own."

"She receives assistance, doesn't she?"

"Yes, and works a full-time job at the bookshop, but it's still hard for her to be self-supporting in today's economy."

"No one would ever doubt that. It's a story I hear almost every day." His eyes peered into mine, and I knew at once what he was thinking. I'd received that same look from Logan more times than I could count, and it was always followed by, 'Just the facts, ma'am. Just the facts.'

"Okay. I'll get to my point. When I pulled into my driveway last night, my car's headlights flashed onto your Airstream. I don't want to say I had a Damascus road experience or anything, but for lack of a better term, I saw the light and had a 'Wow God' moment. I don't say this to influence your decision in any way, and I could be wrong, you know, but—"

"Whoa there, girl," he said, pushing out his palm. "I think I know where this is headed. Remember, you're messin' with my heart now. Daisy and I go back a long way. She was my college dorm room, ya know."

Thinking I'd hit a nerve, I winced and struggled for the survival of my idea. "I know. Olivia told me. But now that you have a house, she just sits there. Wouldn't you like to bring in a little passive income?"

"What? So Natalya lives in our driveway?"

I shrugged. "Well, no. I thought I'd talk to Logan and—"

His palm shot up again before he reached into his shirt pocket and pulled out his phone. "Now, like all good friends, I should probably warn Logan in advance."

I straightened in my chair. "Don't you dare, Chase Evans. Hear me out, please."

He settled back and rocked. "Okay. I'm just jerkin' your chain. I'm sorry I keep interrupting you. Carry on."

"I figured I'd ask Logan if he knows of a spot where Natalya could park the trailer. I thought I heard him say one time that Harbor Realty manages a camper site close by."

"I don't know, Brooklyn. It's a possibility." Chase ran his

hand over his close-shaven beard. "Might be kinda nice to have a little extra income." He leaned forward and rested his elbows on his knees. "I'll talk it over with Olivia and get back to you."

"You will?" I jumped up and hugged him. "Thanks so much for considering this. I'll wait to hear from you before I mention anything to Logan."

He followed me as I walked to the door. "You've got a big heart, Brooklyn. Natalya has a great friend in you."

On Monday, I waited in Logan's office at Harbor Realty and studied the photographs along the wall. There were several of him receiving awards and others showing him with people I assumed to be family. I knew he was the youngest of three children, had graduated with honors from Conway High School, and had received an associate's degree in business before becoming an agent with Harbor. That was pretty much it in a nutshell. As for his personal life, former girlfriends and such, I knew nada. As I reached for the framed black-and-white photo on the desk of his younger self and a pretty girl, I heard him approach the door and jerked back my hand.

"Well, well," he said, closing the door behind him. "To what do I owe this surprise visit?" He leaned over and kissed my hair before taking a seat behind his desk. "You looking to buy a house, condo, or oceanfront property? I have several new listings you might be interested in?"

I tossed my hair over my shoulders and smiled. "Before you put on the hard sell, none of the above. I'm interested in a campsite."

His eyes bulged. "What? You don't strike me as the camper type, but if you're sure, I'll do my best to locate one. I aim to please."

I held up my hand. "No, no, it's not for me. Maybe I should pull the brakes on this runaway train and start from the beginning."

He swiveled in his chair, then leaned back and rocked. "That sounds like a brilliant idea."

"Natalya wants a place of her own, but she can't afford much. So on Saturday, I asked Chase if he would consider leasing her his Airstream."

His chair sprang forward. "You what? You mean Daisy? How did that go over?"

"Very well, actually. He agreed."

Logan placed his arms on his desk, leaned in, and studied my face. "You've got to be kidding me."

I shook my head.

"So Chase Evans said he'd rent Daisy?"

I grinned. "He did."

"Wow! From my conversations with him, I'm amazed he agreed to rent out his pride and joy. Have you ever considered a career in sales? I think you've missed your calling."

She laughed and pressed her index finger to her lips. "Hmm…let's discuss that later and get back to my reason for being here. Do you know of a camp space Natalya could lease? Of course, she'd need to agree. I haven't mentioned any of this to her. I wanted to make sure things were possible first."

"That's wise." He laid his head back on his chair and stared at the ceiling. "Hmm…" After a few moments, he let his chair spring forward. "I just might have something that will work."

I straightened and inched to the edge of my seat. "Really?"

"Harbor manages a campsite, but I might have something better." He tapped his desk with his index finger. "A few months ago, I ran across an older fella who told me he had a quarter-acre lot he'd like to sell. He said if I ever heard of someone who could use something small, I should let him know, and he'd add the needed hookups." Logan pulled his phone from his pocket and scrolled through his contacts. "Let's see, what was his name?" He paused, then continued scrolling. "Oh, yes. Meade. Herman Meade. Here it is." After dialing the number, he waited and then left a message. "I'll try again after a while."

"If it's available, do you think he would lease the space? I feel sure Natalya wouldn't be in a position to buy anything."

"I can certainly ask. The chance of him selling a piece of property that small is pretty slim. He might actually like having a bit of monthly income." He winked. "Kinda like Chase. I'll work on it and let you know."

"Thank you. Thank you so much. I'd better get back to the shop."

He walked around his desk and took my hand. "I'll walk you out. Maybe I can talk you into dinner later."

I laughed. "You won't have to twist my arm, Mr. Corbett. I missed lunch. I'll be famished."

Chapter Nineteen

Saturday, April 24, 1965

Trish danced into the living room with arms held out and twirled. "How do I look, Momma?" she asked as the hem of her chiffon empire-waistline gown settled around her ankles.

Her mother's eyes grew large as she rose from the couch and covered her mouth with her hand. "Oh, sweetheart, you look stunning. Blush pink was the perfect color choice for you."

Trish hugged her. "Thanks for helping me pick it out. I feel like a princess." She locked eyes with her momma as the doorbell chimed. "That's him," she whispered. She inhaled and let her breath out slowly to keep from hyperventilating.

Mrs. Malone looked at the clock. "And right on time. I like a punctual young man." She batted her hand at Trish. "Hurry. Go back to your room while I get the door, then you can make your grand entrance."

Trish giggled, closed her bedroom door behind her, and pressed her ear to it. The screen door squeaked open.

"Why, Billy Ray Jessup. Aren't you a sight for sore eyes?"

"Thank you, ma'am. This is a first for me. I've never worn a bow tie, much less a cummerbund."

"Well, you look very handsome. That white dinner jacket makes you look like you just stepped off the set of Goldfinger. James Bond has nothing on you, son."

"That's mighty nice of you to say, Mrs. Malone."

"Just calling it as I see it. Have a seat while I check on your date." She walked into the hall, cracked open Trish's bedroom door, and winked. "Trish, dear. Billy Ray is here." They both smothered their laughter before Mrs. Malone returned to the living room. "She's on her way."

Moments later, Billy Ray sprang from the edge of the couch as Trish entered the room. "Wow. You look amazing." He set a white cardboard box on the end table and opened it. "I gotcha something."

Heat spread across her face as he pulled out a lovely white orchid. "How beautiful. Thank you."

"Sure," he said as he walked over and fumbled to pin the flower to the shoulder of her sleeveless dress.

"Do you need help, Billy Ray?"

He nodded and moved aside. "I think so, Mrs. Malone. It's a bit whopper-jawed."

Trish giggled, and her heart drummed as her eyes took in her handsome date. "I've got something for you, as well."

Mrs. Malone stepped into the kitchen, returned with a red carnation, and handed it to Trish.

Billy chuckled as Trish sniffed its fragrance and pinned it to his lapel. "Thanks. You're better at that than I am." He crooked his arm. "Are you ready to go?"

She picked up her small purse and elbow-length white gloves from the entryway table and slid her arm through his. "Yes. I'm so excited."

Trish's mother snatched her Polaroid camera from the bookshelf. "Whoa, you two. Stand over in front of the fireplace first. This is your ticket out of here."

Trish rolled her eyes and laughed. "You'll have to get used to Momma's picture-taking, Billy Ray."

"Aww, I don't mind," he said as he wrapped his arm around her waist and pulled her to his side.

As the scent of his British Sterling cologne tickled her nostrils, she found it hard to stop smiling. After their day trip to Sunset Beach last summer, her biggest fear had been one of losing him, but instead, they'd grown closer. Now, for him to take her as his date to the Junior-Senior prom was more than she'd ever dared to wish for. Her granny always told her that she set her sights too low. Granny would be happy with her escort.

Mrs. Malone snapped a photo, pulled the print from the camera, and flapped it in the air to dry before handing it to Trish. "What do you think?"

She held it toward Billy Ray so he could see it. "I like it. Do you?"

"Of course. You're in it, aren't you?"

Trish giggled and laid it on the mantle. After posing for a few more pictures, she hugged her momma and then walked with Billy Ray to the car. His little red Sprite wasn't an enchanted carriage, and her gown may have come from Secondhand Rose, but tonight, the satin slippers fit, and her spirits soared on the wings of the wind. She was on her way to the ball with her handsome Prince Charming, and nothing could bring her down.

Sounds of the band tuning their instruments wafted through the cool night air as Billy Ray and Trish approached Southport High School's gymnasium. She gasped at the transformation as he led her over an arched bridge spanning a shiny foil creek, complete with river rocks and the sound of rushing water. Scanning the room, she admired several midnight blue panels lining the stage. Painted with silvery stars and swirls, Van Gogh's Starry, Starry Night prom theme was unmistakable. As they stepped onto the hardwood floor with the soft glow of twinkling lights reflecting on its polished surface, Billy Ray pulled her closer. "Wow! Pretty cool, isn't it, Trish? It certainly doesn't look like my old basketball court."

"Yeah, it's a huge difference."

Excited chatter filled the air as couples and singles arrived in evening attire. While the girls oohed and aahed over one another's dresses and elegant hairdos adorned with delicate hairpins and baby's breath, the boys tugged at their bow ties, wiped their sweaty palms on their pants, and hovered around the linen-covered tables filled with refreshments.

"Hey, Trish. Billy Ray."

Trish turned and saw Margo making her way through the crowd with Paul McFarland in tow. As the guys chatted, she hugged Margo and peered into her sparkling brown eyes. "I thought you said you were coming with Elise and Rebecca."

"I was, but Paul called me this morning to see if I was going. Said he'd like to pick me up."

"Wow. Good for you. Neither one of us did bad tonight, then, did we?"

"I know. We're lucky girls."

The buzz of voices and loud laughter ceased as Senior Class President Marty Weston leaned into the microphone. As a shrill squeal split the air, he threw his hand to his chest and jumped back. "Wow. Sorry. Let's try this again. Hello, classmates, welcome to a Starry, Starry Night. All of you look amazing. And some of you I don't even recognize." The room burst into laughter. "Let's show the decorating and food committees how much we appreciate them. They've taken this old, worn-out gym, given it an incredible facelift, and presented us with a night to remember." The applause, whoops, and whistles were deafening. "Now I know—" As the mic screeched, Marty winced and backed away. He shrugged. "Now I know you fellas are itching to get out on the dance floor with this room full of beautiful girls, so let's get the night underway." He swept his hand toward a gazebo-like bandstand draped with navy, royal blue, and silver streamers framed with bouquets of blue and silver helium balloons. "Give this up-and-coming group, The Part-Time Party-Time Band, a huge Southport High School welcome, and let's dance the night away."

As applause exploded and then waned, the smooth vocal harmonies of "My Girl" flooded the room, and couples crowded onto the dance floor. Billy Ray reached for Trish. "Come on, dancin' queen, let's show them how it's done." As they zigzagged their way to the middle of the room, she caught Margo's approving glance and drank in the moment. She wanted to remember this night forever. Billy Ray led her in the Shag, and Trish mirrored his every step. Tonight, she couldn't even hear the clicking of her brace. As they moved in sync, he stepped around her and bellowed, "Talkin' 'bout my girl, my girl."

Their dancing was interspersed with trips to linen-covered tables spread with a smorgasbord of delicacies. As they sat on the bleachers with plates piled with finger foods and cups of punch, Marty stepped onto the stage, followed by senior class secretary Rosemary Teague.

"Now, Dolphins, this is the moment we've waited for. The crowning of our prom King and Queen. Thanks for all your votes. It was a tight race, and all our contestants were deserving." He turned. "Rosemary, do you have the envelope with the name of our 1965 Prom King?"

"I sure do."

After she passed him the envelope, he slipped out the card and grinned at the students.

Trish popped a cheese ring in her mouth and nudged Billy Ray's ribs with her elbow. "All the girls I know voted for you,

Billy Ray. I bet you win."

He leaned over and kissed her on the cheek. "Thanks. As long as I have your vote, nothing else matters."

Marty turned toward the band. "Can I have a drumroll, please?"

Trish grabbed Billy Ray's hand and held her breath.

"The winner of the 1965 Southport High School prom king crown is…Billy. Ray. Jessup."

Trish flung her arms around his neck and kissed him. "I knew it. I knew it. Congratulations!"

As the room broke out in a roar of thunderous applause, Billy Ray walked to the stage. Picking up the crown from the table behind her, Rosemary placed it on his head and motioned for him to stand beside a white throne padded with royal blue cushions.

Marty took the second envelope from Rosemary and slipped out the card. "Now for our 1965 Southport High School prom queen." He glanced at the band. "Drumroll again, please. The crown goes to…Susan. Amelia. Yearmont."

Susie clapped her hands to her chest. "Who? Me? Really?" Amid whoops and hollers, she tossed her long blonde hair over her shoulders and sashayed to the stage. Rosemary placed the crown on her head, handed her a bouquet of red roses, and ushered her to her seat on the throne.

Steadying his crown with his hand, Billy Ray leaned over and hugged her.

Trish winced, then reprimanded herself. *Of course, Billy Ray would congratulate her. He's a Southern gentleman.*

Marty turned back toward the students. "Now, as is customary, let's give this handsome royal couple a huge applause as they take to the floor for their coronation dance."

Susie laid her bouquet on the throne and slipped her arm

through Billy Ray's. After he escorted her to the center of the floor, the lights dimmed, and the disco ball was lit. As it revolved above their heads, spraying a rainbow of colors throughout the room, Susie draped her arms around Billy Ray's neck and laid her head on his chest. As they swayed to the smooth romantic vocals of "Unchained Melody," Trish stood frozen and watched with dismay.

Margo pushed through the crowd and slipped her arm around her friend. "Don't worry about it, Trish. It's just one dance. He has to, ya know?"

She nodded as large tears slid down her cheeks. Flicking them to the side, she straightened her shoulders. "I know. It just hurts. Susie is beautiful. She's perfect. Plus, it's no secret that she has a thing for Billy Ray."

"Trish, she flirts with all the guys. You know that. Hold on. He'll be back over here in a few minutes."

As Billy Ray and Susie moved to the soft strains of the music, Billy Ray locked eyes with Trish and smiled.

She burst into tears and ran toward the door.

Margo followed.

"Trish. Trish." Billy Ray walked toward the bench where Margo sat, consoling Trish.

"Here comes your guy. This is where I make my exit."

Trish reached for Margo's arm, but it slid from her grip. She turned her back as Billy approached.

He dropped on the bench beside her, clasped her shoulders, and turned her to face him.

"Baby, please. Please don't cry."

As she fell against his chest, his strong arms enveloped her.

"Trish. It was just a dance. You know Susie means nothing to me."

Feeling like her heart would burst from her chest, she straightened and looked into his questioning eyes. "Why doesn't she? She's beautiful. She's perfect. Not crippled like me."

He held her face in his hands and brushed away her tears with his thumbs. "Stop it. You're the girl I want, Patricia Malone. If I didn't, I would have invited someone else. I'm sorry, Susie and I were thrown together tonight, and you were hurt. Please, put it out of your mind. We're together now. Let's not waste the time we have. The rest of the night belongs to us."

She wiped her tears with the back of her hand. "I'm sorry. You're right. I shouldn't have let it upset me like this, but it was just so hard to see her in your arms."

He kissed her nose and hugged her. "Come on. We need to hurry. I hear Marty announcing the final song." Billy Ray reached for her hand. "We don't want to miss the last dance." As they rushed toward the gym, the lights inside dimmed. Billy Ray grabbed the doorknob, then stopped, and turned around. "On second thought, let's stay out here." He pointed upward. "We have our own starry, starry night, complete with a waning moon. It beats anything that's happening inside."

Trish peered into his eyes and kissed him lightly on the lips. "I agree. Nothing in there matters anymore."

He placed his finger over her mouth. "Shh. Listen. The band's playing the intro to 'The Way You Look Tonight.' May I have the last dance?" As he wrapped his arms around her waist and pulled her close, Trish draped her arms around his neck and cried. This time, it was happy tears.

While they swayed to the harmony of the singers, Billy Ray softly hummed the melody. Then, as the song drew to a close, he whispered, "I love you, Trish. Just the way you are."

Chapter Twenty

Friday, May 21, 1965

Billy Ray opened the door to Willie McKenzie's Ice Cream Parlor and motioned for Trish to go ahead of him.

"Well, well. Look who's here, two of my favorite people." Willie lifted his paper hat from his balding head and plopped it down again. "One grape sherbet and one chocolate nut sundae, comin' right up."

Billy Ray winked, and both laughed as they walked to their usual table in the back of the shop. "Mister Willie, one of these days, we're gonna surprise you and switch our orders…but today's not that day." He sat across the table from Trish. "So what did you think of *The Sound of Music*?"

"It was a little long, but I loved it. How about you?"

"It was okay, I guess. I'm not much into musicals, but I'm happy you liked it. I'm bettin' it doesn't do that well at the box office."

She shook her head. "I say you're wrong. I think it will tug on people's hearts and be around for a long time."

He shrugged. "Okay. You're probably a better judge of it than I am. Time will tell. What I did like was that I got to sit in the dark with my favorite girl for almost three hours."

Trish's cheeks grew hot. "You're hopeless."

Willie set their orders on the table and looked around. "From the looks of my business, the Amuzu Theatre must have been packed tonight."

Trish licked her cone. "Sold out. I think you can count on this crowd every Friday night for a while. It was a great movie. A feel-good one."

His eyes widened as he nodded with approval. "I can go for that. With all the rumblings of the war escalating in Viet Nam and President Johnson's call for more troops this week, we can use some feel-good moments."

Trying to ignore the tightening in his chest, Billy Ray took the cherry from the heaping dollops of whipped cream, popped it into his mouth, and stirred the chocolate syrup and cream together. "This is yummy as always, sir."

Willie flashed a broad smile. "Wonderful." Tapping the table, he shifted his eyes to his wife. "Welp, Missus Anna's givin' me the eye. I'd better step it up before she starts cracking her whip."

"Oh, you love it, Mister Willie." Trish wiped her mouth with her napkin. "Somebody has to keep you straight."

He leaned down and whispered as he walked away. "Yeah, but that's just between us, okay? Wouldn't want to ruin my reputation around here."

Trish sat back in her chair and met Billy Ray's eyes. "That was so good. Thanks for a nice night."

He nodded and scraped the bottom of his bowl.

"Are you sure you don't want to lick it?"

He laughed. "I would if I were home, but I don't want to embarrass my classy date."

"Thank you. She's grateful." Trish glanced at the lighted Hershey's Ice Cream clock over the counter. "It's getting late. Momma won't sleep until I come through the door."

"I know." He walked to the register attended by Mr. Willie's oldest son. The business was becoming a family affair.

Billy Ray pulled his Sprite into Trish's drive and cut off the engine. With one hand gripping the steering wheel, he paused and stared straight ahead.

"You okay? You've been quiet ever since we left Willie's."

He grimaced and slumped back in his seat.

Trish gripped his arm and shook it. "Billy Ray, stop it. What's wrong? You're scaring me."

He shifted his gaze to hers, then leaned over and popped open the glove compartment. As he pulled out a white card and handed it to her, the light in his eyes dimmed.

The card felt weighty in her hand, and her skin tingled. She knew. "Selective Service System Order to Report for Induction. The President of the United States to Billy Ray Jessup, 242 River Drive, Southport, North Carolina."

Trish's voice broke as her eyes shot to Billy Ray's. "Is this for real?"

He pressed his lips together and nodded. "I'd never joke about anything like this."

Her hands shook, and her voice trembled as she continued to read. Her words fell like morsels of hope slipping through her fingers.

"15 May 1965. Greetings: You are hereby ordered for induction into the Armed Forces of the United States and to report at Wilmington Cape Fear Public Transit, 505 Cando Street, Wilmington, NC, on 18 June 1965 at 5:30 a.m. for forwarding to an Armed Forces Induction Station. R.J.Striker, Member or Clerk of Local Board"

She looked up and peered into Billy Ray's glassy eyes. "No. No. I won't let you go."

Billy Ray dug deep to maintain his composure as Trish fell into his arms and wept. "I'm sorry. I've struggled with when to tell you. I figured it would be better to break the news to you tonight than closer to graduation."

"So where are they taking you?"

"I'll go to Fort Jackson in Columbia for eight weeks of basic training."

"And then?"

"From there, I'll leave for six to eight weeks of specialty training. Wherever and whatever that ends up being."

She sat up and wiped tears from her cheeks. "You mean I won't see you for sixteen weeks?"

"Probably about that."

"So when *will* I see you again?"

"I'm not sure. If, like other guys I know, I should have a two-week pass before…"

Her eyes widened as she clenched his hands. "Before what?"

"Before…before, I ship out to Viet Nam."

Stunned, she pounded his chest. "No. No. You can't. I won't let them have you. I won't." She fell against him. "You can't leave me, Billy Ray. You can't."

"Shh. Shh. It's going to be okay, Trish." He inhaled her sweet smell and stroked her hair as his insides roiled. "I'll be in Nam for a year. Probably serve in the States for another. Then, it will all be over. Who knows? Maybe we'll win this war from hell sooner, and I'll be home before my year is up." He kissed her hair and rested his chin on her head. "We'll pray for that, Trish. We'll ask God to shorten this war. He can do that, ya know."

She sniffed. "I wish I could believe He would, but right now, I'm so mad at Him, I can't see straight."

"Hey…I'll make a deal with you."

She popped up and studied his expression. "What's that?"

"I'll believe. You pray."

A slight smile spread across her face. "What about if we

both believe and we both pray?"

"Deal. I love you, Trish." He clung to her trembling body and pressed his lips to hers. He wouldn't dare let her see how frightened he was. He'd heard the horror stories.

Pray hard, Trish. Pray harder than you've ever prayed before.

Wednesday, June 2, 1965

Trish drove her mother's 1958 Rambler American up the long driveway that led to the Jessups' house on River Drive. She'd always admired the Southport homes that fronted the Cape Fear River, but she'd never known anyone who lived in one of them. She'd looked forward all week to attending Billy Ray's graduation party, but now that she was here, her stomach was in knots, and she second-guessed her decision to come. Thoughts of meeting his parents petrified her.

Before she rang the bell of the two-story Southern Victorian home with a wrap-around porch, she heard music and laughter. She didn't know many of the seniors and hoped Margo and Paul were already inside. As she reached for the bell, the door flew open, and Susie Yearmont blew past her.

"Hey, Trish. I'll be right back." She dashed down the steps. "I left Billy Ray's present in the car."

Trish thought of the small, inexpensive gift in her shoulder bag and hoped Billy Ray would like it. She felt sure it couldn't compare to whatever Susie had for him, though.

She stepped into the large foyer that housed a curved staircase leading to a balcony on the second floor. *So this is how the rich live.*

"Trish, you're here."

She breathed a sigh of relief as Billy Ray smiled and walked through the dining room.

He hugged her and gave her a light kiss on the lips. "Come in and get something to eat. I've never seen so much food." He laid his hand on the small of her back and escorted her to the rear of the house and into a large, glassed-in family room adjacent to the kitchen.

"Is Margo here yet?"

"No, she's not coming."

Her eyes shot to Billy Ray's face. "What do you mean she's not coming? Why not? She told me she—"

"Paul called about fifteen minutes ago and said his car broke down on the way. He's having it towed in for repairs."

Trish lowered her head and sighed.

He wrapped his arm around her shoulders. "Come on. You'll be okay. I want you to meet my mother. She's in the kitchen. Dad's out back with some of the guys."

She cringed at his suggestion and tried hard not to let her anxiety show. In social settings such as this one, she wore her leg brace like heavy signage and was conscious of heads pivoting as its clicks broadcast her arrival.

"Mother, I want you to meet someone."

Mrs. Jessup placed a bowl of chips on the long table in the dining room. "Of course—" When she turned, her smile melted, and her eyes dimmed.

"This is Trish Malone, Mother."

His mother's breath hitched as her long, slender fingers, boasting bright red fingernail polish that matched her now pinched red lips, gripped Trish's hand. A strained welcome followed.

"Nice to meet you, ma'am. Thanks for inviting me. Your house is lovely."

She stammered a response. "You're welcome. My son in—"

Billy Ray grabbed Trish's hand and led her out the back door and onto the deck, where a tall, slender man leaned against the railing and joked with several senior boys. He flashed a warm smile as they approached.

"Why, Billy, who's this lovely young lady on your arm?"

"You know, Dad. This is the girl I told you about. Trish Malone."

"Oh, yes, of course. Billy Ray speaks very fondly of you."

Her insides relaxed as she shook his hand. "It's nice to meet you, Mr. Jessup. I could say lots of fine things about your son too."

"Whew. That's good to know." He pulled over a chair. "Have a seat."

"That's all right, Pop. I want her to get something to eat first."

"Oh, sure. Of course. There's a ton of food in there. If you kids haven't come with huge appetites, I'll be eating it for the rest of the month."

Trish laughed and squeezed Billy Ray's hand as they walked away. "He's so kind. Just like you." After Trish filled her plate, Billy Ray carried her punch into the family room, where several tables were set up. "Where would you like to sit?"

She scanned the room filled with familiar yet strange faces.

Susie Yearmont waved her hand above her head from a table by the window. "Billy Ray, Trish can sit with us."

"Perfect," he said as he set her cup on the table and pulled out her chair. "You girls chat while I greet the others."

Trish placed her napkin in her lap. "Thanks, Susie." She looked at Rosemary Teague and one of the cheerleaders sitting across from her. Susie introduced her to them both.

Although they were cordial, she had little in common with them and couldn't shake her discomfort. It hurt to overhear their chatter about the gifts they'd brought for Billy Ray and how Susie planned to write to him while he was in Viet Nam. She knew their exchange was for her benefit and was probably the sole reason Susie offered her a place at their table.

Once she finished eating, she excused herself and walked out to the dock. As she passed Billy Ray's father and several of the guys playing horseshoes, he tipped his Dolphins' cap and smiled at her. She liked him. She liked him a lot.

The traffic on the water was heavy as people took advantage of the beautiful spring weather. Trish marveled at the sleek boats that slowed in passing, making sure they respected the no-wake zone. What she'd give to get a glimpse inside of one. Life from the Jessups' point of view and her family's was worlds apart. It was hard to believe her house was less than two miles away.

"Hey, Trish."

Startled, she turned to see Billy Ray trotting across the yard.

"I've looked all over for you. What are you doing out here?"

"Taking in this amazing view. You're so lucky. Do you ever fish from here?"

"As much as I can, but ball practice and senior events have taken most of my time this year."

"That's a pretty boat," she said, pointing to the one tied to the dock.

"Thanks. Dad bought it a couple of years ago. It's a Sea Ray Runabout. Have you ever been out on the waterway?"

She shook her head.

"I'll take you sometime." He sat on the bench next to her and held her hand. "Let's go back inside. I'm going to open my gifts soon."

"Wait. I almost forgot." She reached into her purse. "I didn't put this on the gift table because I wanted to give it to you in private." She handed it to him. "It's not much, but I hope you like it."

"Thank you. I know I will."

"Wanna open it now?"

"Sure." Billy Ray pulled off the wrapping, reached into the box, and lifted out a white 5x7 frame displaying their picture— one a stranger took with Trish's camera at Sunset Beach the day he'd given her the ring. "Wow. I love this. Thank you." He hugged her. "That was a special day for us."

She nodded. "I know. I hope you'll take it with you and keep it beside your bunk in the barracks."

He laid the frame back in the box. "You bet I will. It's my favorite gift."

"But you haven't opened the others."

He grabbed her hand and winked. "I don't have to. I already know." He kissed her on the nose. "Come on. Let's go inside. I told Pop I'd only be a few minutes." He wrapped his arm around her shoulders and walked toward the house.

Trish leaned into him and choked back tears.

Chapter Twenty-One

Murphy barked and pawed the sand. After stuffing his nose in the hole, he backed away and sneezed. Undaunted, he slapped his broad paws on the ground again, crouched above the ghost crab's safe haven, and dug feverishly, sand flying.

Logan strained to get his attention with two quick yanks on his leash. "Come on, fella. Don't you know by now you can't catch those crabs?"

The tenacious retriever paused, then glanced back and whined.

Logan tugged again. "Give it up, boy. Today's a workday for me." Murphy complied and fell in beside him as they walked along the water's edge. "I know every day is a play day for you, but if you want to keep eating, somebody's got to work." Accompanied by the cry of gulls overhead, his name drifted to his ears.

"Logan. Wait up."

Turning, he saw Brooklyn running toward him, her hand holding her wide-brimmed hat in place. "Good morning," she said, coming to a breathless stop.

He wrapped his arm around her waist and kissed her cheek. "Hi, sunshine. This is a nice surprise. Been stalking me long?"

"A while. I thought you'd never hear me." She leaned over and rubbed Murphy's head. "Hey, fella. I'm glad you slowed your daddy down." She looped her arm through Logan's as they waded in the surf. "Isn't it gorgeous out here?"

"Yep." He brushed her hair from her eyes. "And now that you're beside me, it's near perfect."

She lowered her head. "You're such a flatterer, but I'll take it."

"It's all true. I mean every word of it."

"Thank you. It's nice to see you."

"I'm glad you caught up with me. You were on my call list for today."

"I was?"

"You'll love this news. Herman Meade's lot is ready for hookup. The last of the utilities were connected yesterday."

Her large eyes bulged. "Really? That's fantastic."

"Please tell Chase he can pull his Airstream in any time he wants."

"I sure will, and I can't wait to tell Natalya. She will be over-the-moon excited. We've had such fun buying everything she needs to set up housekeeping."

"I'm happy it all worked out. I think this will be the perfect setup for her."

"I agree." She looked up at Logan. "So, how about you? What's on your plate today?"

"One closing this morning and an afternoon meeting with a potential buyer at an older home on the waterway."

"Oooh…good for you." She pushed her sunglasses up on her nose. "How are things coming along with your house next door?"

"We're on our way. The lot's cleared, and they'll pour the slab this morning."

"Wow. You *are* making progress."

"How about you? Are you working?"

"I am. I go in at ten. Since Natalya works the coffee counter, it will be the perfect time for me to tell her about the lot. I can't wait to see her face. It doesn't take much to make her happy. She appreciates everything people do for her." Brooklyn stopped. "This has been nice, but I need to head back to the house. I don't want to be late for work."

He placed his hand on the back of her neck and pulled her toward him. "Thanks for making my day, Brooklyn Marshal." He lowered his face to hers and kissed her. "Wanna meet at the pier tonight for a hamburger?"

She nodded. "Sure. I'd love that."

"How about six-thirty? That should give me plenty of time after my afternoon showing."

"I'll see you there." She spun on her heels and walked up the beach.

Logan watched. She seemed more relaxed around him lately. Hopefully, she'd worked through the worst of her fears.

Logan drove over the rock-riddled sandy drive toward an old house on the Intracoastal waterway. As he followed the winding drive through thick underbrush and low-hanging water oaks, he wondered about the story behind this property. Tied up in an estate for over a decade, the old home now belonged to an out-of-state heir who simply wanted to be out from under the responsibility of a house to which he had no sentimental ties.

Logan parked at the end of the walk leading to an older, two-story frame house with a long porch that fronted the waterway. He'd purposely arrived an hour before his client to become familiar with the property. This home had great potential but was definitely a fixer-upper. After his walk-through, he sat on the front step and scrolled through social media.

Hearing a car turn into the drive, he checked his watch. *Right on time. Always a good sign.* After parking a late-model Lexus SUV beside Logan's jeep, a man about his age stepped out and waved.

Logan met him halfway on the walk and extended his hand. "Hi, I'm Logan Corbett."

He responded with a firm handshake. "Stuart Wagner. Nice to meet you." He placed his hands on his hips and looked out across the waterway. "This is some view. From the road, I never would have guessed it would be this nice. The pictures on the internet don't do it justice, either."

"That's the way it is with coastal property. You've got to see it and breathe in the fresh salt air to really know how special it is here on the coast. Where ya from?"

"Kentucky." He laughed. "There's certainly nothing like this where we live."

"So you're married? Any children?"

He smiled. "Three stair-step stemwinders. Ages five, seven, and nine. Thought I'd look the place over before I get my family's hopes up. My wife loves the coast and has wanted to move back to North Carolina for a long time. Grew up not far from here. Whiteville."

"Oh, yes, I know it well. As a kid, I loved the glass-bottom boats on White Lake. Have a lot of happy memories from that place." He slapped his hands together. "Okay, now. Would you like to walk the acreage or see inside first?"

"I'm anxious to see inside. It looks like it's going to take quite a bit of work." He chuckled. "But I've never been one to shy away from hard work." He followed Logan onto the porch.

"What's your profession?"

"I'm in software development. Work remotely, so I can live anywhere."

"Can't ask for better than that." He swung open the door. "Step inside and take a look around. Who knows, this may be your forever home."

After they toured the house and walked the property lines, Logan leaned against his jeep and folded his arms. "So what do you think?"

Stuart shoved his hands in his pockets and rocked back on his heels. "I like it. Like it a lot. It has great potential. Must have been a beauty in its day. I particularly like the privacy." He scanned the area and pointed as he spoke. "Wouldn't take much to get the yard in shape. Cut back some of the underbrush. Restore the pier. The kids would love it. They're all good swimmers. Even my five-year-old swims like a fish."

"It's a playground, for sure. For old and young alike. You could rent close by and enjoy the waterway while you work on the inside."

He bit his lip and raised his brows. "You think there's any wiggle room in the asking price?"

"Possibly. I know the owner is more than ready to sell. I think he'd be receptive to taking less as long as it's a fair offer. I wouldn't want to come in with a ridiculous one and tick him off."

"Oh, I understand that." He nodded and offered his hand. "I'd like my wife to see it first. I'll talk to her and get back in touch with you soon. Think you could give me first right of refusal if someone else happens to jump in?"

"Perhaps." Logan pulled a card from his pocket and handed it to him. "My cell number is on here. Call me any time. If you have further questions, I'm always available to answer them."

Stuart walked to the driver's side of his car and lifted his hand. "I'll connect with you soon." After opening the door, he hesitated and tipped his head toward Logan's Grand Cherokee. "I see you got your jeep fixed." As soon as the words left his mouth, he dropped behind the wheel, followed the circular drive, and drove away.

Logan's breath caught in his throat as he watched the Lexus turn onto the road. Squinting, he locked his hands behind his head and mouthed—*car fixed?*

Chapter Twenty-Two

I checked the clock behind the counter at the pier, then breathed a sigh of relief as Logan walked through the door and sat across the table from me. "For a moment, I thought you'd stood me up. Is everything okay?"

"I'm sorry. I should've called. My showing ran later than I'd planned. I got here as quick as I could."

"So, how did things go?"

He grinned. "Good. Very promising."

"Wonderful. Don't keep me in suspense, though. I want to hear all about it."

He dismissed my comment with a wave and turned to look at the specials on the board. "Let's order first. I'm starved. My morning closing took longer than I thought it would, and I missed lunch. What are you having? A burger?"

"Yes. I've tasted it ever since you suggested it this morning."

"Got it." He walked to the counter. After placing our orders, Logan brought our drinks to the table and sighed. "So…how was your day? Did you talk to Natalya?"

I grinned. "I did, and she was ecstatic. Then, I talked to Chase. He's going to pull the Airstream onto the lot tomorrow and hook it up. Natalya's sponsor will be out of town this weekend, so I offered to help her move in. I can't imagine not helping. I've looked forward to this day about as much as she has."

"That's great. You're a good friend. I know she'll appreciate it."

"She's a breath of fresh air, and I always feel good when I'm around her." I squeezed lemon into my tea and stirred it. "What did you think of the property you showed today? Is it nice?"

"It's a pretty location, but it needs a lot of work. For someone who doesn't mind waiting a while to move in, it's a good investment. The land alone is worth the asking price."

"Did the work seem to bother your client?" I noted his expressions as he answered.

"Not at all. He was fine with it. His wife is from North Carolina, and she wants to come back home. They live in Kentucky now."

"I see." After the waitress brought our food, our conversation waned. Logan tried to stay engaged, but I could tell his mind was elsewhere. I laid my hand on top of his. "Please tell me what's bothering you. And don't you dare say that it's *nothing*. I know better."

He peered into my eyes. "It's that apparent, huh?"

I nodded. "Let's just say it's a good thing you're not a poker player."

He tossed his napkin on the table, picked up his soda, and leaned back in his chair. "Mr. Wagner and I got along well. He's a nice fella…and smart. He knows a lot about real estate and asked all of the right questions."

I shrugged. "So…what's the problem?"

He shook his head. "I'm not sure. Can't quite figure him out. Before he got in his car to leave, he looked at my jeep and said, 'I see you got your jeep fixed,' and then he drove off."

His answer puzzled me. "You've never met him?"

"Nope. When he called me to set up the appointment, he

said he'd been in Myrtle Beach for a few days on business and had run across the listing online. He planned to return to Kentucky on Saturday and wanted to see the property before he left."

"Is there anything online that would have clued him into your accident? A police report or something?"

"Not that I know of. That was over a month ago and pretty insignificant in the grand scheme of things."

I sat and mulled things over. "This is weird. What kind of car did he drive?"

"A Lexus SUV."

"And the color?"

"That's what shook me to the core."

My chest tightened, and I swallowed hard. I knew what he was going to say. "It was white, wasn't it?"

He nodded. "Yep. Sure was."

I leaned on the table. "Logan, what's going on? Do you think he's the one who sideswiped you?"

He shrugged. "Could be. I don't know."

"Has anything happened with one of your clients that would make them mad at you?" "Not that I know of. Maybe I should give the police a call."

"I think you should. Did you get his plate number?"

He shook his head. "I was too stunned, but I did notice something."

"What?"

He leaned in and laid his hand on mine. "It wasn't a Kentucky plate."

"What was it?"

"North Carolina."

Saturday, May 27, 2023

I held the door open for Natalya as she carried a cardboard box into the Airstream and set it on the red Formica table. Her wide eyes skimmed the living area as she walked toward the bedroom to check out the rest of the trailer. Afterward, she sat beside me on the couch, hugged me, then dropped back against the cushion. "Thees is wonderful," she said in her thick Ukrainian accent.

"I'm glad you like it. I must say, Chase and Logan went the extra mile to get Daisy cleaned up and ready for you."

"I hope to meet theem and thank theem," she said, tucking a few strands of stray blond hair into her messy bun.

"I'm sure you'll have a chance to do that soon."

"It was nice of all of you. I'm forever indebted to the three of you."

I shook my head. "Please, don't feel like that. You owe us nothing. It was our pleasure. You've been through a lot and have worked hard. You deserve it."

She blushed and, with her finger, traced the words on the pillow I'd bought her. *Home is where you park your camper.* She chuckled and looked at me with tears in her eyes. "Thank you, Brooklyn. I have sometheeng for you also." She walked to the table, reached into the carton, and returned with her gift.

"Thank you," I said, taking the small white box from her hands.

"I'm sorry, I didn't have any wrapping paper."

"That's quite all right, but you shouldn't have done anything."

"I wanted to." She motioned me on. "You've been so

helpful."

After opening the box, I pulled back the tissue and lifted out a beautiful stained-glass sunflower. "Oh, Natalya…this is gorgeous. Thank you."

"You're very welcome. The sunflower is Ukraine's national flower. It's a symbol of peace and resistance—growing in difficulty. There are millions of sunflower fields in my country. My papa produced them and sold his harvest to oil manufacturers." Her eyes danced as she relayed the happy memory.

I held the glass treasure to my chest. "I will cherish this and, in hard times, will try to remember that difficulty produces strength. It's a very thoughtful gift." I leaned over and hugged her. "Thank you again."

"You are welcome, my padrooga."

Leaning back, I furrowed my brow.

She laughed. "Padrooga means friend. You have been very kind to me. I am honored to call you a friend."

As tears threatened to spill from my eyes, I slapped my hands on my knees. "Okay, we've got work to do. I'll get the rest of your boxes from my trunk while you put things where you want them." Unpacking Natalya's few belongings didn't take long, and I was blessed to share in her adventure. The camper's red, black, and white fifties color scheme was the perfect backdrop for her lovely sunflower mementoes. Afterward, we sat at the table, and she served me a cup of hot tea with a slice of Yabluchnyk, a Ukrainian apple cake.

"Mmm." The moist, light cake melted in my mouth. "This is so yummy. Is it a family recipe?"

Her expression brightened. "It makes my heart happy that you like it. I'm not sure where Mama got it, but she made it often.

Sometimes, she'd make it with cherries or peaches. I will share the recipe with you."

"That would be wonderful," I said, stuffing another bite of the delicately flavored cake into my mouth. I pointed with my fork to a photograph behind her of a handsome soldier. "Is that your husband?"

"Yes." She took the frame from the ledge and gazed at it with a sweet expression. Her voice cracked as she spoke. "My Yuri. Such a kind man. So good to me. He promised me a family when he returned. Now I'm alone. As far as I know, all of my family is gone."

I jumped at a knock on the door.

"Anybody home?"

I grinned at Natalya. "It's Logan. Wanna answer?"

"Oh, yes." She returned the picture to the ledge, jumped from the table, and swung open the door. "Logan Corbett, you are my hero. Thank you for this."

He stepped in and embraced her. "Ah…so you approve?"

"Approve? It's perfect. All I need. I couldn't be more excited." She motioned toward the table. "Please. Please sit next to Brooklyn. The least I can do is serve you a piece of cake."

He laughed. "You won't have to twist my arm. I never turn down cake or an opportunity to sit beside a beautiful woman." He chuckled and slipped in beside me. "Hi, sunshine."

My skin tingled as his lips brushed my cheek. "This is a nice surprise."

"I've had you ladies on my mind all morning and want to know if there's anything I can do for you."

I cast Natalya a questioning glance.

She smiled and pointed to a panel of switches. "Yes, there is. After you eat, would you show me what all of these buttons are for?"

"Of course, I will."

While the three of us sat chatting at the table, I tried to take in the sweetness of the moment. Today marked a new day, a fresh start for Natalya. Although my heart broke for her and her continued struggle, she was a living example of a beautiful spirit shaped by difficulty. Her perseverance and optimism challenged me to put my problems in perspective. I laid my hand on Logan's and looked at him with increased gratitude. I prayed I would never take his presence in my life for granted.

Chapter Twenty-Three

Thursday, June 17, 1965
Trish

Sun danced across the ocean waves, and gulls cried overhead as the endless horizon stretched before them. Trish tightened her sunhat under her chin and leaned back in the seat of the Jessup's 1963 Sea Ray Runabout. From behind her sunglasses, she studied Billy Ray in the captain's chair across from her. He looked older at his place behind the wheel, yet in her eyes, he was still very much a boy. Certainly, one too young to face the horrors of a war 10,000 miles away. His bravery astonished her.

As he pulled down on the throttle, the boat's engine roared to life, and a rush of adrenaline shot through her. Looking over, he tilted his head toward the sky, kissed the air, and yelled above the wind. "Whatcha think?"

"It's fabulous. I can't believe how smooth the ride is. Your Bugeye is now my second love."

He struck his chest with his fist. "Oh, pierces like a dagger to my heart."

She shrugged. "Sorry, I cannot tell a lie."

Billy Ray smiled and curled his fingers to form an okay sign.

While cool air brushed against her warm skin and water splashed against the hull, she inhaled the fresh, salty scent of the ocean and propped her bare feet on the console in front of her. "How long does it take to get to Bald Head?"

"About twenty minutes. It's three miles across the Cape Fear."

"What do you know about the lighthouse? Anything?"

"Not a lot, other than it's 110 feet tall and the oldest standing lighthouse in the state. It was built in 1817."

She swept her hair from her eyes and nodded.

"Oh…and in the fourth grade, I learned that in the 1700s, pirates Blackbeard and Stede Bonnet used the island as a safe place to restock supplies and hide their loot."

"Wow. That's neat." She laughed. "We should have brought shovels."

"Ha. Maybe so."

Silence followed as they lost themselves in the beauty of their surroundings and, for Trish, the gravity of her thoughts. Once Billy Ray was trained and deployed to Viet Nam, it would be over a year before he would return home. That might as well be forever. For her to go into her Senior year without his reassuring wink as they passed in the hall, without meeting him at the bottom of the stairs for lunch, or riding home in his red Sprite, was more than she could take in. *And what if he…? No. She wouldn't entertain that. Of course, he would. Wouldn't he, Lord?*

Trish returned to the present as Billy Ray dropped anchor close to shore. The expanse of sand against a backdrop of lush green vegetation on the south beach was how the island got its name. The small dunes reminded mariners of a man's bald head, and thus, the island became Bald Head or Old Baldy. "Nice landing, Billy Ray. You're a pretty decent Captain."

He stood and stretched. "Thanks. It's time to shift gears and see how good of a cook you are."

She laughed. "I'm sure my sandwiches will stack alongside the best of them, but I've gotta be honest, Momma baked the chocolate cake. No one's baking outshines hers."

"Yum. I think I hear it calling my name." He lifted the picnic basket from the stern and helped Trish from the boat and through the shallow water. "You, pick the spot, beautiful. I'll follow."

Trish found a patch of shade cast by a twisted live oak tree and spread out a hand-stitched quilt her Granny had sewn. "This looks like a wonderful place to me."

"I second that." He set the basket on the edge of the quilt so the wind wouldn't lift it and dropped beside it. "Wanna do the honors?"

"Sure." Trish sat next to him and passed out the goodies. "There's another ham and cheese sandwich in here if you want it."

His eyes expressed approval as he twisted the cap from his soda. "Thanks, but I think one will probably be enough. Gotta save room for your momma's cake."

Trish grinned. "We could start with dessert."

He chuckled. "It's tempting, but I like saving the best for last. Kinda like you." He leaned over and kissed her. "I've dated a few girls, Trish. But you're the best...and the last."

Tears welled in her eyes as she returned his kiss. "Thank you. You're last for me too. I know when I've found the best there is."

After lunch, Billy stretched out on his back and motioned for Trish to join him. Lying her head on his outstretched arm, she stared into the Carolina blue sky. The sound of water lapping against the shore and wind whistling through the trees could have lulled her to sleep.

"Trish, are you okay with waiting for me to come home? A year's a long time, ya know, and I hate for you to be tied down in your Senior year."

She followed the movement of fluffy white clouds that dotted the blue canvas overhead. "I'll be fine. There's no one I'd rather be with than you. Don't worry about me. Just be sure you come home to me, okay?"

He rolled onto his side, wrapped his arm around her waist, and peered deep into her eyes. "I will, Trish. I promise." He kissed her, then slipped his arm from under her head. "Come here," he said, pulling her to a sitting position. "Trish, you still have a year of school, so this is premature, but I can't leave here and not know. I probably should have bought a ring, but I didn't want you to feel pressured to say yes or feel guilty if you change your mind while I'm away."

"What are you saying?"

He squeezed her hands. "Trish, when I come home from Nam, will you marry me?"

Her heart drummed in her chest, and her mouth fell open. "Are you serious?"

"Of course I am. I wouldn't joke about something like this."

She moved closer, wrapped her arms around his neck, and peered into his anxious eyes. "Yes, Billy Ray. Yes, I will marry you. I'd marry you right now if I could. If you had asked me sooner, we could have gotten married before you left."

He shook his head. "No. No. It's better this way. Waiting till I return will give me something good to look forward to."

She held his face and gave him a quick kiss. "And it will give me something to plan for while you're away. Oh, Billy Ray, I love you."

He wrapped her in his arms and smothered her with kisses. "I love you, Patricia Malone." He slid off his class ring, reached for her hand, and slipped it on her ring finger. "It's a little big, but it'll have to do for now. Whatcha think?"

She held her hand out in front of her. "With a little bit of paraffin wax, it will be perfect." She furrowed her brow. "Just be sure you remember that a promise is a promise."

He nodded. "I will. I could never forget, nor would I want to." He lifted her chin and pressed his lips to hers.

Trish welcomed them. This moment was what she would cling to until Billy came home to her. *Please, God, let it be so.*

They sat in one another's embrace and said nothing until Billy Ray broke the silence. "You wanna go see Old Baldy?"

She nodded. "Yes. I'd love that. I've never been inside a lighthouse."

"Well, we're about to change that." He folded the quilt, laid it on top of the picnic basket, and led her through thick vegetation toward the white, stucco-covered brick structure.

Before entering the tower, Billy Ray jiggled the doorknob of the vacant light keeper's house. It was locked and had been unmanned since the lighthouse was deactivated in 1935. Its beam once guided ships entering the Cape Fear. Now, the octagonal building was a day beacon and historic landmark—an enduring symbol of Bald Head Island.

As they entered, Trish looked up at the rectangular stairway made of Carolina yellow pine leading to the lantern room at the top of the narrowing tower. "I wish I could climb up there, but my legs would refuse to carry me." She nudged Billy Ray. "Why don't you go. I'll wait for you."

"And leave you down here? No way."

"Hush. I mean it. Go on. We've come all this way. One of us needs to go up there. Then you can tell me how many steps there are."

"Are you sure?"

She smiled. "Yes, I'm sure. I'll follow you around from the outside. You can stop at each window and wave."

He kissed her on the forehead. "You're something else.

Okay…but before you walk out and wait for me at the first window, take a guess as to how many steps there are?"

"Hmm. You said the tower is 110 feet tall. I say there are about that many steps. I guess one hundred and five. How about you?"

"I'll say one hundred and fifteen. Whoever is closest wins."

"Wins what?"

He shrugged. "I don't know. Just wins."

She laughed. "Okay. Deal." Trish followed him to all six of the windows in the octagonal tower. Each time he climbed higher, she stepped back farther so she'd be sure to see him at the next one. It took him about twenty minutes to reach all six windows. Trish was surprised when the last one flew open. "Hey, Trish. There are one hundred and eight steps and a ship's ladder to the lantern room."

She curled her hands around her mouth and shouted. "Yay! I'm closest. I win."

"I guess you do," he yelled. "I'm on my way back down."

"Okay." As she turned to walk to a bench near the keeper's house, Billy Ray shouted. "Hey, Patricia Millicent Malone."

She turned to see him leaning out the window.

"Will you marry me?"

As his words echoed through the air, she laughed. "Yes. I. Will. Billy Ray Jessup."

"Whoopee!" he said, slamming the window. "I'll be right down."

Trish waited on the bench, admiring her surroundings, and tried to make sense of the huge turn of events in her life. Knowing Billy Ray Jessup had changed everything for her. Hearing a door slam, she looked up. Billy Ray sprinted toward her. Oblivious to her limp, she ran to meet him and fell into his arms. She laughed as he whirled her around. "You're going to make me dizzy, Billy Ray."

"You've already made me dizzy, Trish. Dizzy with love for you." He lowered her feet to the ground and kissed her.

She thought her heart would burst through the walls of her chest. "I love you too, Mr. Jessup." Tomorrow, he would leave her. He would be the property of Uncle Sam, but today…he was hers. All hers. Nothing could destroy the thrill of this moment and a day spent in his arms.

Chapter Twenty-Four

Friday, June 18, 1965

Trish peeked at the clock on the nightstand and moaned. Flipping over, she buried her face in the pillow to muffle her sobs. *Gone. Sixteen weeks. The first day of forever.*

"Trish. Are you awake?"

"Yes, Momma." She sat up. "Come in if you want."

Jane Malone eased open the door and sat on the edge of the bed. "Hard morning?"

Nodding, she pushed back tears as a lump rose in her throat.

Her mother wrapped her in a familiar, warm bear hug. "I'm so sorry. I can certainly relate to the pain of missing someone you love."

"I know you can, and as much as I hurt, my pain can't begin to compare to yours. At least Billy Ray and I can write to each other."

Her momma sniffed and blotted her eyes with her apron. "I remember when your father was in Korea. Being apart was hard for us, but time slid by faster than we thought, and when we were together again, our days were sweeter than ever. It will be the same for you and Billy Ray."

Trish dried her cheeks with the back of her hand. "I sure hope so."

Her momma squeezed her shoulder. "I know so. Just try to stay busy and take things one day at a time." She clapped her hands and walked toward the door. "Now, speaking of time and staying busy, you don't want to be late for your first day at McKenzie's. Hop up and dress while I fix you a bite to eat."

"Thanks, Momma. I'll hurry." Trish lifted Billy Ray's picture from the nightstand and kissed it. "I'd give anything to know where you are right now. Maybe you're already at Fort Jackson and having a good time."

Billy Ray handed back the wallet-size black and white photo to Phil Harper, the tall, slender recruit in the seat beside him on the Greyhound bus. "She's really pretty. Looks like we're both lucky guys." He reached into his shirt pocket and pulled out Trish's class picture. "This is my girl, Trish."

He nodded. "You're right. We've both got good incentives to make it back home in one piece." He tucked his girlfriend's photo inside his wallet and returned it to his pocket.

"Where's home for you?"

"Leland."

"Leland?" Billy Ray hesitated and twisted his mouth. "Hmm…Southport played Leland in sports. Were you on the basketball team?"

"I was."

"Ah…I thought you looked familiar. Turns out we beat you in the state finals. I hope you won't hold that against me."

He laughed. "I remember that game well, and now that you bring it up, I remember you. That wasn't our best night, for sure." He reached over and shook his hand. "Well, partner, we're on the same team now."

"You've got that right."

"Do people call you Billy or Billy Ray?"

"Most at home call me Billy Ray, but I'm thinkin' I'll drop

the Ray. Sounds more grown-up." He shifted in his seat and turned his body toward Phil. "Have you lived in Leland all your life?"

"Yep. My parents grew up there. My dad's a builder, and my mom's a third-grade teacher."

"How about you?"

"Always Southport. My father's a loan officer at Waccamaw Bank, and my mother's a homemaker. This is my first time away. You?"

"Same. Other than summer camps."

"I hope we can stick together while we're here."

"That would be nice."

They both sat silent, as did the other recruits on the bus. Billy Ray tilted back his seat and watched the early morning sun peek through a break in the clouds. He didn't have to be a mind reader to know what Phil and the others were thinking. News reports were grim, and President Johnson's recent escalation of troops certainly wasn't a sign that the war was gonna cool down anytime soon.

He closed his eyes and tried to envision Trish on her first day at the ice cream parlor with Mister Willie. His life had been turned on its head and was more than he could wrap his mind around. Yesterday, he was cruising the Cape Fear with his beautiful girl by his side, and today, he was on a bus filled with somber, naive recruits headed toward an obscure, subtropical combat zone 10,000 miles away.

As the bus hissed to a stop at South Carolina's Fort Jackson, a drill sergeant hopped on shouting orders. "First things first. Always answer me with 'Yes, Drill Sergeant.' Do you understand?"

"Yes, Drill Sergeant," the recruits said in unison.

Next, in the crescendo of instructions, "All of you must be

off of my bus in two minutes. Duffle bag in your right hand, paperwork in your left, and standing tall. Got it?"

"Yes, Drill Sergeant."

By now, Billy Ray knew there was but one thing he understood—he wanted to go home. *Yes, Drill Sergeant.*

Home.

Trish

"Sure, Mister Willie, I'll be fine."

As Willie McKenzie walked out the door, Trish dug into the five-gallon tub of cherry vanilla ice cream and dropped two scoops into a glass dish. After drizzling chocolate syrup and sprinkling nuts on top, she swirled whipped cream, dropped on a cherry, and passed the sundae to the girl on the opposite side of the counter.

"Thank you." A tear slid down her cheek as she held up her dish. "This one's for my boyfriend."

"Really?"

"Yes. A chocolate, cherry vanilla nut sundae is his favorite. He gave me a couple of dollars last night and told me to have a sundae on him today."

"Aw…that's sweet."

She lowered her head. "He left for Fort Jackson this morning."

The can of whipped cream slipped from Trish's hand and clanked into the sink. "Oops." She scrambled to pick it up. "He did? Did he leave from Wilmington?"

"Yes."

She slapped her hand to her chest. "Really? My boyfriend

left from there this morning.”

The blond-haired girl’s clear-green eyes bulged as her mouth flew open. “Are you kidding me?”

“Nope.” She motioned toward a table. “You should eat your ice cream before it melts.” Trish walked from around the counter and followed her with a glass of water and several napkins. “By the way, my name is Trish Malone.”

“It’s nice to meet you, Trish. I’m Stella. Stella Merchant.” She smiled as she wiped drips of ice cream from the sides of her dish with a napkin. “Do you have a few minutes to talk?”

She looked toward the door and eased into the chair across from her. “Mister Willie left for the post office, but I’m good until a customer comes in.” Trish leaned back and sighed. “Wow. It feels good to sit down. We were super busy at lunch.” She tightened her ponytail and adjusted her paper hat. “So, do you live in Southport?”

“I do now. We moved from Belville a few weeks ago. My father got a job as a mechanic at the yacht basin. We’re renting a house on Cape Harbor Drive.”

“Cape Harbor Drive? That’s terrific. My mother and I live one street over on North Atlantic. Are you still in school?”

“Uh-huh. I’ll be a senior this year.”

Trish’s heart leaped. “You will? Me too.”

Stella pressed both hands to her chest and sighed. “What a relief. I’ve dreaded starting school in a place where I don’t know anyone.”

Trish leaned in and rested her arms on the table. “Well, now you do. I’m excited. You’re a Godsend. Since both of us have boyfriends in the Army, we should support one another.”

“We definitely should…and will.” Stella pushed her dish to the side and sipped her water. “That was yummy. One for my soldier boy. He’ll be happy I didn’t have to eat it alone. I can’t wait to tell him I met you." Her eyes sparkled as she scooted to the edge of her chair. "Thanks, Trish. You've made a day I've dreaded enjoyable."

"I feel the same way." She pushed a napkin toward Stella and pulled a pen from her apron. "Write down your phone number, and I'll call you soon. We need to get together and talk about our guys."

She laughed and scribbled her number. "We'll need lots of time for that chat."

"I know. Maybe an all-nighter."

"I agree. That sounds like fun."

Monday, June 28, 1965

Trish waited on the front stoop as the mailman strolled up the walk with a mailbag as large as Santa's sack slung over his shoulder. She smiled as he climbed the steps and tried to read his expression.

"Good afternoon, Trish." He sorted through a handful of mail. "Lots of circulars here for you today. All of these Fourth of July sales are making my job a lot harder." He passed her a stack and turned to leave.

Hurriedly thumbing through each piece, she frowned. "Are you sure this is it, Mr. Warren?"

He looked her in the eyes, flashed a wide grin, and whipped an envelope from behind his back. "Oh, it appears there *is* something else. Sorry for the oversight."

Trish squealed, snatched the envelope from his hand, and scanned the return address. "Fort Jackson, Mr. Warren. It's from Billy Ray." She flung her arms around his neck and almost toppled him from the step. "Thank you. Thank you so much. You have a fine day." She hollered as she threw open the storm door and raced past her mother. "It's here, Momma. My letter is finally here." She slammed her bedroom door and bounced onto the bed. "Oh, Billy Ray. I was afraid you'd forgotten me."

She straightened her torso, sank into the billowy soft pillows, and pressed the envelope to her chest. *Breathe, Trish. Breathe.* Gazing at the letter in her hands, she studied every inch of the envelope—the familiar slant of Billy Ray's handwriting, the postmark, and the upside-down five-cent stamp. She grinned and kissed it. "You have no idea how much I've missed you." She started to rip into it, then stopped and grabbed her granny's tarnished, silver letter opener from the drawer of her nightstand. As she carefully slid it under the top edge of the flap, she tried to imagine Billy Ray sitting on his bunk, penning every word. She eased two pages of ruled notepaper from the envelope and unfolded them as if she were handling an ancient treasure that might disintegrate in her hands.

Hi, Baby Doll,

I've only got about ten minutes before lights out, but I'll write as fast as I can. Forgive me. I hate I haven't gotten a letter to you before now, but you wouldn't believe how crazy the days are here. They break before dawn with a drill sergeant shouting, "Get up," at the top of his lungs right in my ear. My stomach is tied tighter than a sailor's knot—a figure-eight follow-through, actually, before my feet ever hit the floor, and my day goes downhill from there. I always knew those slick recruitment brochures were too good to be true. This place is— I don't want to even write it, but it rhymes with...well. Enough whining. I'll survive by thinking about the day I'll be back in your arms.

I'll leave my address at the bottom of the page in case the one on the envelope gets messed up. Please write as much as you can. Mail is beginning to roll in to us now, and it's the best part of our day, at least for the ones whose names are called. The whoops in this tin hut can be deafening. Today was my day. I got a fat letter from Mom. She's still pretty weepy, but it was super to get news from home.

I sure miss her home cooking. Our first meal here was chipped beef on toast in grey gravy. I thought about not eating it until I heard the Sergeant tell the guy who'd made a snarky comment at the next table that he would eat it and another serving just like it. It's best just to open your mouth and hold your breath here or close your mouth and swallow your words.

Welp, there's the rumble of the sergeant's M151 MUTT crunching over the gravel outside the barracks. I'd better sign off. Lights will go dark minutes after he slings back that door. Can't imagine getting my thrills out of yellin' at the top of my lungs all day, intimidating young bucks.

Know I love you. While in boot camp, they strip us of anything that reminds us of home, so your picture is not beside my bunk, but I have your image playing in technicolor every night in my dreams. I love you, Trish. You are the last thing on my mind before I fall asleep. My thoughts and dreams of you are two things Uncle Sam can't take from me.

Good night, Sweetheart. Please write to me as soon as you get this. I'll be waiting.

I love you,
Billy Ray

P.S. I go by Bill here, but to you, I'll always be your Billy Ray.

Trish grabbed her pen and notepaper from the nightstand, clutched the letter to her chest, and laid her head against the headboard. "Stay safe, Sweetheart." *Please, God, keep him safe.*

Chapter Twenty-Five

Monday, June 12, 2023

Logan sat beside the Intracoastal Waterway, breathed in the afternoon salt air, and imagined what it would be like to live on the Lennon property. Since showing the house to his client, Logan had returned several times after a hard day to unwind and relax in the swing. This acreage along the waterway had a totally different vibe from his oceanfront cottage, and his visits were always therapeutic. Whenever this homestead sold, he'd miss it. If he were a rich man, he'd buy the estate himself.

Thinking he'd heard a car pull into the long drive, he turned and looked toward the road. Mistaken, he glanced at his watch, leaned against the arm of the swing, and stretched out his legs. Hopefully, Mrs. Wagner would like the property as much as her husband did. For him to make a return trip from Kentucky to show his wife the house was a good sign. Perhaps they'd even make an offer today.

Later, hearing a car, he looked up from his phone and released a grateful sigh. A white Lexus moved up the driveway. He stood and squinted. With the sun bouncing off the windshield, it was hard to be sure, but there appeared to be one person in the car. As the SUV moved closer, he saw that his assessment was right—only Mr. Wagner had come.

After parking at the end of the walk, he got out and waved. "Good afternoon, Logan. Sorry to keep you waiting."

Logan walked over and shook his hand. "Not a problem. I

couldn't ask for a more beautiful place to wait." His eyes questioned his client's. "Your wife couldn't come?"

He shook his head and grimaced. "No. That's why I'm late. Lynn woke up sick this morning. We thought by this afternoon, she'd feel better, but I had to leave her at the hotel."

Logan's spirits dropped as his suspicions escalated. "Oh no, I'm sorry. I hope it's nothing serious."

"I don't think so." He leaned against his car and folded his arms. "She was really disappointed."

"I imagine so after the long drive from Kentucky. I know how much you wanted her to see the house."

He lowered his head. "It is a letdown."

"Maybe it's a twenty-four-hour bug. Would you like to make an appointment for another day?"

A broad smile spread across his face. "Thank you, but that won't be necessary. Lynn looked at it on your website. She said if I'm sold on the place, she would be fine with it." He laughed. "She's given me the green light to do whatever I think is best."

Logan released a long internal sigh and slapped his hands together. "Now you're talking. She sounds like a fine woman."

"She is." He pointed toward the house. "I would like another walk-through, though." He reached into his pocket and pulled out a small tablet and pen. "I want to make a list of the work that needs to be done. Afterward, maybe we can do some negotiating."

"Certainly. That's a plan I can live with." Logan slipped the front door key from his pants pocket and motioned for the smartly dressed man to walk ahead of him. "Be my guest, sir." He followed his client through the house as he noted areas that needed attention. When they stepped into the kitchen, Logan brushed his fingers over the cracked yellow Formica countertop.

"As with most renovations, the kitchen will be your biggest expense. If it were me, I'd gut this room and start over."

"I agree." Pressing his lips together, Stuart scribbled on his notepad, then looked up and surveyed the ceiling. "Appears they've had a few leaks in here. What shape's the roof in?"

"No problem there. The owner replaced it several years ago. Just hasn't done the interior work."

"Good. Having to replace that would have been a deal breaker." He nodded as he opened the pantry door and looked up. "Water spots in here too. I think you're right. The kitchen needs a complete overhaul. It's a great room, though. My wife's quite a cook, and she'll love this large, airy space." He pointed toward the sink. "Nice big windows with a waterway view. Can't ask for better than that." He spun on his heels. "Yes, Lynn's gonna love it." He walked toward the hall. "If she feels better tomorrow and you have time, I think I will take you up on your offer to bring her out. There's more that needs to be done here than I thought. I know she said to do what I wanted, but I don't feel good about making an offer without her seeing the place first."

Logan nodded as they stepped into the foyer. "You're a wise man. I'll be happy to meet you out here again." He opened the front door and allowed Stuart to walk out ahead of him. "Just call me as soon as you know something."

"I sure will. Thanks for your time." He walked to his car and opened the door. "I heard they have good coffee over at Coffee Chronicles. Would you recommend it?"

"Absolutely. Best on the island."

"Wonderful. I'll see if Brooklyn will whip me up a mocha latte." After dropping into the seat, he lifted his hand and drove off.

Unable to believe his ears, Logan bit his lip, whipped out a business card and pen from his shirt pocket, and wrote down the North Carolina tag number. *Good grief. What's with this guy?*

Brooklyn

I stepped back from the display table and nodded. A sizzling summer sale on the hottest and newest beach reads.

"Very nice…eye-catching?" Natalya wrinkled her nose. "Is that how you say it?"

I turned and smiled at her. "It is. You're a fast learner. You sound more and more like an American every day."

She giggled. "English makes me laugh. Eye-catching makes a funny picture in my head. Think about your language. There is no egg in eggplant, boxing rings aren't round, and why are older people sometimes called spring chickens?"

I laughed and shrugged. "I'm sorry. I have no answers for you. I suppose English can be confusing, but Americans don't think of it as odd. I love seeing life through your eyes. It's refreshing." I hugged her. "Speaking of refreshing, I'm ready for a break and a hazelnut frappe."

"Sure. Have a seat, and I'll make one for you."

"Thank you, but aren't you off the clock?"

She laughed. "There you go again. Yes—Ella's clocking in, but I'll make one for you anyway."

I sat at a table in the corner and scrolled through social media until Natalya placed the cold drink in front of me. "Mmm…that looks good. Thank you."

Pulling a napkin from the holder, she wiped the Formica tabletop and straightened the chairs. "Brooklyn, are you okay?"

I lifted my gaze and stirred my drink with the straw. "Yes. Why do you ask?"

She shrugged. "I don't know. You seem distracted this

afternoon. Not your perky self."

I sighed. "You're not only smart, you're perceptive." I pointed to the seat across from me. "Please."

Her compassionate green eyes studied my face as she eased into the chair.

"I'm worried."

"About what?"

"I haven't been able to get in touch with Logan this afternoon."

"He's working, isn't he?"

I nodded. "As far as I know. But usually, even if he's busy, he'll text me to say he'll get back to me later. Today, I've heard nothing. All I've gotten is his voicemail."

"I feel sure he's fine. He'll get back to you soon."

"You're probably right. I shouldn't worry, but it's out of character for him." I sipped my frappe. "So, are you enjoying your new home?"

"I love it. It's perfect for me. Thank you again for arranging everything with Logan and Chase."

"I was happy—" My phone vibrated on the table. Reading the caller ID, I looked at Natalya and smiled. "You're right. It's Harbor Realty." When I answered, Natalya waved and mouthed goodbye.

"Hi, honey. Where've you been?"

"Sorry, Brooklyn, I couldn't text you back. I just finished a showing. It's too complicated to talk about on the phone. I need you to meet me. Now."

"Logan, what's wrong. Are you okay? You're scaring me."

"Yes, but please do what I ask. Leave the coffee shop right now and come to my house. Tell Courtney it's an emergency."

"Okay. Okay. I'm on my way." I jumped from my seat and burst into the office.

Startled, Courtney looked over the pile of books on her desk.

"Can you cover for me? Something's happened with Logan. He wants me to meet him at his house."

Her eyes bulged. "Of course."

"Thank you." She was close on my heels as I dashed into the storage room and yanked my purse from the file cabinet drawer.

"Are you going to be okay? Maybe Ella should drive you."

I dismissed her offer with a wave and stepped around her. "No. No, thanks. I'll be fine. It's not that far."

"Okay, but when things settle down, call me, okay?"

"I will," I said, the screen door slamming behind me.

As blood pulsed in my ears, I tried hard not to hyperventilate and turned onto West Main. Within minutes, I parked behind Logan's Jeep in the driveway, ran up the steps, and banged on the front door.

Chapter Twenty-Six

Brooklyn

I knew something was terribly wrong the moment Logan opened the door and looked into my eyes. My gut told me that what he was about to say would affect me big time. I wanted to turn and run. Instead, I fell into his arms and hoped we could ride out whatever it was together. Logan placed his hand under my chin and tilted my face toward his. "I'm glad you're here…and safe."

"What? What is it?"

As he led me into the living room, my insides churned, and my knees felt as if they would crumble.

"Have a seat."

I eased onto the sofa, my eyes never veering from his as he sat beside me. Murphy whimpered at our feet.

"Today, I showed the Lennon property for the second time to the man I told you about a couple of weeks ago—Stuart Wagner. Remember?"

"Yes."

"He'd driven from Kentucky with his wife so she could see the property, but he showed up alone. Said he had to leave her at the hotel because she was ill. The showing went well. He seemed interested. He noted the renovations that would need to be made and said he would discuss it with his wife and get back to me. Just before he got in his car, he asked about Coffee Chronicles."

I furrowed my brow. "He did?"

"He said he'd heard the coffee was good. When I said it was

the best around, he said, 'Wonderful. I'll get Brooklyn to whip me up a mocha latte.' Then, like when he was in town before, he hopped in his car and drove off while I stood dumbfounded. Only this time, I had the presence of mind to jot down his plate number."

My eyes widened as an overwhelming sense of dread washed over me. "What? I don't get it. I don't know a Stuart Wagner?"

"Neither of us does."

I pressed my lips together and wrung my hands as my eyes questioned his.

"Brooklyn, the man gave me an alias."

I shook my head as I tried to make sense of it all. "An alias? Why?"

"After I spoke to you, I called the police and—" He held up his hand as his phone jingled and answered it.

I dropped back on the couch and studied Logan's face as he spoke. I could hear a male voice on the other end of the line, but not well enough to make out his words.

Logan nodded a couple of times. "Uh-huh. That's precisely what I suspected. Thanks for getting back to me so quickly." He paused. "Yes, sir, I will. I appreciate your help." He hung up, scooted closer, and cradled my hands in his.

I took shallow breaths and stared while waiting for the hammer to drop.

"That's the call I was expecting. Brooklyn, like I thought, Stuart Wagner isn't the man's real name. The police just confirmed that his name is…Wes Marshal."

Shaking my head, I yanked my hands from his and covered my face. "No. No." I could hear blood thrashing in my ears as images from the past ran rampant through my mind.

"Come here." Logan drew me to his chest and rubbed my

back. "It will be okay. It will."

"You can't know that." I pulled away. "You can't. It will never be okay. He will plague me for the rest of my life." I ran to the back door, yanked it open, and raced down the boardwalk.

"Brooklyn, wait."

Murphy nipped at my heels as I rushed down the steps. Although I hit the sand running, my fastest pace was no match for Logan's long strides. When he grasped my arm, I collapsed onto the sand, and he dropped beside me. Murphy wedged in between us and licked my face.

"Stop that, Murph." Logan pushed him away.

"Honey, I'm afraid for you." Tears streamed down my cheeks. "Wes is unpredictable. Whenever he's drinking, there is no limit to his vindictiveness. We've got to stop seeing one another before you get hurt."

He clasped my shoulders and turned me toward him. "Brooklyn. Look at me."

I lifted my eyes to his—ones that oozed concern.

"Read. My. Lips. I'm not going anywhere. I won't cave to Wes's manipulation or allow him to harass you. Leave it to me. I just need some time to think it through. I'll figure it out. Okay?"

Not knowing what to say, I lowered my head and wiped my tears with the back of my hand. "But, if anything happens to you, I'll never forgive myself."

"Brooklyn?"

I hesitated, then returned to his gaze.

"Please trust me."

I closed my eyes and inhaled. "I want to, but I don't know how."

"Try, okay?"

I sat silent and listened to the gentle lap of the waves and the laughter of children playing in the distance.

"Honey, did you hear me?"

"Yes. I heard." I leaned against his chest. "I'll try."

He embraced me and kissed my hair. "Awesome. We'll take this one day at a time. If you're afraid, I'm sure Olivia and Chase will let you stay with them."

I nodded. "Olivia's already offered, but I don't know. I'll see how I feel."

He grabbed my hand and laughed. "Come on. If we don't move soon, we'll get wet. Let's walk back to the house, and I'll fix you something to eat."

As we followed Murphy's lead to the cottage, Logan wrapped his arm around my shoulders and pulled me to his side. "This will pass, Brooklyn. You'll see. Wes needs to know we won't tolerate his behavior." He stopped, pulled me into his arms, and kissed me. "You're my girl now, aren't you?"

I lowered my eyes. "I wanna be." *How could I not trust him? Logan had proven himself worthy. Wes had stolen ten years of my life. Would I allow him to rob me of my future too?*

Tuesday, June 13, 2023

Logan rubbed Murphy's back. "You be good while I'm gone, big boy. See you this evening." He closed the front door, trotted down the steps, and clicked the remote to unlock his Jeep.

"Hey, Mr. Corbett, you got time to come over here a second?"

He turned and waved at the foreman overseeing the work on his house next door. "Sure." He opened the car door, tossed his briefcase onto the passenger's seat, and walked across the drive. "What can I help you with, Marty?"

The burly young builder, sporting a sleeveless tee shirt and cutoff denim shorts, lifted his branded cap and wiped the sweat from his brow.

Logan grinned. "I know. It's already sweltering out here, isn't it? Typical summertime heat."

"Yep, but I wouldn't trade living around here for nothing."

"Me neither, and I'm happy to hear you say that. Good builders are hard to come by, and your crew is one of the best. Would hate to lose you."

"Thank you, sir. I'll be sure to share that with my boss."

"So what do you need?"

"I'm sorry, but I've got some not-so-good news for ya."

"Oh? What's that?"

"Looks like we had an intruder last night?"

His eyes widened. "No kidding. You serious?"

"As a heart attack." He stepped around a load of lumber and motioned for Logan to follow him into the unfinished house. He pointed to a corner of the kitchen. We lost a few power tools last night and all of our copper wiring and fittings."

Logan put his hands on his hips and shook his head. "Good grief."

"Yeah…we're seeing more and more of this with copper up over four dollars a pound and projected to go higher."

Logan raked his fingers through his hair and scanned the room. "I'm sorry."

"Not your fault, sir. No one's really. The house was locked up, but locks don't mean nothin' to a thief. Just thought you needed to know. It's gonna delay us about a week in the kitchen until we can get the supplies we need back in here."

He nodded. "I understand. Don't worry about me. I hope you find the culprit and don't have any more issues. Any of your other houses get ripped off?"

"Not that I know of, but I wouldn't be surprised. Like I said, in view of the higher prices, theft is ramping up again."

"Sad to say, this is a sign of our brave new world. Totally self-absorbed. No respect for anyone's property." He surveyed the family room. "Looks great in here, though. You're doing a good job. Moving right along. Anything else I can help you with?"

"No, sir. That's about it." He tipped his cap. "Hope you have a good day."

"Thanks, Marty. I appreciate all you're doing."

Logan hopped in his car and turned the key in the ignition. As he backed out onto West Main Street, his thoughts ran amok." *Don't think I'll mention this one to Brooklyn. It might not have been Wes, but I wouldn't put it past him.*

Chapter Twenty-Seven

Friday, July 2, 1965

Trish looked at Stella sitting cross-legged at the foot of her double bed and laughed. "Did you see the look Susie gave me when she turned around in the line at the theater tonight? If looks could kill, I'd be dead and buried about now."

"I did, and I wouldn't put anything past her."

Margo sat with her legs swung over the arm of the upholstered chair in the corner and huffed. "I saw it too."

Smirking, Stella leaned against the footboard and fluffed a pillow behind her back. "She didn't like hearing that you'd received a letter from Billy Ray when she hasn't."

"How do you know that?"

"Because I told her," Margo said, swinging her legs around and dropping her feet to the floor. "I overheard Susie tell Rosemary, and I told Stella. Susie made all kinds of excuses as to why she was sure Billy Ray hadn't written her. I couldn't resist telling her he'd written to you."

"Margo." She wagged her finger in the air. "Shame. Shame on you, girl." She laughed. "But, oh, I'm so glad you did."

She dropped back in her chair. "I probably shouldn't have, but I get so tired of hearing her talk about Billy Ray whenever you're around. She says things just to hurt you. I felt it was time for her to get a dose of her own medicine."

"Yeah…I agree." Stella pulled her hair into a ponytail and secured it with a rubber band. "And it couldn't happen to a more deserving person."

Trish smirked. "Well, I'd say from her grimace, it didn't go down well. Thanks for having my back, Margo."

"Of course. That's what friends are for, right, Stella?"

"For sure." She smiled at Trish. "I know you'd do the same for us. We've got to stick together."

"Stella, Margo and I were talking the other day about how glad we are that you're at Southport this year. And as far as I'm concerned, it's nice to have someone who knows what it's like to have a boyfriend in Viet Nam. I'm happy we've both heard from our soldier boys this week." She placed a stack of Bride Magazines on the bed. "Look. Momma's hairdresser gave her these from her shop so we could look through them this weekend. She said we could keep them as long as we want."

"Really? That was super nice of her." Stella slid one from the stack and thumbed through. "I already know what I want my dress to look like, do you?

"No. I haven't had as long to think about it as you have." She looked at Margo and patted the bed. "Come over here and help me decide."

Margo plopped between them and opened one of the magazines. "Stella, what have you decided on?"

"A satin A-line empire waistline gown, off-the-shoulder neckline with stand-up lace, three-quarter-length lace sleeves, sweep train, and a shoulder-length veil."

Margo's eyes bulged. "Wow. That's what I like. A girl who knows what she wants and goes for it."

Stella turned the page and pointed. "It's kind of like this one without the scoop neck and with more lace across the bodice."

"That's beautiful, but it looks expensive." Trish opened another magazine from the middle and laid it on the bed in front of them. "Here. Let's find something for me."

"Okay, and then we'll search for bridesmaids' dresses. I want you both to be in my wedding, you know."

Trish smiled. "You do? I'd love that. I hope you'll also both be in mine."

"Oh, yes. I wondered if you'd ask."

Margo chuckled. "As long as we've known each other, I knew you'd better ask."

Trish laughed, then dropped back on her pillow and stared at the light fixture above. "Oh, Stella..." Her voice cracked. "How are we ever going to make it through this next year?"

"One day at a time...and together."

Margo nodded. "And I'll be here for you both."

Trish popped up, pointed to the framed quote beside her dresser, and read aloud. *"Obstacles are those frightful things you see when you take your eyes off your goal."* As my Granny Rogers would always say...'and your God.' We've got to keep our eyes on God, trust Him to bring our fiancé's home, and put feet to our prayers by continuing to plan for our futures together." She snatched a magazine and flopped on her stomach. "Stella, Margo and I want to know what color dresses your bridesmaids will wear?"

Friday, July 2, 1965

Billy Ray tossed his clothes in the dryer and returned to his chair in the laundry room on the lower level of the two-story, white-framed barracks on Tank Hill. Stretching his leg across the aisle, he nudged Phil's knee with his foot. Phil's loud snoring had drowned out the sound of the buzzer signaling the end of his wash cycle.

"Hey, sleeping beauty. Duty calls."

"Huh?" He jumped to his feet and saluted. "I mean, yessir!"

Billy Ray laughed and pointed to the washer. "At ease, soldier. Your tidy whities are ready."

Grunting, Phil glared at him, then staggered to the washer and threw his clothes in the dryer before returning to his seat. "A real friend would have let his buddy sleep and handled it for him."

Billy Ray looked over his shoulder and scanned the empty room. "Don't think there's one in here."

Phil batted his hand in the air and yawned. "That sounds about right." He stood and walked to the vending machine, dropped in his coins, and selected a caffeinated soda. After prying off the cap with the machine's bottle opener, he motioned toward the dispenser. "Want one?"

Billy Ray shook his head and glanced at the clock above the folding table. "No thanks. Already had mine. Don't want to be wired when I drop into my bunk in a few."

"After today's five-mile run, there's no chance of me staring at the ceiling tonight."

"You're probably right. Can't believe we've made it through week three. Is it just me, or does it seem like we've been here forever?"

"Forever pretty much nails it." Phil threw back his head and gulped his drink.

Billy Ray lifted his arms, flexed his biceps, and laughed. "Now this is an example of God working all things together for good."

He shook his head and chuckled. "I guess there are some advantages. Being here during the Fourth is a lucky break. Not all recruits get time out in the middle of Basic Training. Sunday's celebration at Hilton Field should be terrific. I can already taste that huge slice of Pepperoni pizza, and of course, I've gotta get my favorite—a chocolate, cherry vanilla nut sundae."

Sunday, July 4, 1965

The mingled aromas of cotton candy and popcorn filtered through the air as Billy Ray and Phil walked down Tank Hill toward Hilton Field. Reminded of Southport's Independence Day celebrations, Billy Ray pictured Trish seated on a quilt at Waterfront Park, laughing with friends and listening to beach bands while waiting for the fireworks to begin.

Billy Ray came to the celebration with a new set of eyes. War was more than playing along the creek bank with a popgun slung over his shoulder. The Fourth far exceeded a fun day down by the Cape Fear River, joking with friends and popping off a few firecrackers. Fort Jackson's in-depth American history classes had given him a new appreciation for what soldiers before him had gone through and for what he and his comrades could possibly experience—and all to keep America free.

He ran his hand under the collar of his combat fatigues and wiped the sweat from the back of his neck. Moisture from the early afternoon rain still hung in the air, making the evening hot and sticky. Maybe Fort Jackson's weather was one more way to ready recruits for the insufferable climate ahead of them. Dense humidity was nothing out of the ordinary for the deep South and was definitely akin to Viet Nam. But dealing with a degree of mugginess wasn't too big a burden to bear on their day off. Most anything beats being on latrine duty or mopping floors in the barracks.

Cars with red, white, and blue ribbons tied to their antennas streamed through Gate 4 and followed the blue line to the parking area. As Billy Ray and Phil neared the field and looked into a sea of men in camouflage, the voice of the commanding general echoed from the PA system and cut through the crowd's buzz.

"Welcome to Fort Jackson's annual Independence Day celebration. Today, active soldiers and trainees gather alongside veterans, retirees, and civilians to celebrate those who defend and protect our nation's freedoms. There's something here for everyone—crafts, food booths, live music, and carnival rides for children and those young at heart. Let's have a great time, and don't miss this evening's grand finale—the 282nd Army Band playing a variety of patriotic music in sync with what promises to be our best fireworks display yet. Now, to kick off tonight's events, if you're not already on your feet, please stand for the playing of our national anthem."

After Billy Ray and Phil saluted and stood at attention during the band's performance, he lifted his cap and wiped the sweat from his brow. As they walked across the field to the food vendors, they passed the bandstand, where the mellow tones of a saxophone and the sweeping sounds of the snare drum played "Take Five" by Dave Brubeck. Phil looked at Billy Ray. "Pretty good, huh?"

He agreed and pushed his buddy's shoulder. "Come on. I'm famished. You get your pizza while I pick up a footlong, then meet me over at the picnic tables." Phil nodded and walked off as Billy Ray took his place in line. Later, when several soldiers got up from a table to leave, he snagged it and spread out the paper wrapped around his hot dog.

Phil plopped a large pizza in front of him. "Wanna slice?"

Billy Ray laughed and reached for a piece. "If you insist. I'm not in the habit of turning down junk food." As the warm cheese melted on his tongue, he moaned and held out his bag of fries. "Here. Help yourself."

Phil grabbed a few and dropped onto the bench across from him. "They've gotta beat the shoestrings served in the mess hall."

After swallowing a couple of bites of his hot dog, Billy Ray watched a pretty blonde put an index finger to her pursed lips and tiptoe up behind Phil. As she reached to place her hands over Phil's eyes, Billy Ray's world went black. He jumped, and his breath hitched as someone's hands covered his eyes as well.

"Guess, soldier boy."

His heart leaped. He'd know that sweet voice anywhere. Jerking around, he met Trish's gaze and dropped his hot dog to the table. He swung his legs over the bench and grabbed her. "What? What on earth…." Pulling her onto his lap, he pressed his mouth to hers, then leaned back, heart pounding. He peered into her moist eyes. "I don't get it. Where'd you come from? How'd you get here?" Without giving her a moment to answer, his lips covered hers again. Turning to introduce her to Phil, he noticed his buddy locked in an embrace with a girl of his own. His eyes questioned Trish's. "What's going on here?"

She slid from Billy Ray's lap, sat on the bench beside him, and looped her arm through his. "Momma surprised us this morning when she said we were coming to the celebration today."

His eyes darted around the area. "Where is she? I've got to give that lady a big hug."

Trish giggled. "She's here somewhere with her friend, Martha. They wanted us to have time alone, so Momma said they'll meet us near the bandstand when it's time for the fireworks display."

He blinked and stared at Trish in disbelief. "Look at you." He kissed her cheek. "I can't get over this, but then again, why would I want to?" He turned toward Phil. "Can you believe it?"

Phil, looking as if he'd seen a ghost, shook his head and motioned to the lovely girl clinging to his arm. "Well, this is Stella, and I'm bettin' the pretty girl beside you is Trish."

Trish cut her eyes to Billy Ray and grinned. "If there's a possibility that it could be anyone else, I want her name and number now."

He leaned closer and whispered in her ear. "You know I only have eyes for you."

"Good answer." She laid her head on his shoulder. "Can we just freeze this moment forever?"

"I would if I could, baby doll." He pulled her to her feet. "Let's get you something to eat." He looked at Phil. "Want anything?"

"Bring Stella back a Coke, will ya? We'll share this pizza. It's huge."

After their meal, they walked hand in hand around the grounds and stopped at a ring toss game, where Billy Ray won a small patriotic teddy bear for Trish. As the sun painted the sky with rich pink, orange, and blue hues, they met Mrs. Malone and her friend, Martha, by the bandstand. After zigzagging their way around excited guests, they found the perfect place to spread out Granny Roger's hand-stitched quilt. Trish sat cross-legged and leaned back against Billy Ray's chest. Burying his face in her hair, he inhaled its sweet fragrance and tried to etch the details of the night into his memory. He hoped they would burrow deep enough to carry him through the daunting days and months ahead.

When twilight approached, and the 282nd Army Band played "America the Beautiful," a sudden burst of fireworks lit up the sky. Amid an explosion of cheers and applause from the crowd, Trish turned around, held Billy Ray's face in her hands, and kissed him.

Now, those fireworks…he'd never forget.

Chapter Twenty-Eight

Monday, November 1, 1965
Oakland, California

Private Billy Ray Jessup of the First Infantry Division sat in the Oakland Army Terminal, waiting to embark on the USS General LeRoy Eltinge for Saigon. Along with his Fort Jackson comrades, thousands of soldiers had descended upon the Pacific coast for the three-week voyage to the Port of Ho Chi Minh City.

The mood of these boys-turned-to-men in twenty short weeks was somber. Although sporting brave faces, they knew not all of them would return—and no one would come home unscathed. There would be wounds. Deep ones. Horrific ones. If not visible, invisible. In order to survive the daunting months ahead, these men of valor banked on being among the lucky ones—those whose feet would return to American soil and whose lips would kiss the ground again.

Phil sat beside him and read Stella's last letter. By God's grace, both of them had remained at Fort Jackson for their infantry training. Still on the same team, they were determined to settle for nothing short of victory.

"Hey, Billy. Stella says for you not to let me out of your sight."

He chuckled. "She does, huh? Next time you write to her, tell her that's a mighty tall order, but I'll do my best, and I hope she'll do the same for me with Trish."

Billy checked his watch. Trish. She would still be in her biology class. She was not only beautiful, but she was smart, and she was his. How did that happen? You bet he'd return. He'd promised Trish he would.

Sunset Beach, North Carolina
Trish

Tears rolled down Trish's cheeks as she sat in her momma's car and waited for the swing bridge to open. Perhaps she shouldn't have come. Should have told her momma. But she hadn't known and hadn't even told Stella. It was a spur-of-the-moment decision. After sitting in the school parking lot for fifteen minutes, trying to pull herself together, she knew there was no way—no way she could sit through classes. She had to be where she felt closest to Billy Ray, and Sunset Beach was that place. It was where they'd shared their first kiss, and it would be their future home. The place where they'd have children and grow old together. She pounded the steering wheel with her fist. How? How could life be so cruel? She hated war. It wasn't fair. Billy Ray was still a boy.

She checked her watch. It was 8:30 a.m. in California. She was sure Billy Ray had been up for hours. Probably sitting in Oakland's terminal, waiting to ship out. *Oh, baby, are you afraid? I wish I was there to hold you.*

She jumped as someone sat on the horn behind her. Turning the key in the ignition, she cringed as the man in the gatehouse hung out the window, yelling and motioning for her to move on. As she passed, she held up her hand and mouthed, "I'm sorry."

As soon as her car tires cleared the bridge and rolled onto the pavement, she stepped on the gas. Catching up to the car in front of her, she slowed and wiped her cheeks with a damp, wadded-up tissue. She was doing the best she could. If people only knew how hard it was for her to move forward. To leave the moments she and Billy Ray had shared and push into the year without him. Thanksgiving. Christmas. New Year's. How would she do it? She had no clue.

At the pier, she pulled into a handicapped parking place, slid her sunglasses from her hair to her nose, and stepped out. After wrapping her coat tighter and buttoning it to her neck, she slipped on her earmuffs, grabbed her tote bag and beach chair from the trunk, and walked toward the water. *Perfect*. Weekdays in mid-November were not days most would choose to sit by the sea. Except for the lonely cry of gulls, the gentle lap of waves, and one lone fisherman farther down the beach, she was alone. Alone with nothing but her thoughts…and her God. Was he enough? Would he really be there to carry her through the year ahead? Granny Rogers never seemed to doubt her God. Why was it so hard for her to trust?

After settling into her chair, she pulled her journal and pen from her bag and stared toward the horizon, where gulls followed a fishing trawler. It was hard to believe this wasn't even the same ocean Billy Ray would sail on. She couldn't comprehend what three weeks on a ship would be like. *Protect him, Lord…and Phil. All of them. Jesus, I'm not even going to Viet Nam, and I'm afraid. How are these young men so brave?*

She opened her journal. Tears fell and splotched the pages as she wrote. Later, she tucked the book that held her heart inside her tote and scanned the beach. The fisherman was walking toward her, carrying his gear. As he neared, he smiled, and she smiled back. He was older than her—thirtyish maybe, and his eyes were kind.

"Good afternoon. You've been here a while. Aren't you chilly?"

She brushed a strand of hair from her eyes. "A bit, but the sun feels good. Did you have any luck?"

"Nothing to speak of, but being out here is not always about catching fish."

She nodded. "I understand."

He moved toward the parking lot. "Well, enjoy your time, and don't get cold. The wind is picking up."

"Thanks." As he stepped away, she blurted, "Sir?" and then swallowed hard. *Why did she do that?*

He turned. "Yeah?"

She opened her mouth and spoke what came up. "If you're a praying man, will you add my fiancé to your prayer list?"

"Sure. What's his name?"

"Billy Ray." She choked out her words. "He leaves for…for Viet Nam today."

He set his bucket and rods on the ground, walked closer, and motioned toward the sand beside her. "Do you mind?"

Unable to speak, she shook her head.

He sat, stretched out his legs, and leaned back on his hands. "I'm sorry. That's a tough one. I remember how it affected my wife when I left for Korea."

"Really? You were in Korea? That's where my dad served. How long were you there?"

"Two years was the average tour, but I contracted malaria, and they sent me home after eighteen months."

She shook her head. "Wow. I thought a year was a long time. I don't know how your wife made it through."

He grinned. "Human beings are resilient creatures. We can do more than we think we can, and with God, more than we ever dream possible." He looked out at the horizon. "When life's seas get rough, there's a quote I remind myself of."

Trish straightened in her chair, ready to inhale whatever it was he had to offer.

"We can't direct the wind, but we can adjust our sails."

Her spirit sighed.

"Just as sailors learn to position their sails so the wind will carry them away from the storm, we need to correct ours and let the wind usher us to a place of peace. Did you read *Little Women* in school?"

She nodded. "Yes. In the sixth grade."

"Well, the author, Louisa May Alcott, said, 'I'm not afraid of storms, for I am learning to sail my ship.' Life isn't as much about what happens to us as it is about the choices we make."

Trish smiled. "Thank you, sir. You're right. Thanks for reminding me that our attitudes have everything to do with how we handle tough times. I need to learn the art of sailing."

He chuckled. "We all do." He stood and brushed the sand from his hands. "I'm glad it helped, but it wasn't just for you. I'm still learning, and I needed the reminder myself." He bent over and picked up his gear. "I'll remember to pray for Billy Ray—and you. I believe you're both going to be fine."

As he turned to walk away, Trish said, "Oh, sir?"

"Yes?"

"My name is Trish. What's yours? I'd like to pray for you too."

He smiled. "It's Bill…Bill Wilkerson."

As he walked away, she scanned the ocean and marveled at how God sometimes sent people into her life at just the right time to be Jesus with skin on. *This* was one of those times.

Somewhere off the California coast

Billy Ray sat in a chair topside, scooted it forward, and propped his feet on the rail. His sidekick, Phil, who'd felt a bit woozy, had turned in early. Billy Ray guessed living alongside the Cape Fear River had given him the advantage and prepped him for this three-week voyage to the Far East. Although no pleasure cruise, their time aboard this reinstated WWII transport ship would outshine MOS training. Sure, they'd have assigned duties and hours of class time to prepare them for what was to come, but there would be a lot more downtime.

This evening, Billy Ray couldn't care less about whooping it up with the guys, playing shuffleboard for a bagful of Cheetos, or slapping down endless hands of Blackjack. All he wanted was to talk to Trish. Knowing it wouldn't be possible now or for months to come, he'd have to make do with writing his thoughts. He slipped a military-issued pen from his pocket and opened a spiral notebook. At the top of the page, he scrawled…Monday, November 1, 1965. Voyage to Saigon—Day One.

Chapter Twenty-Nine

Wednesday, June 21, 2023

Logan opened the Daytimer on his desk, eased into the chair at Harbor Realty, and yawned. A warm mocha latte with a double shot of espresso from Coffee Chronicles was the boost he needed to start his day. Hitting play on his desk phone, he swiveled his chair and listened to his messages. One in particular caught his attention. He replayed it several times.

"Hi, Logan…This is Stuart Wagner. I plan to be at Sunset Beach this weekend and hope we can connect. Would love to sit down and talk with you about the Lennon property. I think Lynn and I are ready to make an offer. Give me a call back when you get a minute, okay? Hope to chat with you soon. Thanks."

Logan groaned. "Well, well…Stuart Wagner, aka Wes Marshal. You've got a lot of nerve, sir. What type of nefarious game are you playing? It's time to call your bluff and put an end to this madness."

He pulled up Wagner's number on his phone, dialed it, and prayed he would answer. Striking while the iron was hot was key to catching him in his own game. He answered on the third ring.

"Logan, my man. Thanks for returning my call."

"Absolutely. What are your thoughts?"

"Was wondering if you'd be around this weekend?"

"Sure will."

"I have a couple of things I want to talk to you about, and if you think all is within reason, I'll make an offer on the estate."

"Terrific. Let's meet at the property. You name the time."

"How's ten Saturday morning?"

"Sounds good to me. Will Lynn be with you?"

"No, but she's on board with whatever we decide."

"Super. I'll look forward to it. Stay safe, and we'll connect on Saturday." Logan leaned back in his chair and sipped his latte. Was Wes really interested in the Lennon estate, or was it all part of his twisted plot?

Saturday, June 24, 2023

Logan pulled up the long drive on the Lennon property and parked his car facing out at the end of the walk. He leaned over the console and pulled a 9mm handgun from the glove compartment. After emptying the chamber, he slid it into his ankle holster and dropped the shells in his pocket—just in case. It wasn't every day that he felt the need to take such precautions with a client, but this one sent cold chills up his spine. He checked his watch, lifted his laptop and notebook from the passenger seat, and walked to the house with a host of scenarios swirling through his head. After entering the foyer, he walked down the hall to the large kitchen. Although this space needed a ton of work, the view of the waterway was spectacular. A shame he didn't have a serious buyer on the line today. This estate would eventually make someone a beautiful forever home.

He laid his things on the bar and unlocked the back door. One never knew, and considering the circumstances, he would take every precaution. While waiting for his client to arrive, he turned on his laptop, helped himself to two bottles of water from the refrigerator, and placed them on the counter. No sooner had he seated himself on one of the stools than he heard the front door open.

"Just me, Logan."

Here we go. Logan stepped into the hall and smiled. "I'm in the kitchen. Come on back." He shook Mr. Wagner's hand, then stepped aside and motioned him in. "I've got us set up at the bar and put some water there for you."

"Nice. I can sure use it. I'm parched." He threw his leg over the stool, plopped down, and slid closer to the counter. "I stopped over at the *Sunny Side Up Diner* in Calabash this morning for breakfast and couldn't resist ordering a couple of country ham biscuits with my eggs." He unscrewed the cap, gulped a third of the bottle, and wiped his mouth with the back of his hand. "So, how's things going with you, Logan? Having a good season so far?"

"I am. Sales are picking up." He seated himself on the stool beside Wes. "The further away we get from the pandemic, the better the sales are. Sure hope we never see the likes of that again." He pulled a pen from his shirt pocket and opened his notebook. "You said you had a couple of things you wanted to talk about. What's on your mind?"

He laughed. "This beautiful property, for one. I'd love to have it, but it's too large. The person who owns this house needs a wife and family. Someone to enjoy it with, ya know?"

Logan tried hard to maintain a poker face and keep his emotions in check. "But I thought you said Lynn was on board with it and that the kids would love the dock?"

Stuart lowered his head and released a sinister chuckle that rose from the depths of his throat. The words that followed were cold and calculated—ones that held no remorse. "Well, yeah, guess I did. I must confess, I haven't been upfront with you." He pushed away from the bar, sat straighter on the stool, and met Logan's eyes. "My name isn't really Stuart Wagner."

Logan cocked his head. "Seriously? Why the alias?"

"Well, I wanted to give you a chance."

"A chance? At what?"

"A chance to convince me that you're the better man for Brooklyn."

"Brooklyn? What does she have to do with this?"

"Everything, Mr. Corbett." He rose from the stool, walked across the room, and leaned back against the sink. "I'm Wes Marshal, and Brooklyn's my wife." A muscle in his jaw twitched. "And…it has come to my attention that you've been seeing her."

Logan held up his hand, blood pulsing in his neck. "Whoa. Perhaps we should get the facts straight. You are right about one thing. I have been seeing Brooklyn, but you're wrong about her being your wife. You divorced her, remember? Told her to get out of *your* house."

"Ha. So that's the story she told you?"

"She did, and I have no reason to doubt her."

"You have no reason to believe her either, and…if you know what's good for you, you'll stop seeing her."

"Is that a threat, Mr. Marshal, or a suggestion?"

He pressed his lips together and shrugged. "Take it however you want."

Logan cleared his throat. "It sure sounds like a threat to me, and I don't respond well to threats." He patted the stool beside him. "Sit back down, sir, and let's talk about this further. Like two adults." He reached for his laptop and tapped the enter key. "I've got a couple of videos here I'd like for you to take a look at."

Wes jammed his hands into the pockets of his jeans, walked

to the bar, pulled the stool farther from Logan with his foot, and took a seat. "Sure. I'll take a look at what you've got."As the screen lit up, Logan searched his files, opened a video, and hit play. "See if this rings any bells with you."

Wes folded his arms across his chest and studied the screen. His jaw clenched, and the color drained from his face.

"Does this bring back any memories, Mr. Marshal?"

He sat sullen.

"Would that be your car, sir? A white Lexus? Do you remember plowing it into my Jeep Cherokee?"

Wes dismissed his question. "There are lots of white Lexus SUVs."

"But there's only one that side-swiped my Jeep."

He puffed out his chest. "You can't prove that's my car."

"Oh, but maybe I can." Logan stopped the video and zoomed in. "Would that be your North Carolina license plate number, sir?"

He shrugged. "I don't know it off the top of my head."

Logan nodded. "I can understand that." He moved his finger across the pad. "Let's pull up something that may be a little more convincing."

As the second video appeared on the screen, Wes chewed his lip and rubbed the back of his neck.

"Isn't that you entering the house I have under construction?"

He sat silent and drew a long breath.

"Isn't that you carrying my drill and copper wiring and throwing it all into the back of your Lexus SUV?"

He hung his head.

"I suppose you forgot that we live in a day where cameras are mounted all around us. That night, mine just happened to catch you in the act."

Wes twisted his mouth and shrugged.

"Are you aware that I could charge you with hit-and-run, breaking and entering, and grand larceny?"

He nodded. "Guess you probably could."

Logan switched off the laptop. "I sure would hate to have to do that. Perhaps we can come to an agreement." He slid his handgun from its holster and laid it on the bar in front of him.

Wes's eyes bulged. "I feel sure we can, Mr. Corbett." He took a swig of his water.

"Well, here's the deal. Take it or leave it. If you walk out of here and don't show your face or interfere in Brooklyn's life or mine again, you walk scot-free. Deal?"

He looked into Logan's eyes. "Deal."

"Great. That makes all of our lives easier." He folded his arms. "Anything else you'd like to discuss, Mr. Marshal? You said you had a couple of things."

He blew out a breath. "Can't seem to remember anything else at the moment." He stood. "Nope. I believe we've covered it, sir." He held out his hand, and Logan shook it.

"Good chatting with you, Wes. Have a nice life."

He tipped his head, walked out of the kitchen, and down the hall.

When Logan heard the front door close, he sighed, wiped the sweat from his brow, and slapped his laptop shut. All in a day's work. A day he hoped he'd never see the likes of again. He slipped his handgun into its holster, his notebook and laptop under his arm, and locked the back door. He paused to stare out at the waterway, then looked around the room. "You were right about one other thing, Mr. Marshal. Whoever owns this place needs a wife." He headed toward the front door. "Yep…a pretty lady to enjoy it with."

Chapter Thirty

Thursday, June 29, 2023

Logan placed several contracts in a neat stack in front of him and pushed back from his desk. Hearing laughter, he swiveled his chair to face the window and noted a young family walking toward the beach. The teenage boy with sun-bleached hair, who perfectly balanced a surfboard on his head, reminded him of his former self. Young and carefree. Today, he was not so young and far less than carefree. He pulled a small box from his pocket and flipped it open. Nestled in the navy-blue velvet-lined case was a brilliant emerald-cut diamond set in a yellow-gold band. He'd found the girl of his dreams and was ready to take the next step. As the saying goes…when you know, you know. He hoped Brooklyn would feel the same.

As the buzz of the phone on his desk jostled him from his daydream, he pressed the button. "Yes, Nora?"

"There is a rather eccentric young lady here to see you, sir."

"Eccentric?"

She lowered her voice. "Yes…not your typical client. She wouldn't tell me why she wants to see you. Should I send her in?"

"Well, now that you've got my curiosity up, how could you not?"

She giggled. "Okay. She's on her way, sir."

He dropped the contracts into the wire basket on the corner of his desk and looked up as a young lady with electric blue hair and a small nose ring strutted into his office. Walking around the desk, he extended his hand. "Good afternoon, I'm Logan Corbett."

"I know who you are." She brushed by him and plopped into the chair in front of his desk.

He returned to his seat and studied her. Pushing back, he placed his hands behind his head and smiled. "So you know me, huh? You'll have to forgive me for not recognizing you. Please…refresh my memory."

She got up and surveyed the pictures and certificates on the wall. "Hmm…impressive. You important?"

He allowed his chair to spring forward and swiveled to face her. "I suppose that's all relative. I'm important to those I help find homes."

She dropped back in her chair, crossed her legs, and smoothed the ripped knees of her jeans. "Perfect. Maybe you can find one for me."

He leaned forward on the desk and folded his hands in front of him. "So you want to buy a house?"

"Oh, no." She laughed. "There's no way I could afford a house. I just need a home."

He cleared his throat and stroked the stubble on his face. "Let's back up a moment. I never caught your name."

"Maybe that's because I didn't throw it."

He cocked his head. "I think you're right, but if you want my help, I need to know what to call you."

She held out her hand, which brandished a "Faith Over Fear" tattoo. "I'm Lacey. Lacey Collins."

"I like that," he said, shaking her hand. "Pretty name, but it doesn't ring any bells with me."

"Well, I didn't say you knew me. I said I knew you."

He gave his head a quick shake. "Now, I'm totally confused.

Care to explain?"

She pointed to a framed picture on his desk. "Can I see that?"

He picked up the black-and-white photo and passed it to her.

"Cool. I can see why Mama liked you."

He froze and swallowed hard. "Say what?"

"I see why Mama liked you."

Blood pulsed in his ears as he slid his trembling hands into his lap. "That's your Mama?"

Her eyes grew large. "Uh-huh…and you're my daddy."

He jolted. "Whoa. Not so fast. Who told you that?"

"Mama."

"You're Amber's daughter?"

She nodded. "And yours. That same picture has been on her dresser for as long as I can remember."

He grimaced as his insides churned. "How old are you?"

"Sixteen."

He did the math, then rubbed his forehead and slid his hand down the side of his face. "Does your mama know where you are?"

She shook her head, and despite her harsh outer shell, her fragile spirit seeped through. "Oh, no. She'd be furious if she knew I came here and told you."

He leaned back in his chair. "Hmm…this is heavy. I don't know what to say. So, tell me again. Why did you come?"

"I need a place to stay."

"You don't live with your mother?"

"I do, but she doesn't want me there."

"Why would that be?"

"She says I don't follow the house rules."

"Is she right?"

She twisted her mouth and nodded. "Pretty much."

"So, tell me. Why would I want to take someone in who doesn't follow house rules?"

"I'd follow them."

"Why would living someplace else make a difference?"

Lacey squirmed. "Do you have a live-in?"

"No. Just a large golden retriever named Murphy."

She smiled. "Well, Mama doesn't either, but her boyfriend is at the house all of the time, and I'm afraid of him."

Logan's eyes widened. "Does he abuse you?"

She shook her head. "No, but he yells and drinks a lot. It scares me."

"So where does your mother think you are now?"

"At my friend's house. I left Mama's last week, but my friend's parents say I need to go home—that I can't stay with them forever."

"I can understand that."

Lacey fiddled with the strap of her slingbag as he mulled things over.

"Can you stay at your friend's house another night or so?"

"Probably."

"Well, you should do that. I'll need time to process all of this."

"Okay." She walked toward the door.

"Whoa. Wait a minute there, missy." He leaned forward and slid a notepad and pen across his desk. "Do you have a phone?"

She nodded.

"All right, then. Don't leave here without giving me your number. I'll need your mother's also. I won't do anything without her approval."

She walked back to the desk, scribbled their numbers on the notepad, and looked up. "Thanks, Mr. Corbett…or should I call you Dad?"

As if gut-punched, he spouted, "For now, let's keep it Mr.

Corbett."

"Sure. I can do that."

He willed himself to remain vertical as he watched her walk down the hall, her exit far more humble than her haughty entrance. Returning to his office, he raked his fingers through his hair and dropped into his chair. He leaned back, stared at the ceiling, and reminded himself to breathe. *Amber, why didn't you tell me you had a child? Our child. A daughter.*

Overwhelmed, he slipped the velvet box from his pocket and flicked it open. As tears threatened to escape his eyes, the sparkling facets of the gem blurred, and the clarity of his future melded with his past. Snapping the box shut, he dropped it inside his desk drawer and stared at the notepad with Amber's phone number scrawled across it.

Logan climbed the steps from the beach and sat in one of the Adirondack chairs at the end of the walkway leading to his house. Murphy sat beside him. "Well, fella, what do you think I should do? Call Amber?"

Murphy cocked his head, whimpered, and sprawled at Logan's feet.

"I know. I feel the same way, but I'm a little old to whine about my circumstances. It's time to move forward." He opened his contacts, sucked in, and tapped on the newly added number for Amber Collins. After the third ring, she answered.

"Hello."

"Hi. Is this Amber?"

"Yes."

"This is Logan. Logan Corbett."

Silence greeted him.

"Amber, are you there?"

She exhaled. "Yes, I'm here. How are you?"

"I'm good? I hope you are?"

"I'm okay."

"Do you still live in Conway?"

"Yeah." She giggled. "But no longer with my parents, of course. Are you still at Harbor? I've read about your awards in the paper. Sounds like you're doing real good."

"It's not hard when you love what you do. You still work at the doctor's office?"

"Yeah. How'd you get my number?"

"I had a visitor at my office today."

"A visitor?" She hesitated. "So, who was your visitor?"

"A young lady named Lacey."

She winced. "Oh, no."

"Does she belong to you?"

"Uh-huh."

"I'm afraid to ask, but does she belong to me too?"

There was a long silence followed by a soft "Yes."

"Well, that's what she said, but I needed to hear it from you."

She muffled her sobs. "I'm sorry. I know I should have told you a long time ago."

"Amber, we need to talk. Are you willing to meet me somewhere?"

She sniffed. "Yes.".

"How about tomorrow in Conway at Rivertown Bistro? I don't have an opening in my schedule until after three, though. Would 4:00 o'clock be okay?"

"That'll be fine. I should be able to get off work a little early."

"Good. I'll get a table upstairs on the porch. Meet me there, okay?"

She whispered an assent and hung up the phone.

Logan stared out at the sea and shook his head. *This is surreal. Straight out of left field. A real game-changer. How will I ever break this news to Brooklyn?*

Chapter Thirty-One

Wednesday, November 17, 1965

"Trish flinched at the soft rap on her bedroom door.

"Honey, may I come in?"

"Sure, Momma." She turned down the radio on the nightstand and laid the letter she was writing to Billy Ray next to her.

Mrs. Malone pushed aside a stack of bridal magazines and sat on the foot of the bed.

Twisting Billy Ray's class ring on her finger, she searched her mother's face and braced for the worst. "What is it, Momma?"

"I just got off the phone with Martha. She said she heard that Billy Ray's father was taken to the hospital today."

"What?" She sat up straight and pulled the covers tighter around her. "What happened? Is he going to be okay?'

She shook her head. "She doesn't know. Someone heard it had something to do with his heart."

"Oh, no. I hope he'll be all right. He's such a nice man."

"We'll find out more tomorrow. Don't worry about it." She patted Trish's leg beneath the bedcovers and stood. "Try to get some sleep, sweetie. Tomorrow's a school day."

"I know. I'll turn out the light in a few minutes. Thanks for telling me."

She leaned over and kissed Trish on the forehead. "Sure. I knew you'd want to know."

As her momma closed the door, Trish fell back on her pillow and let out a long breath. As much as she hated to hear about Mr. Jessup, she was relieved that her mother hadn't come with bad news about Billy Ray. She shook her head. His ship hadn't even arrived in Viet Nam yet, and her anxiety swelled within her like a tidal wave.

She turned off the light. *Jesus, help me, and please, keep Billy Ray safe.*

Thursday, November 18, 1965

Trish pushed open the doors of Dosher Memorial Hospital, picked up the room number from the front desk for Billy Ray's dad, and walked up the steps to the second floor. As she passed the nurse's station, an older, heavyset nurse smiled at her. "Can I help you find someone?"

"I'm looking for Mr. Ron Jessup in room 214. Can he have visitors?"

"Yes. I'm headed that way." She motioned. "Follow me. I'll show you where his room is." When they reached the door, she turned and smiled. "Please try to keep it short. We don't want to tire him."

"Certainly. Thank you." Trish slowly pushed open the door and peeked in. Mr. Jessup appeared to be asleep, and his wife sat on a chair beside the bed. She looked up from her book, sprang from her chair, and placed her hand on the door.

"I'm Trish, I—"

She glared at her. "I know who you are."

"Oh...I thought per—"

"That my memory isn't good?"

Trish cringed. "Oh no, I just—"

She glanced over her shoulder. "As you can see, Mr. Jessup is sleeping and doesn't need visitors right now."

She shrank back. "I'm so sorry. I certainly don't want to disturb him. I just wanted to check in and see how he's doing."

Mrs. Jessup peered over her reading glasses and raised her eyebrows. "He's been better."

Trish lowered her eyes. "I'm sorry to—"

"Grace, is that Billy Ray's girl?" Mr. Jessup pushed himself up in the bed and reached toward her. "By all means, come over here, young lady."

Grace Jessup blew out a long, slow breath as Trish walked around her and took her husband's hand. "Hello, sir. It's good to see you. Momma and I have been worried about you."

"You have? I appreciate your concern."

Mrs. Jessup walked to the opposite side of the bed and patted her husband's shoulder. "Now, Ronnie, you know you should rest."

He kept his eyes fixed on Trish and swatted the air. "I have. I've slept all afternoon. It's nice to have a visitor."

Uncomfortable under the scrutiny of Billy Ray's mother, Trish said, "So you're feeling better?"

"I am." He laid his hand on his chest. "This old ticker decided to act up yesterday." He nodded toward the heart monitor beside his bed. "Today it's behavin'." He pointed toward the chair. "Please, have a seat."

Trish glanced at Mrs. Jessup and knew what her answer needed to be. "Thank you, but I can't stay. Momma will be expecting me for dinner. I just wanted to see how you were." She looked at Mrs. Jessup. "Momma wants to know if there's anything we can do for you."

She let out a heavy sigh. "That's nice. Thank her for me, but I think we're fine."

"Certainly." She laid her hand on Mr. Jessup's arm. "You take it easy now, okay?"

He smiled. "I'll do my best."

"Thanks, Mrs. Jessup." Trish walked to the door and turned. "Is it okay if Momma calls you sometime to see if you need anything?"

Mrs. Jessup stared out the window. "If she wants. We probably won't, but thanks anyway."

When Trish stepped into the hall, she heard Billy Ray's mother scold his dad for inviting her into the room. Would she ever be good enough for the Jessups?

As she walked past the nurse's station, she became acutely aware of her limp.

"Have a nice evening, young lady."

She turned and smiled. "Thank you. I hope you do too." She descended the stairs, tears slipping from her eyes. *Oh, Billy Ray, we have so much to overcome. I need you. Please hurry home.*

Trish closed her bedroom door and flopped across the bed on her stomach. Except for the soft light of a waning moon casting eerie shadows through the sheer curtains shrouding her window, the room was dark and still. No longer did the walls echo the squeals of joy that had filled them weeks earlier when Billy Ray had asked her to be his wife. She felt like a misinformed moviegoer with no way to exit the theater until the bitter end, regardless of how the scenes unfolded. Worse yet, neither could Billy Ray, who had no hope of sitting this one out. Their only option was to press through, pray, and hope to emerge victorious.

After praying for Billy Ray and his comrades, she scooted up on the bed and switched on the lamp. Opening the nightstand drawer, she pulled out her stationery box. Billy Ray's letters would be her lifeline. They would keep her tethered to her one true love. She reached back into the drawer, pulled out a wall calendar already opened to November, and, with a red pen, crossed off day eighteen. Three hundred forty-seven days to go—give or take. Like Stella said, they'd make it through—together. One day at a time.

Chapter Thirty-Two

Tuesday, November 23, 1965
Port of Ho Chi Minh City

Billy Ray followed Phil down the gangway with all of his possessions stuffed in a camouflage duffel bag slung over his shoulder. "Good morning, Viet Nam." He mumbled as a wet blanket of heat engulfed him, and the stench of garbage made his stomach roil. Stepping onto the dock after three weeks of rollin' down the river, they found it hard to get their land legs and keep their footing. Billy Ray threw his arm around Phil's shoulder, and they staggered like two drunken sailors toward a line of blue buses with chain link material covering the windows. They were there to fight the Viet Cong, a formidable communist guerrilla group embedded within the South Vietnamese population.

Billy Ray stopped in his tracks. "Will ya look at that? The enemy knows the terrain, is skilled in ambushes and hit-and-run tactics, and the US Army is chauffeured around in a caravan of pint-sized, blue school buses. God help us." He shook his head. "If we can make it to our base camp, we may have half a chance of making it home from this crazy war."

After Phil and Billy Ray boarded the bus packed with subdued GIs, they threw their bags on the overhead rack and dropped onto one of the few bench seats left. Their driver, a sergeant serving his second tour of duty, shut the doors and revved the engine. As the bus bounced along the hand-hewn dirt road to their base camp, it followed a misty path through thick ground cover, spikey trees, and across narrow creek beds. The tension that hung in the air, like a storm cloud brewing, was abruptly severed by Phil, who erupted into song. *"The wheels on the bus go round and round, round and round, round and round..."* Soon, forty-plus troops joined in the familiar grade school chorus that morphed into rounds from one side of the aisle and then the other. Billy Ray laughed and slapped Phil's leg. "Sung like a pro. My high school chorus teacher would be proud of you, Private. Maybe you need to rethink your calling when we get back to the States."

"What do you mean when we get back to the States? I've been rethinking it ever since I stepped off that ship."

Thirty minutes later, they arrived at the hilltop Fire Support Base. Hidden by dense foliage and surrounded by trenches with sandbag bunkers and concertina wire, it was nicer than Billy Ray imagined, and he supposed far better than their accommodations would be when out on a mission. As one of the larger permanent bases, it contained four 105mm artillery howitzers, a sandbagged munitions storage bunker, a guard tower with a view of the entire trail, a helicopter landing pad for resupply and medical evacuation, a makeshift kitchen, and sleeping shanties called hootches made of wood, tarps, and sandbags. Their assignment from this point, along with their South Vietnamese allies, who had a habit of switching sides when it suited them, was to stop the movement of the enemy and supplies from the north along the Ho Chi Minh trail.

Wednesday, November 24, 1965

Billy Ray lit the kerosene lamp, lifted the top of the small metal ammo chest beside his cot, and pulled out a writing tablet and pen. After stretching out, he pulled up the poncho-lined woobie blanket and tucked it around his tired, aching legs. Their first day out was an eye-opener. The rugged terrain was killer, and the dense foliage made their movements difficult. It was bizarre how, in Nam, a soldier could swelter during the day and freeze at night.

Hi Sweetheart,

I sure do miss you, and I can't wait to get your letters. Delivery is slow here in the bush. As a matter of fact, everything is. Today was our first day humping through the jungle, carrying an M-16 rifle and sixty-plus pounds of supplies on our backs. Disarming booby traps wasn't what I signed up for, but I guess the Army would beg to differ. We saw a little bit of action, but I'll spare you the details. Don't really want to relive it. I'd much rather think about Thanksgiving dinner. Yep, you heard me right. We've got a full-course turkey and dressing feast coming our way tomorrow. I'm sure it won't hold a candle to Mother's with her fantastic stuffing, but anything will beat the C-rations we live off of here. We're twelve hours ahead of you, so my holiday will be winding down as yours ramps up.

How's school and your job going? Tell Mr. Willie hello and that I miss dropping in for a banana split. I wish I had one right now. Phil and I have managed to stick—

Billy Ray's pen slid across the page as explosions shook the earth. Dropping his feet to the ground, he grabbed his rifle from the munitions rack beside the entrance and, along with the other troops, took his pre-assigned position to secure the camp. While the enemy fired mortars into the compound, hoping to strike munition storage bunkers, troops in the guard towers fired high-explosive rounds that burst several feet off the ground, providing a shield of shrapnel around the perimeter. As artillery pummeled in the distance and flares lit up the night sky, images of what could happen flashed through Billy Ray's mind. With lips and chin trembling, he wiped a clammy palm on his pants and returned it to steady his rifle.

After an intense exchange of gunfire, the enemy moved south, and the explosions faded into the distance. Billy Ray looked at Phil and rolled his eyes. "A little close for comfort, huh, pal?"

"Way too close. How does anyone get out of this hellhole alive? We've been in the bush for less than forty-eight hours, and it feels like months."

Billy Ray returned his rifle to the rack and dropped onto his cot. Struggling to steady his hands, he picked up his tablet and continued his letter. He wrote as if what had just taken place was as normal as breathing because here in Viet Nam—it was.

Phil and I have managed to stick together. I wouldn't want to be here without him. Knowing there is someone in the trenches with me that I trust means everything. I know this letter will be late for Thanksgiving, but giving thanks is never too late. I thank my God every time I remember you— which is every minute of the day. I love you, Patricia Millicent Malone. I can't wait to make you my own. It's almost lights out, so I'll sign off. Happy Thanksgiving, beautiful girl. I hope to see you in my dreams. Be there.

341 more days,

Billy Ray

He slid his letter into the envelope, licked the flap, and wrote S.W.A.K. (Sealed With A Kiss) across it. No stamp was needed—compliments of Uncle Sam. After laying the tablet and pen on the ammo box, he snuffed out the lantern and slipped the envelope underneath his pillow. Amid the deafening sounds of insects, he closed his eyes and prayed that a letter from Trish would be in tomorrow's mail.

Chapter Thirty-Three

Friday, June 30, 2023

Logan stirred the ice in his soda with his straw and watched the activity on the street below. It had been a while since he'd spent time in Conway. Many of the buildings in the historic district brought back great memories of his youth.

A soft voice interrupted his thoughts.

"Logan?"

He turned to see a petite lady with coal-black hair and dark eyes. He jumped to his feet and gave her a quick hug. "Amber. I'd know you anywhere. You look great."

"Thank you," she said as he seated her across from him. "You haven't changed a bit."

As Logan struggled to find words, Amber picked up the water glass at her place and swallowed hard.

"Oh…" Logan summoned the server. "Let's get you a drink."

Amber ordered a glass of iced tea with lime and placed her napkin on her lap.

He scanned their surroundings. "This is nice. I've not eaten out here on the porch before, have you?"

She nodded. "I have. Good choice. When I come with my friends, this is our favorite place to sit."

He picked up the menu. "I know it's a little late for lunch and too early for dinner, but I haven't eaten since breakfast. What's good?"

"Everything, but I'm not hungry. Tea is all I need."

He scanned the appetizers. "How about some spring rolls or crab dip?"

She pressed her lips together and tipped her head from side to side before making a decision. "Hmm...the spring rolls *are* yummy." She nodded. "Sure. I can't turn those down. Go for it. I'll eat a couple."

Though their conversation was stilted at first, it didn't take long for them to settle into a relaxed rhythm as they spoke of old times and friends still in the area. Amber sipped her tea and blotted her lips with her napkin. "Logan, I guess we've skirted the issue long enough. I'm sorry you found out about Lacey the way you did. I can only imagine your shock and will understand if you're upset with me for not being upfront with you years ago."

He shook his head slowly. "Shocked is, without a doubt, an understatement." As resentment for how he'd been blindsided by the news mushroomed within him, he struggled to remain calm. "When I walked out of my office yesterday afternoon, pelted with the reality of being a father, it was more than I could wrap my mind around. Why didn't you tell me?"

She hung her head. "I know I should have, and I regret that I didn't." She folded her napkin and rubbed her finger over the folds. "I'm ashamed to say why." She took a deep breath. "I didn't tell you at first because I didn't intend to have the baby." She looked up, tears welling in her eyes. "I'd planned to have an abortion, so I didn't see any reason to upset you."

Logan's heart hurt for her. "So, what changed your mind?"

"Hearing the baby's heartbeat. After my doctor's appointment, I couldn't go through with it. By the time I decided to keep the baby, you were already in college, and I didn't want to upset your life. If my parents hadn't been supportive, I probably would have told you, but with their support, I knew the baby and I would be okay. I didn't want you to feel trapped into marrying me. I thought I was being considerate, but now that I've matured, I realize my actions were selfish. I robbed you of a lot…and Lacey." She slid her hand across the table. "I'm sorry. Will you forgive me?"

Logan laid his hand on top of hers. "Of course I will. At eighteen, neither of us was mature enough to make responsible decisions. However, in the end, you did. You decided to keep our baby. That had to be difficult and was a selfless act. Thanks for doing the right thing. Lacey is a beautiful girl."

Amber smiled. "She is, isn't she?"

He scooted back from the table and crossed his legs. "So what's going on that made her feel the need to come to my office?"

She sighed. "I guess I've slipped back to making poor decisions. I have a boyfriend who's not working out. It didn't take long for me to realize he wasn't who I thought he was, but now he won't let go. He makes our lives miserable." She brushed her bangs from her eyes. "I don't blame Lacey for leaving. If I had a place to go, I'd like to leave, but it is my house, so I can't just walk out."

Logan shook his head. "Wow, Amber, I'm sorry. It sounds like you need to put your foot down. Get a restraining order or something."

"I know you're right, but I'm afraid of how he might respond." She wiped water from the table and the side of her tea glass with her napkin.

"Where do you see me in all of this?" he said, fiddling with his watch. "Lacey has pretty much asked me to take her in."

She shook her head. "I know. I'm sorry."

"No. It's okay. I could probably keep her—short term, but—"

"Oh, it would only be short-term. I'd make sure of that. None of this is fair to her. Her friend's parents have been generous, but it's time she moves on, and I know she won't come home until my situation is different. Do you think she could stay with you for a week or two?"

Logan hesitated.

"It would give you a chance to get to know your daughter. I know her exterior is rough, but she's a sweet girl."

He leaned forward. "Give me time to digest this. I have things I'll need to work out first."

"Of course. I understand." She peered into his eyes. "Thank you for considering it. You're a good man, Logan Corbett. I knew that early on. Sometimes, I wonder how different things might have been for us if I'd told you?"

He shrugged. "I suppose it just wasn't meant to be."

She lowered her eyes. "I guess not."

"Are you ready to go?" He slid back his chair.

She nodded and walked down the steps ahead of him.

"Are you parked close by?"

"Yes, right out front."

Logan paid the bill and escorted her onto the sidewalk.

Before stepping off the curb to her car, she turned. "Logan, thank you for understanding. I hope you and Lacey have great days ahead of you. You deserve the best, and as far as I'm concerned, I know she has the best in you as a father."

As Logan drove down Hwy 501 and crossed the Waccamaw River, memories of days spent with Amber at her parents' home on the river flickered through his mind like scenes on a movie reel. She'd been his first love, and the fact that he kept a picture of them together on his desk after all these years spoke of the magnitude of the bond they'd shared. Seeing Amber today and knowing they'd created a child together stirred something deep within him—feelings that he thought he'd dealt with long ago. He looked forward to getting to know his daughter. It hadn't taken but a few moments with Lacey in his office to see that she had her mother's spunk. He had so much he needed to share with Brooklyn, but breaking the news to her worried him. Did he even know his own heart at this point? He willed himself to tap the phone icon on his steering wheel and prompted Siri to call Brooklyn. Within moments, she picked up.

"Hi Hon…where are you?"

"On my way back from Conway."

"Conway? Do you have a listing there?"

"No. Met someone I hadn't seen in a while. If you're free, I'll drop by and tell you all about it."

"Sure, I'd love that. Have you eaten?"

"Sort of. Had a light late lunch. Don't worry about me, though. I'm not hungry."

"Okay. I'll put on a pot of coffee. How far out are you?"

"About thirty minutes."

"Okay. See you soon. Stay safe."

"Sure thing." He sighed as the call ended. "Thirty minutes to figure this out, Corbett. Tread softly. Don't say anything you'll regret."

Chapter Thirty-Four

Brooklyn

I met Logan at the door with a kiss and motioned him toward the bar. "Have a seat, and I'll get our coffee, then we can settle in on the couch. I know you must be tired."

He nodded. "Yeah, pretty much. It's been a stressful week. Seems like I've had to put brushfires out at every turn."

"I'm sorry. Well, at least it's Friday. Maybe you can get some rest this weekend."

He shrugged. "Probably not much chance of that, but I like the way you think."

I handed him his cup, picked up mine, and walked to the couch. Plopping down, I patted the place beside me. "Here. Sit back and chill."

Logan sighed as he eased in next to me and propped his feet on the coffee table. "Love it. I'm always comfortable here."

I looped my arm through his and kissed his cheek. "As you should be." After we sat in silence for a few moments savoring our coffee, I set my cup on the end table. "So, care to share about your week?"

Logan hugged his warm cup and turned to face me. "On the way here, I tried to figure out a good way to fill you in on my circumstances, but decided the only way would be to just spew it."

"What on earth?" I felt every muscle in my body tense as I tried to brace myself for what would follow.

"There is no way not to shock you. I was shocked myself."

"Logan, you're scaring me. Just say it."

"I had a young lady visit me at my office on Thursday. She told me her name was Lacey Collins and that she…that she…is my daughter."

My mouth dropped open as I clapped my hand to my chest. "Daughter? What do you mean, daughter?"

He sighed. "As in *my kid*. Lacey is *my* child."

I clapped my hands to my mouth and leaped from the sofa. "What? Child? Are you kidding me?"

He shook his head. "No, believe me, I would never kid about something like this."

I walked to the window and looked out at the ocean. "How old is this daughter of yours?"

"Sixteen."

Whirling around, I threw my arms in the air. "Sixteen? And you're just now telling me?"

He rose from the couch and walked toward me with his arms outstretched.

I stepped backward and dropped onto the window seat.

"I'm sorry, Brooklyn. I didn't tell you because I didn't know."

"You didn't know you had a daughter?" I shook my head and dropped my face in my hands. "This is insane and getting crazier by the minute."

"I agree, but it is the truth. What's the saying—*Life is stranger than fiction*?" He sat beside me and cradled my hand in his. "Baby, I'm as shocked as you are about this. Please hear me out."

I clung to his hand but widened the space between us. My desire was to fall onto his chest and sob. Instead, I struggled to maintain my composure and keep my distance. "Okay. Go for it.

I'm listening."

As Logan told me the story of his relationship with Amber in high school, a knot formed in my stomach. I could barely breathe, and Logan's voice grew muffled in my ears. Yes, everyone has a past, and this was his, but his past had now become his present. Our present. I didn't know how to cope with it. How would I ever survive another complex relationship? I'd come to Sunset Beach to escape a painful past and find safe harbor. Instead, I'd run aground and now laid shipwrecked on an island. I needed to learn how to sail my ship, but I wasn't sure it was salvageable—that it would even float.

"Come here."

Logan pulled me closer, and I collapsed in his arms. "This is just too hard, babe. I'm not ready to step back into a firestorm. I don't have the energy. What's your plan? Will Lacey come live with you?"

He rested his chin on my head. "I don't see how I can refuse her. She *is* my daughter, and I want to get to know her. I can't think of a better way."

I sat up and looked into his eyes. "Then that's what you should do. I'll give you both some space."

His eyes questioned mine. "What are you saying? You're the most important person in my life right now. I want you to meet Lacey, and she needs to meet you. I want to get to know my daughter with you by my side."

I took a deep breath. "I'm sorry. I'm being selfish. I know this is harder on you than it is on me. I appreciate you wanting to include me." I clasped his hand. "Yes…I'd love to meet Lacey."

He kissed me on the nose and smiled. "Thanks, babe. I know nothin' 'bout raisin' no girls. I feel better knowing that you're with me on this journey."

Saturday, July 8, 2023

Logan pulled into the drive, cut the engine, and looked over at Lacey. "Well, girl, this is it. Your new digs."

She cut her eyes at Logan. "My what?"

"Oh, pardon me. What would you call it?"

"My new addy."

"Addy?" He raised his brows. "Oh, of course…address. That makes perfect sense. I'll have to remember to use that one with my clients."

She flipped her hair back and grinned.

"Come on. Help me carry in your things." After opening the tailgate, he handed her several totes and lifted out the remaining two suitcases. "Follow me, I'll show you around and introduce you to Murphy."

"This is a super cool place," she said as she followed him up the steps. "You're right on the ocean. How long did you say I could stay?"

He chuckled, turned the key in the lock, and pushed open the door. "Let's take this one day at a time, okay?"

Murphy bounded from Logan's bedroom, eyes gleaming, tail wagging. After circling them, he danced at their feet.

Lacey dropped her bags on the floor, kneeled, and wrapped her arms around his broad neck. "Hi, Murphy. I'm Lacey, your new roomie." She hugged him tight and scratched behind his ears as he pressed into her. "You're beautiful."

"Well, now that you've passed the sniff test with flying colors, follow me, and I'll show you your room."

Lacey followed him down a short hall and into a pale-yellow bedroom trimmed in white that fronted the ocean. She squealed, dropped her bags on the bed, and walked to the windows. "Wow. This is amazing."

Setting her suitcases on the floor, he motioned to an adjoining bath. "This is yours."

Her eyes widened. "What? You mean I have my own bathroom?'

He chuckled. "You do."

She peeked in and then hugged him. "I've never had my own bathroom before. Thanks for letting me come."

"You're welcome. I hope you'll enjoy being here."

She whirled around with her arms outstretched. "I already do. Who wouldn't?"

"Well, let me get out of your way so you can unpack. If you need anything, holler." He walked toward the door.

"Oh, there is one thing."

He turned. "Sure. What do you need?"

"I need to know if I can call you Daddy?"

As warmth spread throughout his chest, he smiled and gave her a thumbs-up. "Yes, Lacey, you can. I'd like that. I'd like that a lot."

Chapter Thirty-Five

Wednesday, December 15, 1965

Billy Ray gave Phil a thumbs up, crouched low, and tried to stay as small as possible while sharp, high-pitched whistles cut through the air inches above his head. As the ground shook from nearby explosions, adrenaline surged through his veins, and chills ran down his spine. The fear among his comrades in the trench was palpable, and every man fought back with a fierce determination to stay alive. Billy Ray coughed. The stench of gunpowder, smoke, and body odor sucked the air from his lungs.

Once the enemy moved farther south and the intensity of the gunfire lessened, Billy Ray surveyed his platoon. All had come out of this skirmish unscathed—physically anyway. The battle to maintain their sanity was a different story. He rose from his belly, rested his back against the mud wall of the trench, and eyed Phil. "Looks like we made it through another one, pal. How do you feel?"

"Numb, but happy to be alive. It's hard to believe we're living this nightmare. How long have we been in this tropical paradise, anyway?"

"Forty-five days. Which means we only have three hundred and twenty more ahead of us."

"What? Impossible. I don't know how anyone makes it out of this hellhole alive." Phil threw back his head and gulped water from his canteen, then wiped his mouth and forehead with his shirt sleeve. "We have to hang on, buddy. Got some pretty young ladies countin' on it." He slipped an envelope from his shirt pocket and pressed it to his nose. Then, flapping it in the air, he said, "I'm convinced this right here is what's going to keep me alive. Did you hear from Trish yesterday?"

"Sure did." He patted the pocket over his heart. "Our girls are full of plans for us when we get home, aren't they?"

Phil clasped the letter to his chest and leaned his head against the muddy wall. "Yeah, wearing this grubby uniform day in and day out makes that monkey suit Stella plans for me to wear on our wedding day sound pretty appealing. What's Trish cookin' up for the two of you?"

"Not sure. It's different in every letter. I think she'll settle for something casual. Right now, she's talking about a simple ceremony by the water at Sunset Beach."

"That's cool. I could go for that, but I don't think Stella's mother would. She's more into a traditional Old South wedding. Something she can impress her—."

Rockets and mortars exploded around them. As Billy Ray and his friends resumed their firing positions, they emptied their M-16s at whatever moved and even at what didn't. Sweat poured from every pore in Billy Ray's body as he ejected an empty magazine from his rifle and inserted another into the well until it clicked into place. When he turned to fire, the air erupted with a deafening roar. The ground shook, and dirt and debris rained on top of them. Phil let out a terrified scream. "Billy, I've been hit. I'm hit."

He lunged toward his friend, and a searing pain tore through his leg. As the smell of smoke and burning vegetation overwhelmed him, Phil's screams melted into the distance. His vision blurred, and the earth spun out of control. As darkness enveloped him, he strained to open his eyes, then realized they were. Spiraling into infinite blackness, he whispered, "Jesus, save me."

Trish…

Trish screamed and shot straight up in bed. As she floundered for the lamp on her nightstand, her mother burst through the door and flipped on the overhead light.

"What is it, honey? Are you okay?" She dropped onto the side of the bed and wrapped Trish in her arms.

"Oh, Momma. It was awful! Just awful." She struggled to catch her breath and pressed her hands to her chest as if to slow down her heartbeat. "I dreamed Billy Ray's platoon was struck by mortar fire. It was horrible. So real." She peered into her mother's worried eyes.

"It's okay, babydoll." She rubbed Trish's back and rocked her. "It was a dream. A bad one, but you're home. You're safe."

"What about Billy Ray? Is he safe, Momma?"

She brushed Trish's hair away from her face. "I wish I could tell you he is, sweetheart, but I can't. One thing I can say, though, is that nightmares aren't reliable barometers of truth. They are kindled by our anxieties and ignited with our worst fears."

She nodded. "I know you're right, but when Billy Ray called my name, it sounded like he was here in the room with me."

"That had to be frightening, but don't borrow from tomorrow, sweetie. If anything happens to Billy Ray, the Army will contact his parents." She squeezed Trish's hands and stood. "Hop up now and get ready for school. I'll have a large cup of hot chocolate waiting for you in the kitchen." She walked toward the door. "And dress warm. It's not supposed to get out of the teens today."

Trish shivered at the thought of climbing out from under the covers and shook off her fears. "Okay, Momma."

"Stella. Wait up." Trish zig-zagged through the crowded hall with Margo behind her and slipped in beside her friend. She shifted the weight of her books from one arm to the other. "How did your Algebra test go? Was it hard?"

"Yes. I know I missed at least one problem, and there were a couple I wasn't sure of. Why did you want me to meet you today?"

Trish motioned toward the library. "Let's find a quiet place to talk."

Stella shot Margo a questioning glance as they followed Trish through the door. "Okay, but you're making me nervous."

Trish placed her books on a corner table in the back of the room and pulled out a chair while Stella and Margo sat across from her. "I don't even know how to explain how real my dream was last night. I hesitate to call it a dream or even a nightmare. Although I've never had a vision, I've heard people talk about them, and I'd say this had to be one."

Stella looked around the room, rested her forearms on the table, and leaned in so as not to disturb students who'd actually come to the library to study. "What? What was it?"

"I'm telling you, it was so real I could smell the smoke from the battle."

Margo blurted. "Battle? What battle? What are you talking about?"

Trish peered into Stella's large, anxious eyes. "I'm scared, Stella. I heard Billy Ray call my name last night. I could have sworn he was in the room with me."

She plugged her ears with her fingers. "I don't think I want to hear this."

"I know. I'm sorry, but I've got to share it. I can't get the sights, sounds, and smells out of my mind." She rested her hands on the table in front of her and fiddled with Billy Ray's class ring. "It was bad, Stella. Really bad. Billy Ray and Phil were in a foxhole and…and both were…both were hit with mortars."

"No!" She slapped her hand over her mouth, looked around, and caught the librarian's disapproving stare. Folding her arms, she dropped back in her chair and lowered her voice. "Stop it. Don't say that." She shook her head. "It's not true. It's not."

Margo slid her arm around Stella's shoulders as tears slid from Trish's eyes.

"I'm sorry. I probably shouldn't have mentioned it, but I've never experienced anything like this and had to tell someone."

Stella laid her head on her arms and sobbed.

Margo rubbed Stella's back as Trish reached over and held her hand. "Forgive me. I hope you're right and I'm wrong. It's probably not true."

Stella's red eyes bulged as she lifted her head and swiped at her cheeks. "Trish…I think maybe it is true."

She blinked back tears and brushed the hairs rising on her arms. "Why do you say that?"

"Because last week I had a similar experience."

"You did? Why didn't you say something?"

"Because I was afraid if I did, I would speak it into existence. I know that sounds stupid, but it was just too scary to repeat. Your dream sounds even more vivid than mine. I passed mine off as fear and a figment of my imagination. But now…now that you've told me this, maybe mine wasn't just a nightmare."

Their tear-filled eyes shifted from one to the other as they gripped one another's hands. They squeezed hard and prayed harder.

Friday, December 17, 1965
U.S. Army Camp Zama, Japan

Billy Ray winced with pain as he reached for his notepad and pen. Although grateful to be out of the enemy's crosshairs, he was plagued with remorse and filled with anxiety about what was to come. As his pen hovered above the thin blue lines, he struggled to find words to describe his condition and the emotions that held him hostage. His life was forever changed, and he knew his future with Trish hung in the balance.

Chapter Thirty-Six

Friday, December 31, 1965

Trish sat on the couch beside Stella, placed her glass on the coffee table, and took a bite of her momma's fabulous cucumber sandwiches. She nudged her friend and mumbled. "Have you even touched your plate?"

Stella shook her head and continued to watch ABC's coverage of Guy Lombardo's New Year's Eve party at the Roosevelt Grill in New York City. Unblinking, she spoke in a monotone voice. "Phil said one day he'd take me to The Big Apple."

"And I bet he will."

She turned her head toward Trish and droned. "Do you really think so?"

"I do."

Tears welled in her eyes. "I wish I had your kinda faith." She picked up her plate, swirled a piece of celery in the creamy white dip, and bit into it. "Have you heard any more from Billy Ray?"

"No, not since he wrote Thanksgiving, and nothing since his parents called to say he'd been injured and that they had few details. The mail doesn't run this weekend, but I'm holding out hope that a letter will come on Monday."

Stella lowered her head. "I've not heard from Phil since Thanksgiving either, and his parents still don't have any word on his location. Maybe we'll both get letters," she said, licking the dip from her celery.

Trish's mother entered the room with a tray of crystal goblets filled with sparkling cider. "Girls, it's getting close. Five more minutes, and we'll be in a brand-new year." After handing each of them a glass, she settled into her husband's easy chair. "The network should cut to Howard Cosell in Times Square any minute now." She pointed to the black-and-white picture on the console TV. "Yes…there's the Allied Chemical Tower and the huge ball. Isn't this exciting, girls?"

Trish glanced over at Stella, who'd slid to the edge of her chair. For the first time in a while, she saw a glimmer of light in her friend's eyes. At 11:59 p.m., the large aluminum ball inched its way down the flagpole. When it neared the rooftop, the crowd in Times Square roared, and the three of them stood. With only ten seconds left in 1965 and with their glasses raised, they joined Guy Lombardo in counting down the final moments. As soon as the glowing ball completed its descent and rested on the rooftop at the stroke of midnight, Lombardo's Royal Canadians Orchestra played his traditional theme song, "Auld Lang Syne."

Once 1966 made its debut, the three of them squealed, clinked their glasses, and downed the cold cider. For a few brief moments, tears of loneliness turned into tears of joy. Trish hugged Stella, then clasped her shoulders and peered into her eyes. "This is going to be a great year. I choose to believe we'll hear from our guys soon and that the war will be over before the year is out."

Stella returned the hug. "Thank you, Trish. What would I do without you? You always help me look on the brighter side of life. I'm going to stop worrying about the dreams we had and, like you say, believe that Phil and Billy Ray are fine and home before the year is out."

Trish squeezed her friend again and patted her back. "There

now, that's the Stella I know."

Stella set her glass on the brass tray on the coffee table and returned to her chair. "Thank you, Trish, for inviting me over tonight. I love that we can bring in the new year together."

She jumped as the phone on the table beside her father's chair jingled.

Mrs. Malone, already on her way to the kitchen, cast Trish a questioning glance and picked up. "Hello." Her eyes grew large. "Sure. She's right here." She held out the receiver.

"Who is it, Momma?"

She shook the phone in Trish's face. "Take it. It's long distance. Person to person."

"What?" She inhaled and put her hand over her heart. "Hello."

"Is this Trish Malone?"

"Yes, ma'am."

"I have a person-to-person call for you from Sergeant Billy Ray Jessup. Will you accept the call?"

Her voice rose an octave as she locked eyes with Stella. "Yes, ma'am. You better believe I will." While she waited for the operator to connect her, she eased into her father's chair and tried to catch her breath. Then came the voice she'd longed to hear.

"Happy New Year, sweetheart."

"Oh, baby, I can't believe it's you. I've been so worried since your father called Momma and said you'd been hurt. Are you all right?"

"Better. And now that I hear your voice, I'm feeling no pain. I'm at a hospital in Tokyo. We're fifteen hours ahead of you, but I figured you'd be up ringing in the new year."

"We are. Stella's here, and we were just talking about you and Phil." She giggled. "But, then again, what else is new? We're always talking about the two of you." She blurted without taking a breath. "What happened? Your father didn't know a lot when he called Momma. Are you okay?"

"I have a leg injury, Trish, but I'm alive, and that's what's important. Didn't you get my letter?"

"No. Not since Thanksgiving."

"Well, you should have another one soon. It will tell you everything. We only have a couple of minutes now, babe, so we've got to make this quick. How are you? Good?"

"Yes. Yes, I'm fine. Just stay worried about you."

"I know. I called to tell you that in a few weeks, I'll be transferred to Walter Reed Army Medical Center in D.C."

Trish yelled and sprang from her chair. "You will? That's wonderful news. Will I get to see you soon?"

"Not for a while, I'm sure, but at least I'll be in the States, and we can talk more often."

She glanced at Stella sitting with her head laid back, and eyes closed. Grateful for the long phone cord, Trish picked up the base and walked into the dining room out of earshot. "I love you, baby. It's so good to hear your voice. How's Phil? The last we heard, his parents were waiting to hear about his location."

His hesitation sent shivers down her spine. "Billy Ray, what is it?"

"He was also wounded in the ambush, but isn't here at the hospital."

"He's not? Why? Where is he?"

"I wish we knew. Phil's still missing and is now listed as a POW."

"A what?"

His voice broke. "A prisoner of war, Trish. The Army believes he was captured by the Viet Cong and…"

Trish strained to hear as static popped and crackled in her ear. "Billy Ray? Billy Ray…can you hear me?" She yelled into the vacuum. "Sweetheart, can you hear me?" Sighing, she carried the phone back into the living room and set it on the end table. She lifted her eyes to Stella's.

"What?" She shot straight up. "Trish—what is it? Are Phil and Billy Ray all right?"

She pressed her lips together and struggled with what to say. Her words would sting, but with them could also come hope— hope in the possibility that Phil was alive. *Wasn't hearing from their soldiers what she and Stella had hoped for? Part of their prayer had come true within the opening moments of the new year.*

Monday, January 3, 1966

Trish sat on the front step and checked her watch every few minutes. She knew Mr. Warren's route would be heavy after the holiday, but... Hearing his truck round the corner, she ran and met him on the sidewalk.

Laughing, he hopped out and handed her a letter. "Is this what you're looking for, young lady?"

Noting the Tokyo, Japan postmark, she hugged him. "Yes. Oh, yes, it certainly is. Thank you. Thank you so much." She took it with the rest of the mail toward the house, then hollered over her shoulder. "Oh... and Happy New Year, Mr. Warren."

Pulling off, he shouted, "You too, Trish. I hope it's a good one."

As much as she wanted to tear into the envelope, she sat on the top step, carefully slid her nail along the flap, and pulled out Billy Ray's letter. A waft of British Sterling cologne accompanied it.

Wednesday, December 29, 1965
My dear, sweet Trish,

I'm sorry I haven't written sooner, but I've been pretty much out of it. I'm at Camp Zama, an army evacuation hospital near Tokyo. My pain, though constant, pales in comparison with the nightmares that keep me awake and the images that haunt me throughout the day. I can't begin to describe the horrors of Viet Nam…, and believe me when I say you don't want to know.

On December sixteenth, the surgeons here finished the job the Viet Cong started and amputated my left leg…

Trish slapped the letter to her lap and gasped. "What? They've cut off your leg? No…Billy Ray. No. Why didn't you tell me on the phone?" She blinked and continued to read, tears welling in her eyes.

…amputated my left leg, just below the knee. When my medication wears off, I deal with phantom limb pain. It's a weird but common phenomenon often faced by amputees after surgery. My doctors say that, although the pain should decrease over time, it could continue for several years or even remain for a lifetime.

Baby, I'm not sure how you will feel about us now, and I won't blame you if you choose to move on without me. You don't deserve less than what you committed to that day on Bald Head Island. How I cherish those memories. I find it hard to believe I'm the guy who ran to the top of the lighthouse and was Southport High's prom king and star athlete. What a joke…but at least I'm alive, right?

I'm not sure when I'll get to come home. I have extensive rehab and therapy ahead of me—physical and mental, before being fitted for a prosthetic limb and learning how to walk again. Hopefully, that part of my journey will take place at Walter Reed Army Medical Center in D.C. Please pray for that. I want to be back in the States. I don't ever want there to be an ocean between us again.

Even more than my ordeal, I agonize over Phil. There is still no word of his whereabouts—whether he's living or dead. For now, he's listed as MIA. I let him down, Trish. I tried. I really did try to get to him. Please, tell Stella I'm sorry and that we were talking about our wedding days when the ambush happened. He loves Stella as much as I love you—if that's even possible.

I've got to close. The doctors are making their rounds, and my doc is a couple of beds over. Please know that I love you and will understand whatever you decide. I do have one request, though. Please write and let me know your decision—good or bad. I believe I could cope with anything except never hearing from you again. I love you, Trish, and I hope to see you in my dreams. Be there.

Billy Ray

Oh…and Happy New Year, Sweetheart! Wow, it will soon be 1966. I don't know what next year holds, but I know Who holds it, and I pray it finds me holding you.

Chapter Thirty-Seven

Never in his wildest dreams would Logan have predicted this shift in his life. He stacked the last of the dishes in the dishwasher and joined Amber and their daughter in the living room. After stepping over Murphy, who was sprawled on the floor beside Lacey, he eased into the wicker swing that hung in the corner.

Lacey's face glowed as she sat at her mother's feet and shared her seashell collection. She lifted a whelk shell from the coffee table and handed it to her mama. "Look at this one. Isn't it pretty?"

Amber turned the near-perfect shell over in her hands. "Yes. I'm impressed. This is quite a treasure."

"I know. I was lucky to find one that wasn't broken. I found it after Tuesday's storm on Bird Island, not far from the Kindred Spirit mailbox."

Amber held it over her ear. "Ahh…I hear the roar of the ocean like in a conch shell. Hearing that always fascinated you as a child. Every time you'd hold a shell to your ear, your eyes would grow as large as saucers." She lowered her head. "Such sweet memories."

"I know. It's so cool."

Her mother laid the shell on the table and picked up a smaller one, "This one is nice, as well."

"That's one of my favorites—a calico scallop shell. I just

love the different shades of coral, don't you?"

Amber glanced over and smiled at Logan as she spoke to their daughter. "My, my, you've become quite the shell expert."

Lacey slid a book from the shelf beneath the table. "Daddy had this on his bookshelf. It tells all about the different types of shells found along the North Carolina coast."

"That's terrific. It sounds like you're having a good time. And it looks like Murphy approves of you living here. You've always wanted an indoor dog."

Lacey reached over and stroked his silky golden coat. "Yeah, he pretty much sticks to me like glue." As soon as she stopped rubbing him, Murphy lifted his head and nudged her hand. The three of them were laughing at his antics when the doorbell rang.

Logan leapt from the swing and opened the door. "Brooklyn, what a nice surprise."

"Surprise?" She stepped inside. "We agreed the first of the week that I'd come over this evening to meet Lacey, remember?"

He stood silent, then nodded. "Oh, yes, today *is* Thursday, isn't it? I'm sorry. I lost track of time. It's been a hectic week with getting Lacey settled in."

Brooklyn looked into the living room. "It sounds like everyone's having fun in here. I heard the laughter before I ever reached the steps. I hope I'm not interrupting anything."

"Oh, no. This is perfect timing. Lacey's mother is here. You can meet both of them."

With a reserved smile, she took Logan's hand and followed him into the spacious room. After greeting Amber, she turned and handed Lacey a small gift bag. "Welcome to Sunset Beach."

"How nice. Thank you." She sat on the couch beside her mother while Brooklyn sat in an adjacent chair. After pulling out the tissue paper, she found a wooden plaque with a painted seascape and a quote—*Sometimes, in the waves of change, we find our true direction.* She looked up at Brooklyn. "Aww…thanks. I love this."

"I'm happy you do. That quote rings true for me. Coming to Sunset Beach was an unexpected blessing. I hope it will be for you."

Logan's eyes shifted from Brooklyn to Lacey and then to Amber. How he'd come to sit in the same room with these ladies was hard to process. All three held a prominent place in his heart. Scripture states, *…and a child shall lead them.* But where? That was the question. Where would finding Lacey lead them? Lead him? He reread the plaque on the table and prayed for divine direction.

Friday, July 14, 2023
Brooklyn

I lowered an armload of books onto a shelf in the fiction section and pulled my cell phone from my pocket. "Hey, Logan."

"Hi, babe. Hope you're having a good day. I'm sorry about my mess-up last night and hate we didn't have a chance to talk privately."

I dropped into a chair at the window and looked across the street to the ocean. "That's okay. It was getting late, and I knew I had to come in early this morning to key a shipment of books into our inventory. What time did Amber leave?"

"A little before midnight."

"Oh?" I ran my finger along the dusty windowsill and frowned. "You two must have found lots to talk about."

"Well, Lacey was excited to see her mother. It has been a

long time."

"How about you?"

"How about me? What do you mean?"

"Were you excited to see Amber too?"

He huffed. "Brooklyn, that's not fair." Silence followed.

"You're right, hon. It's not. I'm sorry."

"By the way, thanks for your thoughtful gift for Lacey. She put the plaque on the shelf in her room along with her shell collection."

"Good, I'm glad she likes it."

"I've had you on my mind all day. Do you think you could meet me at the pier after work so we can talk?"

"Sure. Chase is out of town, and Olivia and I have plans for dinner at seven, but I can come for a while. I'm off at five, so we can meet at our usual bench shortly after. Is that good?"

"It's perfect. I'll see you then, babes."

My imagination ran wild, and my insides rolled into a ball as I slipped my phone back into my pocket. Insecurities that I'd thought were in my rear-view mirror had reared their ugly heads again. They now stood like sentinels, front and center, threatening to block my path to happiness with Logan. How had life gotten this complicated so fast?

As the sun dipped lower in the sky, I slipped my sunglasses on and walked toward the end of the pier. Logan was already seated with his legs propped on the railing. I slipped up behind him and placed my hands over his eyes. "Guess."

He straightened and dropped his feet to the ground. "Hmm…voice sounds familiar."

"I would hope so." I walked around the bench and sat beside

him.

He gazed into my eyes. "How are you?"

I shrugged. "Pretty good. I guess."

"What do you mean, I guess?"

I looped my arm through his and laid my head on his shoulder. "Still reeling a little from all that's happened the last couple of weeks."

"Yeah. I can relate to that."

"I'm sure you can." I stared at a trio of fishing boats on the horizon and squeezed his arm. "How long do you think Lacey will stay?"

"I don't know, but if things haven't smoothed out by the end of the summer, I'll talk to Amber. Hopefully, she'll get things straightened out soon with that jerk she's involved with."

"I hope so, and the sooner, the better. Take it from one who knows. Tell her she can't waffle on her decision, either. Not even once. Men like him don't understand anything but a heavy hand." For a while, we sat silent, staring out at the water. I shook his arm. "How about you? How are you doing?"

A slight upward curve at the corners of his lips spread wider as he turned to face me. His dark eyes sparkled. "Wonderful. I'm having some proud papa moments."

I chuckled. "Well, I'd say after all these years, you deserve more than a few."

"Lacey really is a swell kid. Amber's done a great job with her. She's a good mother."

I laid my head on his shoulder. "Logan?"

"Yeah, babe."

"Do you still have feelings for Amber?"

He stared straight ahead and then answered. "Well, if you mean as in romantic…no, but I do care about her. After all, she's the mother of my child. How could I not?"

I nodded. "I understand." I brushed my wind-whipped hair away from my face. "Just checking."

He lifted my chin and gazed into my eyes. "Brooklyn, you must know by now how I feel about you."

I smiled. "I do. I think. No…I do. I'm sorry. I know I'm my worst enemy. I'm sorry for doubting you."

He rose from the bench and dropped to one knee in front of me. When he pulled a small box from his pocket and snapped it open, I gasped.

"Brooklyn Marshal, will this help? Will you marry me?"

I sat stunned…unable to move…then threw my hands over my mouth. "Oh…oh…" My eyes shot from the sparkling diamond to Logan's questioning eyes. "Heavens, I can hardly breathe."

He chuckled. "You can breathe later. Just answer."

I shouted and threw my arms around his neck. "Yes. Oh, yes." I pulled back as he slipped the ring from the box and slid it onto my trembling finger. "It's gorgeous."

He stood, lifted me from the bench, whirled me around, and kissed me. "You're what's gorgeous. Brooklyn, I love you and can't wait for you to be my wife."

As he lowered me to the ground, I stroked his face and peered into his eyes. "And I can't wait to be Mrs. Logan Corbett." My insides quivered as he pressed his lips to mine.

Chapter Thirty-Eight

Saturday, July 15, 2023
Logan

"No! No, you can't. You just can't." Lacey leaped from beside Murphy on the rug, dashed into her room, and slammed the door.

Logan followed with the retriever at his heels, knocked lightly, and peeked in. "Honey, let's talk about it."

Standing red-faced, she placed her hands on her hips and her large eyes reduced to slits. "I have nothing to say to you, and there is only one thing you can say to me, but you're not willing. Until then, I never want to speak to you again." She darted into the bathroom and slammed the door. The lock clicked.

Logan cringed as a picture slid down the wall and crashed to the floor. He eased onto the foot of the bed, rested his elbows on his knees, and hung his head. "Lacey, please. This will accomplish nothing. Come out, honey."

"Go away. I have nothing to say to you."

He released a long sigh and returned to the family room, where Brooklyn sat huddled on the couch. Her shoulders shook as she wept.

He raked his fingers through his hair. Good grief. From bachelorhood to fatherhood. From hero to zero in milliseconds, and an explosion of rants fueled by hormones. As he eased onto the couch, Murphy nuzzled his leg and dropped across his feet with a whimper. Logan rubbed the large retriever's head, then fell back on the sofa and wrapped his arm around Brooklyn. "Sweetheart, I'm sorry. I never saw this coming."

With her head buried in her hands, she shrugged.

Surrounded by sobs, Logan sat silent. How? Why? All he'd done was try to love one woman and a young girl. He raised his hands and lifted his eyes. *If you're trying to tell me something, you'll need to speak a little louder. I can't hear above the roar.* He rubbed his face with his hands, laid his head back on the cushion, and closed his eyes.

Logan yawned, shot to a sitting position, and looked out at the setting sun. Brooklyn was asleep on the end of the couch. Except for Murphy's snores, the house was still. He leaned back and moaned. *What a mess.* He nudged Murphy with his foot and put his finger to his lips. Shh! Rising from his place on the sofa, he entered the kitchen and dropped a pod into the coffee maker. After pulling a mug from the cabinet, he sat at the counter and waited.

His phone vibrated in his pocket.

"Yes, Amber."

"Hey, how are you?"

"I've had better days, but things will level out."

"Oh…I'm sorry. Is Lacey available? She's not answering her phone."

"I don't hear her, but I'll check. She's probably taking a nap." He walked to her room and tapped on the door. "Lacey, you awake?" Turning the doorknob, he peeked in and then backed away.

"Amber, she's asleep. Do you want me to have her call you

when she wakes up?"

"Sure. No rush. I'll be here for the rest of the evening."

Once he returned to the counter, Brooklyn pulled out a stool and sat beside him. Looping her arm through his, she kissed him on the cheek. "I'm sorry I reacted like I did. I can understand why Lacey wouldn't be thrilled about me marrying her daddy. She doesn't know me, and when she came to your office, I know she had high hopes that you and her mother would get back together. I've lain there for a while, thinking and praying about what I should do." She slipped the diamond from her finger and held it out to Logan. "In light of what happened with Lacey, I think this is premature."

He pushed away my hand. "No, Brooklyn, I won't take it."

She laid the ring on the counter in front of him. "Then I guess it will just lie here."

Logan swiveled his stool to face her. "Brooklyn, listen—"

She put her finger to his lips. "Shh. No. I'm not through." Her voice cracked. "I think the most important thing right now is for you to get to know your daughter. She's at a fragile and vulnerable age. She needs the influence of a good man in her life, and you're that man. I don't want to do anything to come between you and Lacey. This should be an exciting time for you both." She choked back tears. "Please, put her first right now. I'll understand."

Peering at her with blurred vision, he clasped her shoulders and pulled her to his chest. "Brooklyn, please. Surely, we can work this out another way."

She shook her head and pushed back. "I'm sorry, but I'm confident this is the only way. Lacey needs time with her daddy. She needs to get to know your heart and see for herself what is best for all of you. It may be me, and maybe not, but our time apart will allow truth to rise to the surface."

Logan sat stunned and tried to process the fiasco.

Brooklyn wrapped her arms around his neck and kissed him. "I'm sorry. I love you and want to be with you, but the timing is all wrong."

He cupped her face. "Brooklyn, please reconsider."

"I can't." She pushed back her stool. "And the longer I stay here, the weaker I'll become.

Let's give it a few days and see how things go with you and Lacey. We'll take it a day at a time." She kissed him again. "Tell Lacey I love her and understand." She picked up her purse from the table by the door, then turned and blew him a kiss.

When the door clicked behind her, Logan heard her burst into tears as she ran down the steps. He lifted her ring from the counter and tilted it back and forth, allowing the light to cast a rainbow of colors on the wall. *Well, Lord, I think I heard you this time—loud and clear. Next time, perhaps you could turn the volume down a bit?* He folded his arms on the counter, lowered his head, and wept. Murphy whimpered at his feet.

Logan placed a serving of heat-and-serve lasagna on Lacey's plate and put it beside her dinner salad on the counter. Murphy whined. "No, Murph. You know where your bowl is. You've got plenty." He wiped his hands on a dish towel hanging on the oven door and walked to Lacey's bedroom. "Lacey. Dinner's ready." Moments later, he placed his ear on the door and tapped softly. "You hear me, Lace?" He put his hands on his hips and shook his head. "You can stop the silent treatment now. It doesn't become you, sweetheart." He turned the knob, peeked in, and wrinkled his brow. She was still asleep—*but in the same position?*

He raised his voice. "Lacey?" His breath quickened as he entered the room and walked around her bed. "Lace?" His voice elevated as he shook her. "Lacey?" He fell to his knees beside her. An overwhelming sense of dread washed over him. He shook her hard. "Lacey, answer me." He put his trembling fingers on the side of her neck. *No? Yes?* He tried to steady his hand. *Heavens, I don't know.* He closed his eyes, pulled his phone from his pocket, and dialed 911. As the phone rang, he put his phone on speaker, then sat back on his legs and blinked. The hair on his neck and arms lifted as he slid an empty medicine bottle from underneath the bed. His heart raced. "No, Lacey, no. No, you didn't." *Oh, Jesus, please. Don't let anything happen to my baby girl. I just met her.* He leaped up and rolled her onto her back. Placing the heels of his hands over her heart, he pumped and prayed.

Chapter Thirty-Nine

Friday, January 21, 1966

Trish opened the mailbox, snatched Billy Ray's letter, and clutched it to her chest. Once inside, she dropped her books on the sofa, threw off her coat, and greeted her momma in passing. She slammed her bedroom door and used her Granny's sterling silver letter opener to slit the envelope. Billy Ray's letters were what she lived for—outside of his return, of course. The wait was hard, but she had his words, words that spoke of plans for their future—so much more than Stella, who didn't know if Phil was dead or alive. Neither she nor Stella could watch the news. The stories of the way POWs are treated were too horrific to think about. The best they could do was pray that the war would soon be over and the prisoners would be released.

Fluffing her pillows behind her, she settled back to savor every word that Billy Ray scratched out.

Tuesday, January 11, 1966
My dear Trish,

How are you? I imagine your Senior activities are ramping up. A few more months, and you'll be a Southport High School graduate. I hope I'm home in time for your graduation, but my progress is slow, and I doubt I'll make it. I don't want to be a pessimist, but I'd rather disappoint you now than later. That way, if I do make it, we'll both have a pleasant surprise.

There is still no news as to Phil's whereabouts...or if he's even alive. Many of the POWs were taken to a camp in Hanoi dubbed the Hanoi Hilton. I've lost a leg, but at least I'm here in the States in a warm and secure hospital where people attend to my needs. My heart breaks for my friend. Although it would be hard knowing he's in a camp being mistreated, there would be some comfort in the hope that he's still alive. I know Stella is worried sick.

I am so sorry. I wish I could have reached him. I have so many regrets about leaving him alone in the jungle and continue to fight depression with the help of therapists here at Walter Reed. My story is just one of many soldiers who sit in that circle with me each week. Our physical injuries are far easier to treat than the psychological wounds that plague us all. As much as I want to be with you, sometimes I feel you'd be better off moving on without me.

Trish slapped the bed and screamed. "Billy Ray Jessup, stop it. Have you forgotten who you're talking to? Don't you think I know a bit about living as a cripple and having to war against depression? Don't you ever think you're not good enough for me. Don't you ever."

She collapsed on the bed and sobbed. "Oh, if only I could be there with you. If only I could hold you. Kiss you. Show you that you're all I care about. All I want. Please. Please don't pull away from me, Billy Ray. Let me love you like you did me under the stars on prom night. You said, 'I love you just the way you are.' Well, the same goes for me. I love you just the way you are and always will. Please, keep fighting for us and find your way home to me. Please."

There was a soft rap on the door. "Trish. Trish, are you okay?"

She swiped the tears from her cheeks. "Yes, Momma, I'm fine. You can come in."

Mrs. Malone entered carrying two steaming mugs. "I thought you might like a cup of hot cocoa. With the cold wind blowing in off the Cape Fear today, I find it hard to stay warm, even indoors." She handed Trish a cup, then sat on the foot of the bed. She nodded toward Billy Ray's letter. "Did you get bad news?"

"Not really? Not new bad news anyway." She sipped the warm cocoa. "I get so frustrated with Billy Ray thinking he's not good enough for me." She gazed into her mother's compassionate eyes. "I don't care that he's missing a leg. I mean, I do care, but it doesn't make him any less of a person. I, of all people, should know."

"You're right, but you also know you didn't come to grips with your disability overnight. It's a journey. A long one filled with plenty of ups and downs. Give him time. He'll make it. You both will."

"I hope you're right, Momma."

After finishing their cocoa, Mrs. Malone carried the mugs into the kitchen, and Trish reread Billy Ray's letter.

Wednesday, July 6, 1966

Trish sat on the couch with her arm around Stella's shoulders as the evening news broadcast the Hanoi March. With still no news of Phil's whereabouts after six months, they willed themselves to watch the horror unfold before their eyes. Stella hugged herself with her forearms pressed into her belly and tears streaming down her cheeks. Fifty-two American prisoners of war were forced to walk handcuffed in pairs through the streets of Hanoi before angry crowds. Cameras zoomed in on the grim faces of gaunt, emaciated men in dirty gray jumpsuits, flanked on either side by Viet Cong soldiers with M-16s ready to eliminate any moves of defiance.

Trish fought hard to be strong, as did her mother, who sat on Stella's other side. Neither could hold back their tears as the crowds hurled insults at the humiliated soldiers. Less than thirty minutes into the march, a grainy, black-and-white image of Phil's face flashed onto the screen. Emitting a blood-curdling scream, Stella broke from Trish's hold and lunged for the TV. As the camera spanned the parade of men, Phil's face vanished as quickly as it had appeared. Stella collapsed onto the floor, and Trish and her mother dropped to her sides. "Oh, Stella. I'm sorry. I'm so so sorry."

As loudspeakers in the streets of Hanoi blared insults, the march turned violent, and the POWs were attacked and beaten. Trish crawled to the TV, switched it off, and then knelt beside her friend. When she opened her mouth to pray, only groans spilled out.

After what seemed like an eternity of Stella refusing to move, Trish and her mother helped her from the floor and eased her onto the couch. Lying back, she covered her eyes with her forearm and reached for Trish, who sat on the floor beside her. "I can't stand this, Trish. I can't stand knowing my precious Phil is suffering in some hellhole on the other side of the world. How will I ever make it through this? How will he?"

Trish prayed she could offer her more than empty platitudes. "The same way Phil is surviving through unimaginable conditions. I'm sure it's with prayer, sheer grit, and his determination to return to you. As horrible as it was to see his face on that screen hours ago, at least we know he's alive. You now have the hope of seeing him freed one day. Only God knows the time or the hour, but we'll pray He has mercy on these brave soldiers and brings them home soon. You've got to be strong, Stella. You have family and friends who love you and will be here to support you every step of the way. Keep on believing and remember the promise of Hebrews 10:23, *"Let us hold unswervingly to the hope we profess, for He who promised is faithful."*

"Hold on, Stella. Hold on for Phil."

Chapter Forty

Saturday, October 15, 1966

Trish studied her face in the dresser mirror, leaned in closer, and squinted. Stepping back, she cut her eyes toward her reflection and turned her head from side to side. Would Billy Ray think she'd changed? She felt like she'd aged ten years in the past 484 days. Their separation had been longer than the year they'd anticipated, but she wasn't about to complain. For her soldier boy to come home from this horrific war was an answer to the prayers of many. She pulled her navy cardigan from the closet, grabbed her purse from the bed, and walked into the dining room.

"Morning, Momma."

Mrs. Malone looked up from her place at the table and laid her pen on the stack of bills in front of her. "Look at you, honey. You're glowing. I know you're excited."

"And nervous." She placed her hand on her stomach, hoping to settle the fluttering. "I can't wait to see Billy Ray, but I don't look forward to seeing his mother again. She'll be more protective of her son now than ever."

Her momma stood and hugged her. "Just remember this isn't your problem—it's Mrs. Jessup's. Try to let whatever she says roll off your back. You're there for Billy Ray. He wants you there, and that's what matters. Just be polite and let him handle things with his mother."

"Thanks, Momma. I know you're right. I'll try my best to do that." She slipped on her sweater fand pulled the car keys from her purse. "I refuse to let anyone or anything steal my joy today." She kissed her mother on the cheek and left through the kitchen door.

In less than five minutes, she'd traveled the short distance to the Jessups' house. As she eased the car up the familiar drive and drew closer to the house with the stunning view of the Cape Fear River, her breath caught in her throat, and tears clouded her eyes. There he was—waiting for her on the porch. The moment she feared she would never see was here. Billy Ray was home.

He waved one hand over his head. At first glance, her eyes were so fixed on his broad smile and sweeping wave that she failed to notice the long ramp leading to the porch. Then, beyond that, the wheelchair. He'd told her about it, but seeing him in the chair brought a heartbreaking finality to his disability.

Parking the car at the end of the drive, she threw open the door and rushed up the steps with her arms outstretched—her emotions a mixture of tears and laughter. "Oh, honey. I can't believe—" She was only moments away from feeling the warmth of Billy Ray's embrace when he pushed out his hand.

"Stop."

Her heart plunged, and she all but tripped over her feet as she froze. "What are you—?"

"Wait." He lifted his index finger and grinned. "Give me a moment. We're going to do this right."

She held her breath and watched in disbelief as he gripped the arms of his wheelchair, winced, and pushed himself to a standing position.

A bit wobbly at first, he steadied himself, stretched out his arms, and winked. "Come here, Trish Malone. I've dreamed of this moment since the day I left you."

Laughing and mindful to not upset his balance, she rushed into his arms. As she leaned into him and their lips met, the warmth of his body assured her that she wasn't dreaming. Billy Ray was home. He was really, really home. As she savored the familiar comfort of being wrapped in his arms, the world around her evaporated. Later, she pulled back enough to peer into his eyes, then swiped a tear from his cheek. "Welcome home, soldier boy. I missed you so much. Don't you ever, ever, ever leave me like that again."

He caressed her face and kissed her forehead. "I don't plan to. All I want from here on out is to be with you." Lowering himself into his chair, his hands slid down her arms, sending chills through her body. He patted his lap. "Sit here."

Her eyes questioned his. "You sure?"

He laughed. "I may be short a leg, but I still have a lap." He tugged on her arm and toppled her into the chair. "Don't worry. I won't break."

"I know you won't." She wrapped her arms around his neck and kissed his cheek.

"You're stronger now than you've ever been. I'm so proud of you. You're my hero."

His eyes sparked. "Wanna go for a celebration ride?"

She scrunched her face. "A what?"

"Hold on tight." He unlocked the brake on his wheelchair, rolled it to the end of the porch, and pushed.

As his chair flew down the ramp, Trish squealed. "Billy Ray Jessup, don't you dare dump me out on the ground."

"No chance of that, sweet girl. I'm not about to let go of you." He laughed as they sailed onto the concrete drive. "What's the matter? I thought you liked my driving."

She clung tighter and buried her face in his shoulder. "Billy Ray, stop. What are you doing?"

Grabbing the wheels, he slowed down the chair, rolled it down the walk, and onto the dock. "What's wrong, babe? Don't you trust me?"

She straightened and yanked his ear.

"Ouch."

"You're mean, Billy Ray. I can see your time in Nam made you fearless."

He cupped her face, brushed her cheeks with his thumbs, and kissed her nose. "Trish, when you look death in the eyes and watch it slink into the night, you see life differently. You realize how fragile our time on earth is and understand the importance of living in the space between breaths. We're in that space now, and I intend to make the most of it." He pulled a linen handkerchief from his pocket, unfolded it, and lifted out a sparkling solitaire diamond ring. A broad smile crept over his face. "Honey, I'll trade you this diamond for that clunky class ring on your finger."

Her hands flew to her chest as her heart drummed in her ears. Then, sliding his ring from her trembling hand, she dropped it into his palm.

"Patricia Millicent Malone, I may not be the man I used to be, but I love you more this year than last. To the best of my ability, I promise to stay by your side for the rest of my life. Will you marry me?"

Tears flooded her eyes. "Billy Ray Jessup, you're right. You aren't the man you used to be." She paused and shook her head. "You tower far above him." She outlined his lips with her finger and kissed them. "I love you, sweetheart. Yes, I would be thrilled to be your wife."

Warmth radiated throughout her body as he slipped the ring on her finger, pulled her to his chest, and covered her lips with his.

While resting in Billy Ray's embrace, a cool breeze blew off the Cape Fear River. She slipped her arms around his waist and laid her head on his shoulder. As her eyes fell on the stately home, a shadowy figure stepped away from the window.

She gasped and straightened. "Billy Ray, your mother has been watching us from the house."

He glanced back and rolled his eyes. "I'm sorry, Trish. Don't let her worry you. She'll adjust. We can't let her steal this moment from us."

She smiled. "Thank you. You're right. This is our moment." She stood. "I'll give your legs a rest." Sitting on the bench in front of him, she clasped his hand and searched his eyes. "Tell me…do you hurt?"

"Yes, but I try not to focus on it…and when I'm with you…I feel no pain."

She kissed his fingers. "What did I ever do to deserve you? I love you, Billy Ray."

His eyes widened. "Returning to the subject of love…when are you going to let me make you my wife?"

She smiled. "When would you like to?"

"As soon as possible. We've waited a long time and have survived a lot. I don't want to waste another day."

Pensive, she held out her hand and allowed her diamond to capture the light. "I had hoped to have an outdoor wedding at Sunset Beach. It will be too cold if we marry before spring."

"Hmm…you're right. I'd rather not wait that long, but I like your idea. It was during our visit to Sunset Beach that I first knew I wanted to marry you. I'll do whatever you want. You're the bride, and I want you to have time to plan the wedding of your dreams. A spring wedding is fine with me."

She leaned over and kissed him. "It will be worth the wait. I promise."

He chuckled. "Of that…I have no doubt."

Chapter Forty-One

Sunday, March 5, 1967

Trish held onto Billy Ray's arm as he ascended the steps of the Sunset Beach oceanfront house. "I'm so proud of you. You always rise to the challenge, and I love you for it."

"You're my inspiration, Trish." He kissed her cheek. "I've learned from the best." Billy Ray leaned on the handrail as he stepped up with his good leg and then brought his prosthetic leg to the same step. "You've dreamed of living in a house on the beach since our first visit to Sunset, and there aren't many houses here without steps, especially on the oceanfront. I won't let a few steps rob you of your dream." After stopping on the landing to catch his breath, he walked up the final flight to the porch.

Trish turned and pointed out to sea. "Turn around, honey, and look at this view." She gazed at the Atlantic and fought back tears as she thought of the obstacles they'd had to overcome to get to this point. "This is incredible. Can you imagine bringing our coffee out here in the mornings to watch the sunrise?"

He breathed in the salt air, leaned against the railing, and scanned the beach. "It would be phenomenal, but don't get your hopes up till we hear what the realtor has to say. It all depends on what the owner will do."

A car door slammed beneath the house, and an attractive lady sporting a navy blazer with a gold NC Realtors' pin on the lapel trotted up the steps. "I'm sorry I'm late. The last showing took longer than I thought it would." She shook their hands. "I'm

Kalista Cartwright. I hope you haven't waited long."

Trish swept her windblown hair from her face. "Not at all, but even if we had, I would not have objected to a few more moments to enjoy this breathtaking view."

She laughed. "I know what you mean. It's hard to beat, isn't it?" She jingled the keys. "Let's go inside. I think you'll be happy with the interior as well." She pushed open the door and motioned for them to go in ahead of her. "It is an older home. One of the first ones built here on the island. It's not fancy, but it's very comfortable and well-maintained. As you can see, it's a traditional layout—the living area runs through the center, with the bedrooms on either side. And the best part is, as a rental, it comes fully furnished."

Trish admired the vaulted knotty pine ceiling and the kitchen, located on the ocean side of the house. She walked to the sink. "Oh, yes, I love this kitchen with a view." She looked at Billy Ray. "I might actually learn to cook in here."

He chuckled. "And clean fish?"

She cringed. "Now you're pushing it."

Kalista lifted her hand. "No worries, Trish. I've got your back. There's a sink in the carport under the house for the *men* to clean their fish."

Trish gave an affirmative nod to Billy Ray and grinned. "I'm liking this place more and more."

After going through all of the rooms, Billy Ray sat on an ottoman in the living room and looked at Kalista. "So, what did you find out from the owner? Is he willing to come down on the rent?"

She nodded. "He said he'd come down fifteen dollars a month, but that's as much as he could do."

Trish's pleading eyes met Billy Ray's.

He grimaced. "I don't know Trish. That's still $85 a month.

With me settling into my job at the bank and you with nursing school at Cape Fear, I think it's more than we can commit to." He turned to Kalista. "Have you got anything else you can show us? Maybe in the $60 a month range?"

Shaking her head, she glanced out the window and held up her hand. "Whoa." Speaking of the owner…" Kalista walked to the door and opened it. "Hey, I thought I heard a car door slam. Come join us. Your timing couldn't be more perfect." She motioned. "This is the young couple I told you about yesterday. The ones getting married next month."

"Oh, yes." He shook Billy Ray's hand. "Nice to meet you, son. I'm Bill."

"Well…that's easy enough to remember. Mine's Billy Ray?"

"How about…" He shifted his eyes toward Trish and stopped mid-sentence. "Billy Ray?" He pointed. "Are you Trish?"

Knowing he looked familiar, she laughed. "Oh, my, of course. You're Mr. Wilkerson?"

He nodded. "I am." He tapped his forehead. "Now it's all clicking in. We met on the beach a couple of years ago?"

Her heart leaped. "You're right. We did." She whipped around to Billy Ray. "Honey, this is Bill Wilkerson. We met here at Sunset Beach, and he was a huge encouragement to me."

He gave his head a quick shake and furrowed his brow. "Huh?"

Bill told him of how they'd met on the beach the day he'd left for Viet Nam and of how he'd prayed for him. He looked at Kalista. "So this is the couple that wanted me to lower the rent?"

"Yes, sir, I told them you would come down fifteen dollars a month."

"My goodness. I absolutely will. And from one veteran to

another, I can do better than that."

Trish watched as Billy Ray's eyes grew large. "You can?"

"I'll take off another ten dollars, which will make your rent seventy-five dollars a month."

Billy Ray's eyes shot to Trish's.

"And if you commit to a year's lease, I'll bring it down to sixty-five."

Trish grabbed Billy Ray's arm. "Oh, honey. I know you were hoping for even less, but with your disability pay, don't you think we can do this? I know it won't be a lot, but I can throw in my weekend check from McKenzie's."

He smiled and looked at Mr. Wilkerson. "Sir, thank you for your kind offer. I believe we can make this work."

Trish bounced on her toes and clapped her hands. "Oh, thank you. Thank you."

The agent smiled. "Well, now that the rent's worked out, let's sit at the kitchen table and sign some papers."

Billy Ray shook the owner's hand. "Thank you."

Mr. Wilkerson strengthened his grip. "You're the one who deserves the thanks, young man." He saluted. "It's my honor to serve you, sir."

Friday, March 24, 1967

Trish glanced at the clock on the wall above the soda fountain, locked the door, and shouted into the back room. "I'll get the tables tonight, Mr. Willie."

"Thanks, girl. I've got all I can do back here."

She grabbed a clean towel and a spray bottle from behind the counter and started with the table in the back corner—the one she and Billy Ray always sat in. Trish loved working for Mr. Willie. Although she didn't earn a lot at the ice cream parlor, she'd been able to set a little money aside to help her mother with the cost of her wedding. After April 22nd, she'd be able to help Billy Ray with the rent.

The sound of someone banging on the door startled her.

"Trish. Trish. Let me in." Stella peeked in the glass. "Hurry up. Let me in."

As soon as she ran and turned the deadbolt on the door, Stella burst into the shop, rushed past her, and spun around. "Trish." She bent over and tried to catch her breath. "You won't…you won't believe what's happened."

"What? What is it?"

She bounced on her toes and clapped her hands. "Phil has been found. He's alive, Trish. He's coming home."

"What?" Dropping the bottle and cloth, she embraced Stella. "He really is?" She pulled away and peered into her friend's sparkling eyes. "How? When? What happened?"

"Phil's parents called Momma a little while ago and said he'd escaped from the Viet Cong and was picked up beside the Ho Chi Minh trail by a troop of our soldiers. He'd walked and hidden in the jungle for days."

Trish rubbed her arms as a shiver ran through her body. "This gives me goosebumps. I can't even imagine. How is he?"

She lowered her head. "Mr. Harper didn't have all of the details, but was told Phil was thin and suffering from wounds inflicted by his captors. The Army was flying him to the hospital in Japan that day. The one where Billy Ray was treated." She hugged Trish's neck. "Oh, Trish. Can you believe it? Our prayers have been answered. Maybe he'll be home in time for your wedding next month. Wouldn't that be fabulous?"

Their conversation was interrupted by Mr. Willie darting from the back room. "Trish, what's all the commotion out here?

Is everything okay?"

"Better than it's ever been, Mr. Willie." She rushed over and hugged him. "Phil has been found. He's coming home soon."

His mouth dropped open, and his bulging eyes cut to Stella. "You mean it?"

"Yes, I do, Mr. Willie. My hero is coming home. He's coming home."

He embraced her. "That's amazing news. I want to hear all about it." He held up his hand. "But first…this calls for a celebration in Phil's honor." He motioned. "Go on, girls. Grab a table. Three chocolate, cherry vanilla nut sundaes coming right up."

Chapter Forty-Two

Saturday, April 22, 1967

Trish gazed out of the window at the wedding guests gathering on the beach and squealed. "Momma, guess what. Aunt Mabel's here. She made it. She really made it." She placed her hands over her heart. "Now Granny feels so much closer."

"Wonderful, honey. Her friend told me she'd get her here if at all possible." Standing in the doorway of the bedroom, she smiled. "Hurry up, now. Stella and Margo are almost ready. It's your turn."

Trish walked toward the bedroom she'd soon share with Billy Ray and glanced up. *You were right, Granny. There's no end to life's possibilities when we keep our eyes on our goal...and our God.* When she entered the room, Stella and Margo twirled, their lavender chiffon dresses swirling and settling about their ankles.

"Heavens. You two look amazing. Wait till Phil and Paul see you. I can hear the wedding bells now."

"Uh, yeah, silly, and they happen to be yours." Laughing, Stella lifted the hanger with Trish's wedding gown from the back of the door. "Your Prince Charming awaits, girlfriend. Let's get you ready to meet him."

As they helped slip the white chiffon dress over her head, Trish slid her arms into the wispy bell sleeves, gave the empire waistline a tug beneath her bust, and allowed the layered chiffon skirt to billow to the floor.

Tears welled in her mother's eyes as she adjusted the off-the-shoulder lace neckline and kissed her daughter on the cheek. "I've never seen you look more beautiful."

Trish hugged her. "Thank you, Momma. You've always made me feel pretty in spite of my disability."

"It's because you are, dear. Just ask Billy Ray." Mrs. Malone picked up her mother's pearls from the dresser and smiled. She motioned for Trish to turn, then hooked the strand around her neck and patted her shoulder. "There now, sweet girl…the pièce de résistance. Perfection."

Trish looked in the full-length mirror and swished the skirt of her dress from side to side. "I can't believe the girl in the mirror is me and that this is my life."

"It's been a long journey, dear. You and Billy Ray are both overcomers. You will make a great team." She glanced at the clock on the nightstand. "We need to hurry. It's almost five. Let Stella help you with your headpiece."

As Stella positioned the wreath of yellow and lavender gerbera daisies mixed with baby's breath on Trish's head and straightened the long white streamers, the soft strumming of "Unchained Melody" filtered through the partially opened window. Trish's eyes widened, and her breath caught in her throat, as she placed her hands over her chest. "Oh, my goodness. There's our cue."

Mrs. Malone gathered Trish and her bridesmaids in a circle and prayed with them.

Billy Ray

While the soft chords of an acoustic guitar blended seamlessly with the rhythm of the ocean waves, thoughts of a future with Trish swirled through Billy Ray's head. Standing barefoot in the warm sand, his prosthetic leg visible beneath the loosely rolled-up hem of his khaki pants, he shifted his eyes to Paul and Phil and gave them a thumbs up.

Phil, still frail, with his arm wrapped in a sling, flashed a broad smile.

They'd made it. Regardless of a growing antiwar movement surrounding the legitimacy of the Viet Nam War, they both stood proud, wearing their battle scars as badges of honor and courage. They were talking about this day moments before mortars screamed into their foxhole and threatened to steal their futures. For Billy Ray to have his friend by his side at his wedding was a dream he'd almost given up on. Phil's presence was a reminder that with God at the helm of their lives, all things are possible.

His eyes teared as he surveyed the intimate crowd of guests seated in front of the floral arch where he and Trish would soon repeat their vows. They were family and friends who never gave up, never stopped praying for his and Phil's safe return. Even his mother, who'd witnessed how much Trish loved her son, had begun to accept her as her soon-to-be daughter-in-law.

The evening was warm but not too warm for the guests to sit beneath a cloudless blue sky. As a light breeze carried an intoxicating scent of salt mingled with floral sweetness, joy and excitement permeated the atmosphere. It was electric and everything that he and Trish had hoped for.

Beyond the guests, Billy Ray scanned the row of beach houses and fixed his eyes on the one that he would soon share with Trish. His heart raced, and he struggled to steady his breathing as he anxiously watched for the door to open and for his bride to appear on her mother's arm.

As the music transitioned from "Unchained Melody" to the velvety chords of "Can't Help Falling in Love," anticipation mounted, and the chatter of guests came to an abrupt halt. Heads turned, and the screen door opened. Stella, barefoot and dressed in her lavender chiffon gown, walked down the boardwalk, descended the stairs, and followed the sandy path lined with seashells that cut its way through the center of the guests. She glanced at Phil and kissed the air. He winked. Margo, Trish's maid-of-honor, followed. As she passed Billy Ray, she whispered. "I hope you're ready, big guy. She's gorgeous."

At his first glimpse of Trish, his legs grew weak. Her beauty was more than he could take in. Her auburn hair shone beneath her floral crown. She looked like an angel, her white chiffon dress catching the breeze as she descended the steps with her mother. His heart raced as she approached the arch covered with colorful gerbera daisies. Stopping at her mother's seat on the front row, Trish kissed her cheek, then turned and stepped toward Billy Ray. As their eyes met, and she slipped her hand into his, tears rolled down her cheeks.

Billy Ray couldn't pull his gaze from his bride's face. He loved her more than life itself. Standing with her before the minister, who would soon pronounce them man and wife, produced unspeakable emotions. Surrounded by the beauty of the ocean and the warmth of their loved ones, the minister opened the short and simple ceremony with the invocation. Then, following their declaration of intent and the presentation of the rings, Billy Ray slipped a gold band on Trish's finger and led with his vows.

"Trish Malone, from our first day here at Sunset, I knew you were the one with whom I wanted to share my life. Just as the tide is constant and unwavering, so will my love be for you. With this ring, I promise to support you, laugh with you, comfort you in times of need, and cherish our moments together. I give you my heart, my soul, and my love, now and forever."

Trish struggled to keep her composure as she slid Billy

Ray's ring on his finger, peered into his eyes, and allowed her words to pour from her heart. "Billy Ray Jessup, my love for you is as steadfast as the rising and the setting of the sun. With this ring, I vow to be your partner in adventure, your confidant, and your biggest supporter. I will celebrate your successes and walk with you through your challenges. I promise to create a home filled with love, joy, and peace. With all that I am, I give you my hand and my heart forever."

As several sighs emanated from the female guests, the minister addressed the starry-eyed couple. "You have pledged your faith to each other in the company of your family and friends. By the power vested in me by the State of North Carolina, I now pronounce you husband and wife. Billy Ray, you may kiss your lovely bride."

After he embraced her and they sealed their vows with a tender kiss, the minister directed them to turn toward the guests. "Family and friends, it is my honor to present for the first time as husband and wife, Mr. and Mrs. Billy Ray Jessup."

Cheers and applause erupted as the newly married couple walked down the aisle. Afterward, the celebration continued with a seafood buffet, and guests dancing barefoot to songs written by The Lettermen, The Beach Boys, and The Beatles. While music blared from a portable stereo record player, a bonfire and tiki torches lit up the night.

Billy Ray and Trish danced cheek to cheek as waves crashing against the shore drowned out the voices of their guests and squelched any fears that threatened the future they dreamed of.

Chapter Forty-Three

Saturday, July 15, 2023
Myrtle Beach, South Carolina
Brooklyn

I sprinted through the parking lot of Grand Strand Medical Center and stopped short of the emergency room entrance to catch my breath. I wanted to know how Lacey was, but, at the same time, was afraid to find out. I didn't know what to say or do, and I knew interacting with Amber would be awkward. After all, wasn't my relationship with her father the reason Lacey tried to take her life? Afraid my legs would buckle, I stepped closer and leaned against the wall of the building. From my vantage point, I could see inside the well-lit ER waiting area. Logan was seated with his back to me, and Amber was in the chair beside him with her face in her hands. Logan rubbed her back and, at times, would lean closer to say something to her. *Jesus, what do I do now?* I considered leaving, but couldn't bring myself to walk away. I needed to know if Lacey was all right—if they were able to resuscitate her. My heart broke for Amber as I watched her through the glass. She straightened and spoke to Logan. It was then that he pulled her to his chest and rocked her. Had they received bad news, or were they still waiting to find out if there was anything the doctors could do for them?

I pulled my phone from my crossbody bag and stared at the screen. It didn't seem appropriate to intrude on Logan and Amber, and yet, I'd come this far. I couldn't leave without knowing something. I had Logan's number on speed dial, so I tapped the key and watched as I waited for him to answer. He didn't acknowledge the first ring or the second, and he almost didn't respond to the third, but then…

"Hello."

"Hi, babe."

"Hey, Brooklyn, can you hold a minute?" He lowered his head and said something indistinguishable to Amber. After straightening, she leaned back against her chair while Logan stood and walked across the room. "Yeah, doll, whatcha need?"

"Have you heard anything about Lacey yet?" A man ran past me on his way to the entrance, and the automatic doors opened.

Logan turned and scanned the room. "Where are you, Brooklyn? I heard doors open through the phone. Are you here? Are you standing outside?"

"Yes."

"Why on earth are you doing that? Come in here."

"I came intending to, but as I neared the entrance, I questioned whether or not I should. Although I didn't want to upset Amber, I had to speak to you. Logan, I'm so sorry. I can't imagine your pain."

"I want to see you, sweetheart. Wait a minute." He walked over and spoke to Amber, then headed toward the doors. "I'm on my way out." As he stepped into the entrance, the doors slid open, and he ran toward me.

I fell into his arms and laid my head on his chest.

"Thank you for coming, honey. I needed to see you."

I pulled back and looked into his tear-stained face. "And I had to see you and hear how Lacey is without upsetting her mother."

He kissed my nose. "That's why I love you like I do. You

always put the needs of others before your own.

"Have you heard anything yet?"

He shook his head. "No, the doctors are working with her now."

"I wish there was something I—"

"Logan?"

When I looked up, Amber's eyes pierced mine. She didn't have to say anything to me. Her expression said it all.

At the sound of Amber's voice, Logan released me and turned. "What is it?"

Her lip trembled as she shifted her eyes from mine to his. "The doctors want to speak to us."

He grabbed her hand, walked indoors, and never looked back.

It hurt, but I understood.

After pacing along the walk for a while, I decided to wait inside. If Amber and Logan were gone very long, I'd text him, or perhaps he'd think to text me. I tried to pass the time with a magazine but mindlessly turned its pages. At least it gave my fingers something to do. After staring at the double doors that led to the examining rooms for what seemed like hours, they opened, and Logan entered the lobby. As he walked toward the exit, I ran and grabbed his arm. "Logan, I'm over here." I led him to my seat, and he sat in the chair beside me. "How is she, babe?"

He shook his head and sighed. "Better but not out of the woods."

"Were you able to talk to her?"

"No. They've intubated her while they remove the toxins from her body. She'll be in the hospital for another day or two."

"So things look hopeful then?"

"Yes, but she's on suicide watch. Lacey needs counseling. According to Amber, this isn't the first time she's tried to take her life." He leaned his head back and sighed. "I wish she'd told me."

"Wow. I'm sorry. Lacey's a sweet girl. I'm happy she's improving and going to get the help she needs." I kissed his hand. "I should go and let you get back to Amber and Lacey."

He nodded. "You're probably right." He wrapped his arm around my shoulders. "It's dark. I'll walk you out."

"Thank you. That would mean a lot." I looped my arm through Logan's and leaned into his side as we walked to my car. The events of the day had sucked the air from our lungs, and we moved in silence. How would Lacey's fragile state of mind affect my relationship with her father? Young girls can be manipulative when it comes to their daddies. I know. My father could do no wrong, and losing him was the hardest day of my life. Would Logan feel like he had to choose between the daughter he'd just found and me? *Oh, Jesus, help us.*

Sunday, July 16, 2023

It had been a while since I'd been to the mailbox and even longer since I'd risen before the sun, but today, I needed to experience both. For me, there was no better place to sort through the events of the last couple of weeks than the solitude of the Kindred Spirit mailbox. Because mid-summer was peak vacation season at Sunset Beach, it was important for me to arrive long before sightseers would come to experience the tranquil beauty of this unique place.

As I rolled Olivia's lavender bike to the packed sand where the waves kissed the shore, I noted the first blush of dawn above the horizon. If I kept a steady pace, I could settle with my coffee on one of the benches at the mailbox and enjoy the sunrise. There was a serene beauty about these predawn hours, known as nautical twilight. Although the sun's center is twelve degrees below the horizon, the sky begins to brighten, and the light is a mix of deep blues and pinks, which combine to create a lavender hue. This time of day is referred to as the "blue hour." Still, when conditions are right, like they are today, I call this a lavender tide morning—one that is dreamlike and profoundly peaceful—a morning hushed and still, as if holding its breath in anticipation of a new day.

As I neared the box, I slowed my bike and squinted. My heart sank. I wasn't alone. Someone had beaten me here. I couldn't discern if the visitor with stooped shoulders was male or female, but the person had a slow and uneven gait. I slipped off my bike and wondered whether I should proceed. I wasn't up for company or conversation, and yet, my curiosity egged me on. There *were* two benches. I could greet the person and then block them out, or I could sit on the shore and wait for them to leave. I lowered the bike's kickstand and sat in the cool, dry sand. Wrapping my arms around my knees, I hoped they wouldn't stay long.

Chapter Forty-Four

The visitor to the Kindred Spirit stayed longer than I had hoped, but the beauty of the sunrise that morning was not lost on me. As the sizeable golden orb peeked above the horizon and rose higher in the sky, I inched back a little farther from the rising tide and breathed in the sacredness of the moment. Typically, I'm a sunset person, but whenever I've taken advantage of the opportunity to greet the morning with the sun, I've not been disappointed and have always been happy I made the effort. The day not only starts off brighter, it starts lighter. Even if I don't have the answers to the problems that weighed me down throughout the night, suddenly, they seem surmountable in view of a God who summons the sun from the deep and paints the sky with a broad and multicolored brush. In the moment, I'm reminded that night never has the final say. Light always overcomes darkness.

Inhaling the coolness of the morning air, I watched the world wake up and glanced down the shoreline. The Kindred Spirit visitor walked toward Sunset Beach. I stood, brushed the damp sand from the seat of my britches, and rolled my bike toward the dunes. Although I didn't come to leave a note in the box, I wasn't ready to let go of the beauty of the morning.

As I settled onto one of the benches to seek God's wisdom concerning my relationship with Logan, my eyes fell on the mailbox. I reflected on the visitor and wondered why the person had come so early. Like me, had they simply come to enjoy the morning's solitude, or had they left a note? Hmm… The last time I took the liberty of reading some of the entries, I learned about

Natalya and acquired a new friend. As hard as I tried to ignore the pull of the Kindred Spirit, I couldn't dismiss the desire to know more about the visitor and the reason the person had come to the box so early.

Succumbing to my curiosity, I opened the mailbox, pulled a yellow journal from the top of the stack of notebooks, and returned to my place on the bench. I paged to the final entry and noted the date. Yes, the visitor had left a note.

Sunday, July 16, 2023
Hi, Kindred Spirit,

I'm a widow. Heavens—did I just write that? Today is the first time I've used that word in a sentence—spoken or written. After being married to my true love for 56 years, he died in March, and I'm lost without him. Since we couldn't afford to own a home at Sunset Beach, we rented a house here for our entire married life. Because our landlord knew we were "lifers" and that our rent would be a steady income, he kept our rate affordable and way below what the market suggested.

After our landlord's death a few years ago, his children honored the rent set by their father. Now that my husband is gone, the three siblings have decided to update the house, sell it, and divide their inheritance. They've asked me to be out by the end of August. So far, I haven't found anything I can afford.

Kindred Spirit, I don't blame his children, but I have no place to go and can't imagine leaving this beautiful beach and all that I've shared with my husband. We weren't able to have children, so I am totally alone except for a few friends, who dwindle as the months roll by. I hope by writing here, someone will see my note and know of a reasonable rental, or maybe I should say an unreasonable one. Although it's more challenging at this age to make trips to the box, I'll check back next Sunday.

I thank God for the many good years I've spent on this beautiful beach, and I pray I'll have several more.

Fondly,

Desperate at Sunset

I slapped the notebook shut, returned it to the box, and ran to my bicycle. After pushing it through the loose sand to the water's edge, I jumped on and peddled hard. I had hoped to catch up with the lady who'd left the note but never saw her. I'd waited too long. She was gone.

As I neared Logan's house, I struggled with whether or not to stop. Would he even be home? It was early, and he'd probably stayed overnight at the hospital. I couldn't imagine him leaving Amber alone. That's just not who he was. Drawing closer, I slowed my bike as I neared, hopped off, and propped it against the steps leading to his house. I stomped the sand from my feet as I climbed the steps and walked up the boardwalk to the kitchen door. Murphy barked before I even had a chance to knock. I was surprised when I heard Logan tell him to settle down and then opened the door.

He smiled while Murph danced at my feet. "Well, well. To what do I owe this early morning visit from my favorite girl?"

"Ask me in, and I'll tell you." I tapped my cheek as I passed.

He kissed it and closed the door behind me. "It's already muggy out there, isn't it?"

"Yes. It's going to be a scorcher."

"How about something cold to drink?"

"Got any tea?"

"I do. Have a seat, and I'll bring it."

I settled on the couch in the living room, and within moments, he handed me a glass of iced tea and sat beside me. After taking a couple of swallows, I set the glass on the coffee table. "That's just what I needed. Thank you. I wasn't sure you'd be home. Thought you might still be at the hospital."

"If you'd come thirty minutes earlier, I would have been."

"Any improvement with Lacey?"

"Yes. The doctors are pleased with her progress. She's still intubated, but they'll gradually bring her out today."

"That's great news. I'm sorry things turned out this way for you."

"Thanks. It's difficult, but we'll work through it." He clasped my hand. "Now, what's up with you?"

I told him about my trip to the Kindred Spirit and the entry I'd read in the journal. "I hate that I missed her. Since you know a lot of people on the island, I thought you might have a clue as to who the lady is."

He stared out the window and tapped his index finger on his lips. "No one comes to mind. I'll need to think about it for a while. What do you plan to do if you find her?"

I grinned and bit my lip.

"Oops. I've seen that look before. Why do I get the feeling this will involve me?"

She tipped her head from side to side and spoke softly. "Maybe because it does?"

"I knew it." He dropped back against the cushions and rested his left leg on his knee. "Go ahead. Let's hear it."

I straightened. "How's the house next door coming?"

"Uh…good. Why?"

I relayed the lady's need for a house. "Have you decided to sell or lease it?"

"Leaning toward leasing."

"Oh, that would be perfect." I clapped my hands, then shrank back on the couch. "But of course, it's not going to do the lady any good if I can't find her."

He shrugged. "Well…if it's meant to be, it will work out." He reached over, lifted my hand, and stroked my ring finger. "Let's talk about us. I think this hand needs a bit of bling, don't you?"

"What's changed? Anything?" I picked up my tea glass, sipped it, and wiped my mouth with my napkin. "You talk. I'll listen."

He shifted and leaned against the end of the couch, stretching his arm across its back. Taking a deep breath, he smiled. "Let me start with what's *not* changed…my love for you and my desire for you to be my wife. That remains constant, regardless of what goes on around me."

Tears welled in my eyes. "I want that too."

"As for all that's happening with Lacey, her mother and I will see that she has the help that she needs. I want her to be happy about our engagement, but whether she is or isn't, we don't need Lacey's approval to get married. My actions aren't dependent on her response to my life choices. So…." He dropped to his knees at my feet and slid the diamond ring from his pocket. "I was going to come and talk to you today, but it looks like God sent you to me. Brooklyn, will you marry me?"

I caressed his face and kissed his lips. "Yes. Yes, Mr. Corbett, I will."

As he slipped the ring on my finger, I knew Logan was the man I wanted to spend the rest of my life with.

He returned to the couch and wrapped me in his arms. "I love you, Brooklyn. I don't want to do life without you."

"And I don't want you to." I melted in his embrace as he

buried his hands in my hair, and the warmth of his lips met mine.

Chapter Forty-Five

Sunday, July 23, 2023

As soon as I reached to knock on Olivia's kitchen door, she opened it and put her index finger to her pursed lips. "Shh. Chase is still asleep."

"Okay, I figured he would be."

Yawning, she sat on the step and slipped on her shoes. "He's where I wish I was. I can't believe I let you talk me into a trip to the mailbox this early in the morning."

"Aww…what's happened to you, Olivia? You used to love an early morning run."

She pulled Chase's bike from the wall and rolled it across the porch while I followed with her lavender one. "That was before I worked from dawn till dusk. Don't get me wrong, I'm not complaining. I'm grateful for my business, but I have little energy left over for anything else."

"Well, the ride should energize us, and like me, you'll be glad you made the effort."

On our way to the Kindred Spirit, Olivia asked about Lacey and my relationship with Logan. "I'm happy to see his ring back on your finger. Have the two of you set a date?"

"Nothing is on the calendar yet, but we're talking about next May. It's such a pretty month, and it will give Lacey a little more time to adjust to the fact that Logan is not going to marry her mother. She's doing better with the idea of our marriage, but more time won't hurt." I swerved to miss the tide as it rushed ashore. "I've asked her to be one of my bridesmaids, and I think that helped. She's excited about going with me to pick out dresses. Which brings me to ask if you'll be my matron of honor."

Olivia's eyes sparkled as a huge smile spread across her face. "You know I will. I would have been hurt if you hadn't asked."

"Awesome. Plus, I need your decorator's eye to help me with all of the details. Logan and I have decided we want something other than a beach wedding. I'd like to have a garden wedding. There is nothing prettier than an Old South wedding among cypress trees dripping with Spanish moss."

"I agree. That would be spectacular and would eliminate a large florist bill. I have a couple of ideas and will ask my designer friends for their suggestions, as well." Olivia zig-zagged her bike in and out of the surf. "So, how do you know your lady will show up this morning?"

"I don't, but she did write in one of the Kindred Spirit journals that she would come back today. I just hope she keeps the same schedule as last week."

"I know. I'm not up for a long wait."

I laughed. "Maybe you can curl up on one of the benches and take a nap."

She rolled her eyes. "Not if I plan to walk again. I'm all for a firm bed, but the bench would be a little over the top."

As we pushed our bikes toward the dunes, I sent up a quick prayer. "Since we didn't pass the lady on the way, maybe she's already here, and we won't have to wait at all."

"I hope you're right."

After we laid our bikes in the sand, I held my breath and walked over the dune. My spirit dropped. We were alone.

Olivia released an audible sigh. "Well, this isn't a good sign."

"Let's not count her out yet. We're here earlier than I was last week. Maybe she's on her way."

"Maybe." Olivia sat on one of the benches. "It *is* beautiful here. I haven't been to the box in so long I forgot how peaceful it can be."

I glanced at my watch. "The sun will break the horizon in less than four minutes. I'm always amazed by the consistency of God's creation. Scientists can predict the exact time the sun will rise on any given day years in advance."

"You do know the same sun rises on our end of the beach, right?"

I smirked. "Yes, smarty, but it's not nearly as peaceful as on this uninhabited island."

"I know. I'm kidding you. This is a remarkable vantage point."

As the sun broke above the horizon and its brilliance reflected in the placid water, we sat speechless. Vivid oranges and pinks mingling with soft lavenders and blues created a display second to none. After waiting for our mailbox visitor for nearly an hour, I could tell Olivia was antsy. I worked the afternoon shift at the bookstore, but as Olivia said earlier, her hours as an interior designer are from dawn to dusk. "We should go. I know you have a busy day ahead." As we rose from the benches and Olivia followed me over the dune, I threw out my arm to block her.

"What? What's wrong?"

"Hurry. Turn around and go back. She's coming."

"Seriously?"

I waved her on. "Yes. Hurry."

As we rushed to return to the benches, I fell, and when Olivia tried to pull me up, her foot slipped, and she landed in the sand beside me. We laughed so hard we couldn't get our footing and crawled to the bench. The more we tried to regain our composure, the more we laughed. I sat straight and swatted her arm. "Hush, now. Look nonchalant."

She stifled a laugh. "I'm trying. I really am."

After waiting longer than we expected, she looked at me and mouthed. "Where is she?"

I shrugged and shook my head, then grabbed her arm. "She's coming." I cleared my throat. "The sunrise was gorgeous this morning, wasn't it?"

Olivia nodded. "One of the prettiest I've—"

"Good morning, young ladies." The woman's greeting was sandwiched between breaths. "I hate to interrupt you, but…"

I dismissed her comment with a wave of my hand. "That's quite all right. You're not bothering us. We're just sitting here enjoying this beautiful morning." I motioned to the other bench. "You're welcome to join us."

She panted. "Thank you. I think I'll take you up on that invitation." Leaning heavily on her cane, she plodded through the sand, then dropped onto the bench opposite us. She let out a long breath and tucked several loose strands of white hair into her disheveled bun. "This is nice."

"It is, and the best place ever to enjoy the morning."

She nodded. "I agree. I've come here for years, but the walk is not as easy for me as it used to be."

"It is a hike. That's why we like to ride our bicycles."

"That's smart, but I'm afraid my bike-riding days are over." She grinned and tugged on the brim of her hat to shield her eyes from the sun. "And…it appears my walking days will soon follow." She propped her cane on the edge of the bench and leaned back. "I couldn't help but notice your bikes. Especially the lavender one."

Olivia's eyes brightened. "Yes. It's sweet, isn't it? It was a wedding gift from my husband."

"Nice." A slight smile crept across her face as she gazed into the distance. "I had a lavender bicycle once."

Olivia and I replied in unison. "You did?"

"Yes. When I was a young girl. It was a fifteenth birthday present from my granny."

I straightened and moved to the edge of the bench. "What happened to it?"

Her smile faded. "Wish I knew. After I was in an accident with it, it disappeared from the repair shop. Its whereabouts have been a mystery ever since."

Olivia brushed her hair from her eyes. "How sad. When I came here a couple of years ago, I leased this one from Surf Daddy. That's where I met my husband, Chase. The bike brought us together, and the rest is history."

The lady shifted on the bench. "What a sweet story." She twisted to stretch out her back. "I know this is a long shot and may sound crazy, but have you ever looked at the column underneath the basket?"

Olivia scrunched her face and shook her head. "No. Can't say I have. Why do you ask?"

"My bike had a distinctive mark."

"It did? What was it?"

"There was a small stainless steel plate with an inscription on the column that read, *Happy 15th Birthday, Trish. I love you! Granny Rogers.*"

Olivia's eyes bulged as she jumped from the bench. "Goodness. Wouldn't it be something if this is the same bike?"

I stood and watched as Olivia shuffled down the dune toward the bicycles. Pulling her lavender one from the sand, she stooped and lifted the white wicker basket.

I waited. "Well?"

Her mouth dropped open as she laid the bike back down and trotted up the dune.

"What?" I turned to the lady whose eyes questioned mine, then looked back at Olivia.

Stunned and unable to find words, she simply nodded.

Our visitor's eyes widened. "I'm not believing this. I never thought I'd see my bicycle again."

My eyes shot to hers. "So…you're Trish?"

Tears slid from the lady's eyes. "I am. I'm sorry, I should have introduced myself." She looked up at the sky. "Well, Granny, take a look at your girl now. How I wish you were here to experience this moment with me."

Olivia and I sat on either side of Trish and wrapped our arms around her as she cried. After regaining her composure, she insisted we come to her house for a cup of tea. As we walked toward Sunset Beach, we pushed our bikes alongside her. Our pace was slow, but neither Olivia nor I cared. Trish was a delight, and our conversation was rich and engaging.

Chapter Forty-Six

Brooklyn

Olivia and I followed Trish up the steps to the small beach cottage. She apologized for her slowness and explained that she'd developed complications from childhood polio.

"I have more muscle weakness and pain now, but I'm not complaining. I've gotten along well through the years—better than most." As we followed her into the kitchen, she motioned with her cane toward the dimly lit paneled living room. "Have a seat while I put the kettle on for our tea. And if you don't mind, will you open the blinds in there? No sense sitting in a dark room on a beautiful day like today."

"Of course." After letting the golden rays of the early morning sun shower the mid-century décor room, I sat on the couch beside Olivia. "How long have you lived at Sunset?"

"Ever since I married in 1967. My husband had just returned from Vietnam."

I pointed to a picture on the wall beside several medals. "I'm guessing that's your husband?"

"Yes, that's my sweet Billy Ray." She carried a tray with our tea and set it on the coffee table in front of us. "Please help yourself to the cream and sugar." Welcoming the opportunity to talk about her husband, she picked up a cup and a linen napkin and eased into a gold corduroy recliner across the room. Gazing at his picture, she sighed. "He passed suddenly back in April. A few days after our fifty-sixth wedding anniversary." She brushed a tear from her cheek. "We had a good life. Didn't have a lot of material things but had an abundance of love, and that's all that mattered." She tipped her head toward us and peered over her wire-rim glasses. "Just a little piece of advice for you both…and your young loves—love doesn't dominate, it cultivates. If you remember that, you'll do well."

Olivia smiled at me, then sipped her tea and asked, "Do you have children?"

"No. It was just the two of us. Billy Ray lost part of his leg in the war and suffered injuries that made children for us an impossibility."

"I'm sorry." I glanced at the wall of medals that included the Purple Heart. "I'm happy he was recognized for his service. I can't imagine how hard it was for you while he was away."

She nodded. "Yeah, not an easy time, but at least Billy Ray's injuries took him out of harm's way and brought him home. His friend had it worse. Suffered in a war camp. Phil never could overcome his demons. Ended up taking his life." She shook her head. "Such a sweet fella. Sad. Really sad. 'Bout killed my Billy Ray and Phil's wife Stella."

Olivia placed her empty cup on the tray. "Is Stella still alive?"

She smiled. "Yes. One of the few remaining older friends I have. She lives with their daughter in Leland. That was Phil's hometown." She wiped her mouth with her napkin. "She comes to visit me every month with her daughter."

"How nice."

Trish stared out the window and then chuckled. "I can't get over you having my bicycle, Olivia. Knowing that is a sweet blessing from above for me today."

"It is, isn't it? I should give it back to you."

She held up her hand and shook her head. "Oh no. You're

kind, but I wouldn't think of it. That bike needs to be enjoyed. It makes my heart sing to know it brought you and your husband together. Can't ask for better than that. No, no. I wouldn't think of taking it back. It's the way God wants it." She scrunched her face. "I wonder how it got to the surf shop. Guess there's no way I'll ever know."

Olivia squinted. "I could ask Chase. Maybe there would be some record of the purchase."

She shook her head. "I doubt it. It happened so long ago."

"You're probably right, but it won't hurt to try."

I scooted to the edge of the couch. "This is nice, but I suppose we should go, Olivia. We both have things we need to do today."

Trish frowned. "Oh…it's been such a pleasant morning, I hate to see it end. Can't you stay a little longer?"

I looked at my cousin. "It's up to her. I don't have to be at work until three. Olivia is the one with the pressing schedule."

She laid her hand on my arm. "It's okay. I'll work a little longer tonight. Besides, didn't you have something you wanted to say to Trish?"

I questioned her with my eyes, then jolted. "Oh, yes. You're right, I did. I was so lost in our conversation that I almost forgot why Olivia and I rode to the box in the first place." Settling back on the couch, I confessed. "We went to the mailbox this morning to meet you."

"Meet me?"

"Well, of course, at the time, we didn't know it would be you or if anyone would show up at all. I read your entry in one of the Kindred Spirit journals last Sunday about your need for a place to live."

Her face brightened. "That's why I went to the box this morning, but after I learned about your bike, I forgot to check the journal." She chuckled. "Of course, that's not unusual for me, at this age. Just one of life's daily challenges when you live this long." She grinned. "Forgive me, girls, but your forgetfulness makes me feel better." She giggled and shook her head. "Oh, dear, I'm sorry, I keep rattling on. Please, what were you about to say?"

"Olivia and I came to the box this morning hoping you'd show up. My fiancé, Logan, has a two-bedroom house he's building on the oceanfront and wants to rent it. When I read about your need, I hoped his house would be the answer to your prayers. It even has a small elevator."

Tears flooded her eyes as she stammered. "I…I…can't even believe God would have another blessing for me this morning."

Olivia and I smiled. "We hope it's something that will work for you, but of course, you'll have to take a look at it and talk to Logan. Actually, it sits beside his cottage and isn't far from here. We passed it this morning on our way to your house."

Her small eyes widened. "You don't mean it?"

We nodded.

"You ladies are something else. Thank you. This all sounds too good to be true, but I'd love to take a look at it and talk to him."

"All right then, I'll call Logan and have him meet us there today."

She slapped her hand to her heart. "Heavens, this is unbelievable. God never ceases to amaze me."

Olivia and I smiled at one another. "We stand amazed right along with you."

Logan met us at the house around lunch, and Trish couldn't have been more pleased with the smaller size and location. When he was able to adjust the rent enough to accommodate her, she was thrilled and ready to sign the contract. Logan had another client to meet afterward, so he handed me the key and said we could stay as long as we liked. Trish wanted to sit on the deck for a while, so the three of us settled into the rockers facing the ocean.

She leaned her head back against the chair. "Whew. What a good day this has been. Thank you both so much."

"Our pleasure. It appears our meeting this morning was divinely orchestrated."

"I'm convinced of it." She shifted in her seat. "There's something else I've been thinking about today, and I'd love to talk to you both about it."

I looked at Olivia, and she nodded. "Sure. We've got time."

"There is another part of my life with Billy Ray I want to share with you."

"Of course." I leaned back in the chair and rocked.

"The day Billy Ray left for Vietnam, I was a senior at Southport High School. I couldn't stop crying long enough to go to class, so I decided to drive here to Sunset Beach, the place where Billy Ray and I fell in love. I sat by the water and journaled. Poured my heart out to God about my love for my soldier boy and begged Him to keep him safe and bring him home.

"While he was in Vietnam, this beach became my place of solitude. It was here I felt closest to Billy Ray. I'd spend hours by the water journaling. Several months after he came home, we got married on the beach in front of the house that would become our forever home. The one I still live in. Although we loved each other very much, we weren't immune to life's problems. I've filled more journals on this beach than I can count, and hardly have room to store them all.

"In 1975, on our eighth anniversary, Billy Ray surprised

me. At that time, Bird Island was separated from Sunset Beach by Mad Inlet and could only be accessed by boat or by wading across at low tide. Billy Ray planned our entire day. After he packed our lunch, we took our small jon boat to the island. It was a beautiful spring day, and after we ate, we had a wonderful time lying on one of my Granny Roger's quilts, talking, laughing, and spying cloud formations. When Billy Ray carried our picnic basket back to the boat, I thought we were going home, but he returned with a long piece of driftwood he'd hidden beneath a blanket in the boat. He laid it in the sand beside the quilt, winked at me, and walked back to the boat. This time, he brought his toolbox and a shovel, set them down, and went to the boat a third time. He walked toward me with a broad smile, carrying a large item wrapped in another blanket. 'Billy Ray Jessup, what on earth are you doing? What is all this?' His eyes sparkled as he laughed, unwrapped the object, and set it in front of me. It was a mailbox."

Hardly taking a breath for fear I'd miss a word of her story, my eyes shot to Olivia and then back to Trish. "A mailbox?"

"Yes…with *Kindred Spirit* written across one side."

"You mean the Kindred Spirit mailbox was Billy Ray's idea?"

"It was. For years, he'd watched me haul my chair and journals to the edge of the water to work through problems and record my joys. Sometimes, I'd be out there for hours, but he said I always came home a happier person. Now, that's true. I did. Billy Ray knew that writing down my conversations with God was cleansing for me, and he wanted to give others the opportunity to jot down their experiences—good and bad. He hoped it would be a source of joy and healing for them also."

"So you put the Kindred Spirit mailbox in the dunes that day?"

A sweet expression enveloped her face, and her eyes

glistened. "We did. Planting the mailbox was so much fun. However, we could never have dreamed that fifty years later, people would still come to the Kindred Spirit to pour out their hearts."

"What a legacy. There's no way to know how many lives have been touched or perhaps forever changed because of an unsuspecting trip to the mailbox. The Kindred Spirit has certainly played a pivotal role in Olivia's and my life."

She shook her head and sighed. "God works in mysterious ways, doesn't he? While we can't think past the moment in our own lives, God sees the complete picture and does something extraordinary."

"What an amazing story. Thanks for sharing this with us."

"There is only a handful of people who know our story, but hopefully, it won't end with us. We've cared for the box all of these years. We've come every week or so to swap the filled notebooks with fresh ones and remove trinkets left by visitors. But, as you witnessed today, it's hard for me to make the trip now. If the Kindred Spirit's legacy is to continue, the baton needs to be passed, and that's where I hope you sweet ladies come in."

"Us?"

"Yes. It's evident you both have an affinity for the box and believe in its value. I wonder if the two of you would consider becoming keepers of the Kindred Spirit mailbox?"

I was stunned by Trish's offer, and from the look on Olivia's face, she felt the same.

It wasn't hard for her to read our thoughts. "I don't need an answer now. Take time to discuss it. I realize it's a lot to consider, but for Billy Ray and me, it was the joy of our lives. We didn't have children, and the Kindred Spirit was our baby. The connections we developed with kindred souls throughout the country filled the void in our hearts." She chuckled. "Just look here at the three of us. Connected by the Kindred Spirit, and I dare say we'll remain in one another's hearts forever."

Chapter Forty-Seven

Friday, August 25, 2023
Brooklyn

I lifted the large box from the elevator and peered around it. "Where does this one go, Trish? I can't see the label."

She placed a soup tureen in the corner cabinet and turned to read the large letters on the side of the box facing her. "That's the linens. They go to my bedroom. The one on the right."

"Got it."

Olivia followed me with a smaller box labeled Fragile and set it on the antique dresser.

Chase said to send the elevator back down one more time. He thought they could get all of the remaining cartons inside."

"Whew! That sounds good to me." I put the box on the bed, stepped into the hall, and hit the button. "This has been a lifesaver. An elevator was the best addition Logan made when he selected this house plan. Thinking ahead to the influx of baby boomers. Smart." I returned to the living room and plopped onto the couch. "Your place is really starting to come together, Trish."

She walked in from the kitchen, released a long sigh, and eased into her gold recliner. "It is, isn't it? I've dreaded this day. Just couldn't imagine leaving all that I'd shared with Billy Ray, but with my four sweet friends, I feel like I've gained a family. Thank you all for helping me through this difficult time."

"We're glad we can and are grateful the Kindred Spirit brought us together."

"Yes. I feel the same and want to tell you again how much

I appreciate both of you considering my offer and agreeing to be keepers of the mailbox."

Olivia and I looked at one another and smiled. "We're honored you asked. Neither of us takes the responsibility lightly."

Olivia nodded. "We'll do our best to carry on your and Billy Ray's legacy and keep this beautiful tradition alive for years to come."

Noticeably moved, Trish rerouted the conversation by pointing to the wall opposite her chair. "I figured that would be a good place to hang Billy Ray's pictures and medals. What do you think, Olivia? You're the one with the designer's eye."

"I think it would be perfect. With the exception of your beautiful ocean view, that's your focal wall." She pulled several books from a box and put them in the tiger-oak bookcase with leaded glass doors.

"Good." Trish pressed the button on her recliner and leaned back. "Now, sit down and rest a while, girlie. We don't have to get everything put away this afternoon. I'll unpack a couple of boxes a day until it's done. I'm too old to stress over a mess. As long as I have most of the kitchen, one of the bathrooms organized, and sheets on the bed, I'm good."

Olivia sat in the bamboo chair and put her feet up on the ottoman. "You don't have to twist my arm." She looked around. "This is the perfect house for you. I think you'll be happy here."

Logan laughed as he and Chase entered the kitchen door. "Who wouldn't be happy here with that wonderful fella next door for a neighbor?"

I rolled my eyes. "Yeah. And he's modest."

Logan tugged on the bill of his cap and tilted his nose in the air. "One of my greatest virtues."

"Says who?" Chase smirked and slapped him on the back. "Keep on believin' that while you can, big man. Marriage will soon make that yesterday's news."

Olivia huffed. "Leave them alone, Chase Evans. No one asked for your opinion."

"Since when do I wait to be asked?"

Olivia shook her head and shrugged. "Truth. I give up. You're hopeless."

Attempting to get the boxcar back on the rails, I cleared my throat. "Ahem. There are still cartons that need to come off the elevator, guys."

Logan chuckled. "Yeah, yeah. Crack that whip, Brooklyn."

Trish waved her hands in the air. "Now, children, let's not get snippy. If you're good, there's cake once all the boxes are in the assigned rooms."

Olivia laughed. "Now that should put some pep in our steps."

After the five of us sat around the trestle table built by Trish's father and enjoyed the most heavenly chocolate cake I've ever put in my mouth, the men headed back to their real jobs and left the fine-tuning to us ladies. Olivia and I put the sheets on Trish's bed while she organized the bathroom linen closet. Folding a throw, I laid it across the arm of her chair. "What's next?"

Trish walked in from the bathroom and scanned the room. "Looks wonderful to me."

Olivia and I sat beside her on the bed, and I checked the clock on the nightstand—5:10 p.m. "I'd say we've put in a good day's work."

"We certainly have." Trish rose, lifted the box marked fragile from the dresser, and clutched it to her chest. Returning to the bed, she pulled the tape from the seam and carefully lifted out a rosewood box with a carved border on the lid.

"Is that what I think it is?"

Struggling to keep her composure, she stroked the top of the box with her arthritic fingers and nodded. Then, attempting to speak, her voice cracked.

I patted her hand. "It's okay. No need to say anything."

She took a breath. "I haven't been able to part with this."

Olivia wrapped her arm around Trish's shoulders. "Why do you think you should?"

Tears slid from her eyes. "Because I've not done what Billy Ray wanted." She lifted her eyes to the window and stared out at the sea.

"There's plenty of time. You don't need to do anything until you're ready. Billy Ray would understand, and truthfully, I think he would be fine with whatever makes you happy."

She sniffed. "But I'm not happy."

Olivia pulled a tissue from a box on the nightstand and handed it to her.

"And I won't be until I carry out Billy Ray's wishes." She wiped her eyes and blew her nose. "The truth is, nothing will make me happy. I'll simply have a clear conscience, knowing I've done what he asked."

Olivia and I sat in silence, giving her time to share whatever she wanted.

"I understand Billy Ray's wishes and told him I'd honor them, but it's not easy." She traced the border on the box lid with her finger.

"Is there something Olivia and I can do to help?"

She closed her eyes and inhaled. "No, I could never ask."

I rubbed her back. "You're not asking. I am." Her tired eyes met mine as I brushed a tendril of hair from her face. "Trish, Olivia and I will help you. Let us have the privilege of walking this road alongside you. We'll do whatever we can to help you make Billy Ray's wishes a reality."

She wiped a tear from her cheek. "What did I ever do to

deserve the two of you?"

"Believe me, you're worthy of far more. God has his eye on you, Trish. He'll see that you have everything you need to accomplish what's necessary."

She whispered. "I know you're right. He always has."

"And He's not about to stop now."

Olivia pulled her closer. "Take time to think about what we've offered. Nothing has to be decided now. This is an emotional period. Give yourself some grace and time to settle into your new surroundings. As you told us earlier, I believe we're all too old to stress. Things will fall into place when the time is right."

She patted Olivia's hand. "You're precious." She stood and set the box on the dresser. "As Scarlett O'Hara said, 'I'll worry about that tomorrow.'" She turned. "I think today has taken its toll on me."

I rose and hugged her. "I know it has. It's to be expected." I pulled back and looked her in the eyes. "Olivia and I will slip out so you can get some rest. Is there anything else you need before we leave?"

She shook her head. "I can't think of a thing. You've all done so much already."

Olivia hugged her. "Okay, give us a call then if you need anything, and we'll come running. You hear?"

Trish brushed out the wrinkles in the bedspread. "I hear."

"And, of course, there's a 'wonderful fella' living next door that can be here quicker than we can. I think we've got you surrounded." I hugged her again. "We love you, sweet lady. You rest well tonight, okay?"

She laughed. "After today, I don't think I'll have an ounce of trouble falling asleep." She walked to the window and cracked it open. "I'll simply listen to the surf's lullaby and be off to never-

never land in a heartbeat."

"Oh, my goodness, listen to the surf. I think I'm going to drop right here." I tapped Olivia's shoulder. "Come on. Let's get home while we're still upright."

"I'm behind you, cuz. Lead on."

Chapter Forty-Eight

Sunday, September 17, 2023

"Hop in, beautiful lady." I placed Trish's canvas bag in the back of the fire-engine red golf cart, helped her in, and buckled her up. After she handed Olivia her handicapped tag to hang on the mirror, I gave her a peck on the cheek. "You good?"

She nodded. "I am, and I'm so excited. I couldn't ask for anything better than for my two special friends to accompany me on this maiden voyage."

"You mean you've never ridden in a golf cart?"

"Nope. Always thought I'd like to try golf, but I knew my legs wouldn't cooperate."

"Well, that makes this trip all the more special." I dropped onto the seat behind Olivia and tapped her shoulder. "Okay, madam chauffeur. You have precious cargo on board. Watch the speed limit and don't bounce us out of here."

"Not planning on it. I have strict orders. Chase knows I have a heavy foot and said he wants his vehicle back in one piece." Her eyes met mine in the rearview mirror. "Should I take offense that he didn't mention his wife or her passengers?"

Trish smothered her giggle with her hand.

"If you don't, I will." I shook my head and mumbled. "So typical. Wait till I see him."

A hint of fall was in the air, and cooler temperatures were a welcome reprieve from the stifling summer heat. As Olivia plowed the cart through the loose sand toward the water's edge, gulls soared lazily overhead, their cries blending with the rhythmic lap of waves. While she zigzagged around vacationers who were still savoring the elusive days of summer, I hollered above the wind and the pounding surf. "So, Trish, what do you think?"

She turned her head to the side and cut her eyes toward me. "Now, this is the way to travel. Reminds me of riding with Billy Ray in his red Bugeye Sprite on our first trip to Sunset Beach. I had never felt so free. Today echoes that same sense of freedom."

"Aww…we're so happy you're enjoying it. We weren't sure we could get the city's okay to bring the cart onto the beach, but after hearing our story, they wished us well. You're a real VIP, Trish."

Little more was said as we enjoyed the warmth of the sun on our faces, inhaled the salty scent of the sea mixed with sunscreen, and breathed in the distant aromas of beachside barbeques. Once we crossed into the remoteness of Bird Island, the carefree sounds of summer melted into the background, and the enormity of a poignant season soon to be put to rest toyed with my emotions.

As we drew closer, Trish pointed to the American flag that slapped the air above the place where the Kindred Spirit stood. Despite the persistent battering of storms through the years, Billy Ray had always made sure the flag still waved to welcome those who sought the solitude of the Kindred Spirit.

Olivia slowed the cart and stopped at the water's edge. "How's this spot, Trish?"

"It's perfect." She tugged at the seat belt.

I jumped from the back. "Here, I'll get that for you. It can be a little tricky." I unfastened the belt, helped her from the cart, and noted the sun lowering in the sky. "We couldn't ask for a prettier evening."

Olivia agreed, pulled off her sandals, and laid them in the cart. Once Trish and I did the same, I lifted the canvas bag from the backseat and clasped her hand. "How do you feel?"

She nodded. "I'm okay."

When she reached for the bag, I held it open so she could lift out the rosewood box. Large tears welled in her eyes as she clutched it to her chest. "Here we are, Billy Ray. I'm doing my best to do what you asked."

She looked back toward the dunes. "I'll always remember the day we planted the Kindred Spirit." She chuckled. "I know you got a little miffed with me because I kept telling you the post was crooked, but in true Billy Ray fashion, you bit your tongue and did your best to please me. From that day on, you never stopped pleasing me. You made me the happiest woman in the world, and I was blessed to be your wife. The one thing I regret is that we didn't have more time together. I suppose God had His reasons for taking you from me, but I don't have to like them."

While Trish poured out her heart to Billy Ray, Olivia and I kept to the side and held hands, trying to maintain our composure. Later, after a short and somber ceremony spoken by Trish, we helped her wade into the water, where she prayed and gently released Billy Ray's ashes. Olivia and I followed by sprinkling white rose petals over them, and with tears streaming down our cheeks, the three of us held one another and watched the waves carry away his ashes. When we could no longer see them, we walked back to the shore. I passed around a box of tissues from the cart and glanced at the dunes. "Trish, would you like to spend time at the Kindred Spirit before we go back?"

"No. Not today, but if you and Olivia have time, I'd love to sit here and wait for the sun to set."

"Of course. I can't think of a better way to close out this beautiful evening."

After Olivia and I helped Trish into the cart, we took our places and waited for heaven to paint the western sky. As usual, God's handiwork was breathtaking. During the trip home, Trish sat with the rosewood box holding Billy Ray's remaining ashes in her lap and stared straight ahead. No one ventured to interrupt her sacred silence.

Monday, September 18, 2023

On my way home from the bookstore, I stopped by Trish's house. When she didn't answer the front door, I passed through the carport beneath the house and climbed the back steps to the deck. When she failed to respond to my knocks, I tested the door and cracked it open.

"Trish, it's Brooklyn. Are you here?"

I'm not accustomed to snooping through people's homes, but I needed to know if she was okay. Concerned when I didn't find her, I prayed she'd be on the beach and walked out to the deck. Scanning the area, I saw clusters of people enjoying the beautiful day, and several chairs sprinkled along the surf. I spotted a lady wearing a sunhat and rushed down the walkway, calling out Trish's name until she turned. Pressing my hands to my chest, I sighed. "Oh, thank goodness, Trish, it's you." I dropped to the sand beside her and leaned back on my hands, trying to catch my breath.

"Hi, Brooklyn. This is a nice surprise."

I rolled my eyes. "A nice surprise is an understatement. When you didn't come to the front door, I was worried, but then, when you didn't answer the back door either, I panicked. I'm relieved you're okay."

She clasped my arm. "Honey. I'm sorry I worried you. I came out to reflect on yesterday." She pointed to her tote bag.

"And record some things in my journal."

"Oh. I don't want to disturb you."

She dismissed my concern with a smile. "You're not. I've been here a while and have already had my alone time. It's wonderful to see you. I can't thank you and Olivia enough for taking me to the Kindred Spirit yesterday. It was hard, but a fulfilling evening, and one I couldn't have experienced without the two of you."

"Trish, it was a blessing. Olivia and I were honored that you shared such a special time with us. You've been on my mind all day, and that's why I stopped by. I wanted to make sure you were all right."

She smiled. "Yes, dear. I'm more than all right. A huge weight was lifted from my spirit yesterday. Knowing I've done what Billy Ray requested has given me peace."

"That's good to hear," I said, checking my watch. "I hate to run, but now that I know you're okay, I need to meet Olivia. She's helping me plan my wedding."

"Well, by all means, run along. I don't want to stand in the way of that…and tell your sweet cousin I love and appreciate her."

"I certainly will." I hugged her. "Holler if you need anything, and of course, you know your wonderful neighbor, Logan, is always on call."

She laughed. "Yes, he's the best. He's kept a close eye on me."

"I bet he has, and soon you'll have four eyes tracking your every move." Giggling, I gave her a thumbs-up and walked back toward the house.

Trish dug into her tote bag, pulled out her journal, and smiled as she reread what she'd written.

Chapter Forty-Nine

Monday, April 22, 2024

I took another sip of my morning coffee, placed my cup in the holder, and hopped on Olivia's lavender bike. "You do have the notebooks, right?"

"Yes. They're in my basket with several new pens."

"Good. Just checking." I breathed in the moist, salty air and noted low-hanging clouds that made a lavender-tide morning an excellent possibility. As Olivia's tires cut ruts in the damp sand, I tried to stay in her tracks. It was a game we played as children whenever she'd come for extended summer stays. Since neither of us had siblings, our early bond as cousins was stronger than most. Although I was never good at our game, I still find following in my older cousin's tracks, on or off the beach, a worthwhile challenge.

As we grow older, it's easy to drift from those who've meant the most to us throughout the years. Performing our combined role as caretakers of the Kindred Spirit fostered the renewal and deepening of our relationship. We had sweet Trish to thank for that, as well as her husband, Billy Ray, who had connected us all through the Kindred Spirit mailbox. Even Granny Rogers' lavender bike had played a crucial role in our journey and was now a familiar and delightful sight to islanders who knew its history.

After Olivia and I arrived at the box, we replenished the

notebooks, placed the filled ones in a bag to be archived at the university library, and spent time writing in the journals. I chose a lavender one to match the mood of the morning.

Dear Kindred Spirit

My cousin and I have been keepers of the mailbox since August of last year, when Trish, the wife of the Kindred Spirit's founder, Billy Ray Jessup, passed the baton to us. Being caretakers of the Jessups' fascinating legacy is one of the greatest honors of our lives and one we hope to enjoy for years to come.

We've had the pleasure of visiting this beautiful spot on Bird Island at sunrise and sunset, in midday and evening, at nautical twilight, and beneath the silvery moon. We've made the trip at low and high tides in the winter, spring, summer, and fall. We've opened the Kindred Spirit mailbox when it was too hot to touch, encased in ice, and, on rare occasions, blanketed in snow. We've laughed and cried here and have met our next-door neighbors, as well as people from around the world. And my cousin literally bumped into her husband-to-be on her first visit to the Kindred Spirit in 2022.

Today, April 22, 2024, marks another milestone—the anniversary of the Kindred Spirit mailbox. Forty-nine years ago today, on the Jessups' eighth wedding anniversary, Billy Ray surprised his beloved Trish with a mailbox. Yes, a mailbox he'd named the Kindred Spirit and planted in the dunes of this remote island. Billy Ray's unique present to his wife has become a gift to us all, uniting kindred spirits around the globe.

Last week, Trish asked Olivia and me to come to the

dunes today to celebrate and chronicle the origin of the Kindred Spirit mailbox in one of the journals. Although this recognition is filled with bittersweet history and emotions, it's one we're all invited to participate in. May the tradition and legacy of this beautiful couple and the hours of pleasure they've given to this barrier island live in our hearts and lives forever.

Sincerely grateful in Sunset Beach,
The Keepers of the Kindred Spirit Mailbox

As I closed the journal, I observed Olivia on the opposite bench writing to the Kindred Spirit, and a lump rose in my throat. She noted my movement with a wave of her hand and continued to write. After we returned both journals to the box, I followed Olivia down the dune to our bicycles. She set the small bag of notebooks on the sand and picked up another bag we'd brought with us.

I swallowed hard. "I don't think I can do this."

"I feel the same way, but yes, we can. With God's help, we'll accomplish this together." She held open the canvas bag.

I took out the all-too-familiar rosewood box and clutched it to my chest. "What a difference a week makes. We just never know, do we?" The rapid beat of my heart pulsed in my ears, drowning out the rush of waves crashing against the shore.

Olivia's tear-filled eyes gazed into mine. "It's what she journaled, Brooklyn. This is what she wanted."

I nodded. "I know, but—" I dropped my forehead onto the box and wept.

Olivia and I walked hand-in-hand to the water's edge. While gulls overhead yielded a forlorn cry, we waded into the tide with the rosewood box that held the beloved couple's ashes.

After scattering them onto the rolling sea, we blanketed the area with fragrant lavender rose petals. As sea spray dispersed a sweet, intoxicating scent that saturated the air, I remembered. Today, Billy Ray and Trish would celebrate their fifty-seventh wedding anniversary in heaven.

Together.

"Let not your hearts be troubled. Believe in God;
believe also in me. In my Father's house are many rooms.
If it were not so, would I have told you that I go to prepare a
place for you? And if I go to prepare a place for you,
I will come again and will take you to myself,
that where I am you may be also."
John 14:1-3, ESV

A Note from the Author
and Kindred Spirit History

Dear Readers,

It seems like only yesterday that my husband and I visited the Kindred Spirit mailbox for the first time with our oldest daughter and son-in-love. At that point, the premise of a story started to percolate in my mind's eye. Today, as a result of our visit that beautiful June evening in 2022, there are now two novels in my Summer Is Tomorrow series. *Waiting for Sunset* and *Lavender Tide* are both split-timeline fictional stories rooted in Kindred Spirit history.

If you're reading this, I assume you've read both books. I would like to thank you for accompanying Olivia, Chase, Brooklyn, Logan, and me on our journeys to the Kindred Spirit. If you haven't visited the box, I encourage you to walk or ride a bicycle to this landmark that has captured the hearts of tens of thousands of kindred souls since its inception.

In 1975, Sunset Beach resident Frank Nesmith happened upon Claudia Sailor from Hope Mills, straining to erect a mailbox on the northern tip of Sunset Beach at Tubbs Inlet. After finding a piece of driftwood lying on the shore, he helped her stabilize the box. Since then, seekers who make the pilgrimage to the mailbox leave behind their heartfelt and often therapeutic messages in small notebooks placed inside the box by its caretakers. Though many of these entries are written anonymously, their words of hope, grief, gratefulness, joy, and sorrow have inspired others to do the same. The original metal box, weathered by the elements, has been replaced several times, but Frank's driftwood base remains.

In 1983, time and tides eroded the land, and the Kindred Spirit was relocated to Bird Island, situated on the opposite end of Sunset Beach. At that time, the two islands were separated by Mad Inlet, and visitors accessed the island by boat or wading through the brackish water at low tide. Since Hurricane Bonnie filled in the inlet in 1999, visitors can now make the 1.4-mile trek from Sunset Beach to the mailbox on foot.

Claudia and Frank's initial meeting at the box led to a sweet romance and a lifelong friendship that included 30 years of shared responsibility for the Kindred Spirit. After Claudia died in 2013, Frank cared for the box until he was no longer able to make the trek. Since his death at the age of 92 in 2020, friends have carried on the couple's legacy.

Those who continue to care for the Kindred Spirit keep Frank and Claudia's love and friendship alive by maintaining the box, replenishing it with pens and notebooks, and collecting trinkets left inside. To them, we owe a debt of gratitude. The filled notebooks and items are later taken to the University of North Carolina at Wilmington, where they are cataloged and stored in a unique collection at the Randall Library.

The final scenes in *Lavender Tide* describing the scattering of Trish and Billy Ray's ashes are fictional and bear no resemblance to Claudia and Frank's story. The federal Clean Water Act, overseen by the EPA, mandates that the scattering of human ashes must occur at least three nautical miles from land. Although a permit isn't required, the EPA must be notified within 30 days of the scattering event. These regulations are in place to protect marine life and prevent pollution of coastal waters.

If you enjoyed Brooklyn and Logan's story in *Lavender Tide*, please consider leaving a review on Amazon, Goodreads, Barnes & Noble, and your social media accounts. I'd love for you to stay in touch. You can contact me through my social media pages or my website, which are listed below. Additionally, if you'd like to receive updates on my future book releases, please enter your email address in the subscription link on my website.

Blessings,
Starr Ayers

Website: www.starrayers.org   www.instagram.com/starrayers2
www.facebook.com/starr.ayers.9   www.x.com/StarrAyers2

Discussion Questions
For Book Clubs

1. *Whatever you do, Corbett, don't look guilty.* In Chapter 2, Logan Corbett is questioned at the hospital by a police detective. Why? When you learned Brooklyn Marshal was missing, what did you think had happened to her? What were your thoughts concerning Logan?

2. *How can things look incredibly promising one minute and in the next—Snap! Gone.* What was Logan referring to when he had this thought? Can you relate to his fear of losing something you love? Explain.

3. In Chapter 3, you meet 15-year-old Patricia (Trish) Malone. What was her disability? Who was her biggest encourager? Her encourager had given her a framed quote by Henry Ford— *Obstacles are those frightful things you see when you take your eyes off your goal.* What ending did she add to the quote?

4. What was Trish's birthday present from her Granny Rogers? Have you ever received a special gift from someone that you cherish to this day? What was it? What life-altering event happened on Trish's birthday? When you were younger, did you experience a life-altering event? If comfortable, share.

5. In Chapter 6, Logan and Brooklyn walk to the mailbox. What does Brooklyn find inside the box?

6. Who did young Trish meet at the cemetery? As their relationship grew, what did he give her on their first visit to Sunset Beach? Later, Billy Ray was drafted and met Phil. Do you know anyone who fought, was killed, or was a POW in Vietnam? Can you relate to the pain of being separated from someone you love for a long time? Share, if comfortable.

7. Who showed back up in Brooklyn's life one evening on the beach? Later in the story, what did this person do? Did you guess Stuart Wagner's true identity? What did you think of the way Logan handled the situation? Have you ever had to deal with a stalker? When it was hard for Brooklyn to trust again, she chose to remember Olivia's advice. *You don't have to build a fortress, only a shelter—a place where love can take root and thrive.*

8. Later in the story, who showed up in Logan's life? Have you ever had a family member you didn't know about contact you? Lacey hoped Logan and her mother would get back together. Would you have liked for a romance between Logan and Amber to blossom?

9. At the end of the story, Brooklyn and Olivia ride their bicycles to the Kindred Spirit mailbox. Who did they meet, and what did the person reveal? Were you surprised? How did you feel about the ending of the story?

10. The overarching theme for *Waiting for Sunset* was letting go. *Lavender Tide's* theme is overcoming hardship and moving forward. In a nutshell—Hope. How do you find the power to persevere through trials? The theme verse for *Lavender Tide* is Hebrews 10:23. Is there a Bible verse you cling to in times of difficulty?

11. What stood out to you most about the book? Were you satisfied with the ending? Who was your favorite and least favorite character, and why? What was your most surprising moment? Is there a character or characters you'd like to read more about?

12. Did you know about the Kindred Spirit mailbox before reading the Summer Is Tomorrow series? Have you been to this mailbox at Sunset Beach? If so, share your experience. If not, do you think you would like to visit?

13. Would you recommend *Lavender Tide* or the two-book Summer Is Tomorrow series to a friend? If so, please consider sharing it on your social media sites and writing a review on Amazon, Goodreads, or both. A review is one of the greatest gifts you can give an author.

www.ingramcontent.com/pod-product-compliance
Lightning Source LLC
Chambersburg PA
CBHW071208210726
48293CB00002B/337